SWITCHED

Kiana Bay

contents

CHAPTER 1

A merica

As a Princess, I've learned that any time I wanna spend with my friends has to be scheduled.

I've also learned that as a Princess, you do not make very many friends. At least not ones that aren't paid to work for you.

You suffer a lot when you're a princess. Your feet hurt constantly from the walking you do in heels all day. Your lungs burn from being trapped in a dress that is three sizes too small from dawn till dusk. Your cheeks are sore from the fake smile you plaster on your face every-time you see another living being. Your heart aches from rarely seeing your family and never having a soul to tell about it. If your me, your back stings from the few times you do see your family.

But I live my life in dresses that took three people each to make. I have makeup and beauty products shipped from foreign country's that cost more than some Sixes rents. I have rings that were fitted specifically for my finger and shoes that were molded for my feet. I have never missed a meal and each meal I have had has been 3 courses. My skin is always glowing and my nails are never chipped. My hair shines and my figure has been perfectly sculpted to everyone else's liking.

How can you complain when your the luckiest girl in the world?

Right?

I gasped, all my air leaving my lungs with a swift pull. "Can you pull any tighter?"

"Sorry, America," Mary apologized. Her nimble hands pulled the strings again as she laced the back of my dress up. I gasped as my lungs cried for help. This particular gown had a drop waistline and a bodice that extended down to my thighs, which meant the strings seemed to never end.

"The human body was not made for this," I whined.

"Your body was," Anne disagreed. She not so gently grabbed my head, turning it side to side as she judged my face.

"No—," I cut myself off as my lungs struggled for air with a new wrench of the dress strings.

"Sorry," Mary laughed, not sounding sorry at all.

"Are you done yet?" I yelped.

"Almost...." Mary trailed off. My organs were shifted around one last time as Mary jerked the strings of my dress and then tied them together in a polished bow.

I gulped air into my lungs as she finally let go of those wretched strings.

"Don't move," Anne reprimanded. "Smile."

I flashed her my teeth.

"Smile not growl," She repeated.

I softened my face into a gentle grin. She griped my chin and held me still as she lined my lips with liner and then gloss.

"I've got it!" Lucy squeaked as she entered the room. She shut the door behind her and leaned against it, smiling brightly. "I've got it! I've got it! I've got it!"

"What?" I laughed as Lucy did a little bounce over to us.

"These m'lady, are custom made high heels."

She held them out and presented then dramatically. Anne and Mary squealed, looking more like Daphne and Nicolette than my usually composed maids.

"High heels?" I asked.

"Yes high heels," Mary said. She grabbed the silver heels from Lucy, admiring them. "Aren't they beautiful?"

"Custom made,"Anne added.

"To add to the rest of my collection of custom made high heels," I said sarcastically. I fisted the skirts of my dress in my hands and walked over to my closet, pushing the door open. Rows of high heels revealed themselves to us.

"No. No. No," Lucy began. "You don't understand."

Mary handed the shoes to me and stood at my side so she could admire them over my shoulder. "They are custom fitted to your feet and lined with a special padding so that they feel like walking in your favorite slippers."

My eyes widened. "Are you joking with me?"

All three of them shook there heads simultaneously. I set them on the ground and they surrounded me. Anne and Mary held the skirts of my gown back as Lucy gently eased one of the shoes on to my foot and then the other. They all lined up beside me, silently urging me to test them out.

I took a hesitant step forward and my shoe nestled gently into the padding underneath.

"These are amazing," I admitted.

Lucy came up behind me and placed a necklace against my skin, fastening it.

"You look lovely, Princess," She complimented.

"It is what I am hear for," I sighed. I gave them each a pointed look. "You do know that I am not going to be able to eat in this dress, correct?"

"Lay off the tarts for a night," Mary advised, checking the hems of the dress. "Beauty is pain."

"Starvation is also pain," I agreed.

Mary rolled her eyes. "Have a nice night at the ball America."

"I will not."

I waved them goodbye and then headed out the door.

~oOo~

I sipped my wine politely in the corner as people danced around the room. My signature lip gloss was smeared across the rim of my glass and the nail polish my maids put on this morning was chipped. Luckily, I had stopped spilling things on my gowns many years ago so my dress at least survived the night.

"Hey Amy," Somebody chirped, appearing next to me.

"Good Evening Amara," I greeted, sloshing my wine around my cup.

"Not having fun?" She asked.

"Of course not. I'm having a great time," I said automatically.

"There is no amount of wine that would make me believe that," Amara laughed. She flicked a long perfect curl over her shoulder and laughed. She would make a gorgeous princess if she ever had the chance.

"No I am," I argued half heartedly.

She began running her fingers through her hair absentmindedly, separating her brunette curls into smaller pieces. "My mom says that you should dance with some guys."

"Silvia always thinks that I should dance with a guy," I said.

"Maybe she's right," Amara shrugged. "There is a cute guy over there."

I followed with my eyes to where she was gesturing. I shook my head.

"That is the Prince of Spain. He is a bit of a slob and also two years younger than I."

"I am also two years younger than you. And if you don't want him than I will have him."

"But he's a complete—."

She handed me her glass of wine and pulled out a compact mirror, checking her makeup. Than she grabbed the skirts of her dress and strutted on over to him.

I shook my head. She never listens.

Amara wasn't a princess. She wasn't really....... anything. She is the daughter of Silvia and Sylvan Santos, two of the most important staff members of the palace. Silvia is the royal planner and plans basically every ball, event, and anything else that's held in the palace. She also organizes all events that we go to outside of the palace. Thats her formal job title but honestly she does everything.

Sylvan is my mother's closest advisor and expert on all things etiquette. She is loud, bossy, and annoying. He is refined, quiet, and stoic. But I have a bit of a soft spot for both of them. She was my teacher as a child. And he taught me which spoon to eat soup with. They taught me everything I know. They made me a successful Princess. If only they could implement the same values in their daughter.

Amara is a sassy, uncontrollable bundle of many crushes, no manners, and a lot of makeup and hair products. Growing up, her parents must of been so busy teaching me that they forgot to teach her. Either that or she just never listened to them when they tried.

Because her parents worked and lived here, so did she. I've grown up with her tagging along on tea parties, showing me up at dance lessons, and sitting with me while I play piano for hours. Once upon a time, I found her annoying. But eventually I realized that this palace is really lonely when the maids no longer want to play with you because your not a cute toddler anymore. I kind of got used to her being around and eventually she stopped being annoying. She's my best friend.

"Have you danced with anyone?"

I looked up as my mother approached. Her hair was pulled back and her dress sparkled as she walked. She looked beautiful as always. Her skin was tanned where mine was pale. Her hair was golden brown where as mine was bright red. I've heard are noses where the same but I'm pretty sure that's just what people tell you when you look nothing like your parent.

"No one has asked me to dance, Mother," I replied.

"Well of course not, dear. Your hiding in a corner. No one knows your here," She teased.

I smiled guiltily.

"I'm sorry, Mom."

She stroked my hair, grinning fondly. "I know this isn't really your thing. But you are a force to be reckoned with during meetings."

"If by force you mean a nuisance to all advisors," I sighed.

"They're just threatened. You know what you want to do with this country and they don't agree."

"Neither does Father."

"You should lighten up on your father, America. He's under as much stress from the advisors as you are," She commented.

"The advisors are afraid of him Mother."

She leveled me with a reprimanding look. "And they'll be afraid of you one day."

My dad was suddenly at my moms side, his arm resting on her waist.

"Clarkson," Mom greeted.

He kissed her cheek. "Would you care to dance Amberley?"

"I would like to, but I'm feeling a tad bit under the weather. Why don't you dance with America?" She suggested.

Father turned his eyes to me. "America should be dancing with suitors."

"No one has asked for my hand in a dance, Father," I said giving him a tight smile.

"That's because you are hiding in a corner."

"That's exactly what I said!" Mom cut in, poking his chest. "I'm going to go lay down upstairs but I'll see about coming back down later."

I knew she wouldn't be coming back.

She walked away and I noticed she wore flats tonight. She must be having headaches again. And she came to the ball anyways. I wonder if I'll ever be as strong as she is.

"Would you care to dance?" Father asked, extending his hand.

"Of course," I agreed, bowing my head and taking his hand. He stiffly led me out to the center of the dance floor and placed a hand on my hip and kept the other in my own. I grabbed the skirts of my dress in one hand and held his hand in the other. He didn't smile. He never smiles.

"You look nice tonight," He said approvingly.

"Thank you, Father. My maids do wonderful work."

"Well I'm glad they do more than just talk to you. I do not pay them to be your friends," He said.

"They know that, Father. They work very hard."

"Humph," was all he said. He never listens.

We continued to dance in silence and it seemed like the song may never end. It may seem like my relationship with my father isn't very good. And I suppose it isn't. But I do love my father. I respect him. He is a hard worker and he treats my mother well. He is a good King. But what he does as a King, I do not agree with. He can be cruel and the way that he governs this country is not well. People are scared of him. And he thinks that makes him a good king. I disagree with most of my fathers principles. Father doesn't like it when I disagree with him. Especially when I do it in front of others.

I love my dad though.

I respect him.

My dress got caught underneath my heel and I tripped through the next few steps of the dance. I quickly recovered, avoiding my fathers eyes.

He stopped. When someone stopped during a dance it messed up all other dances on the floor. But he was a King. He could do what he wanted.

"Your supposed to look at people when you dance," He corrected. "And you are not supposed to trip over yourself. Work on it."

I watched him walk away, leaving me by myself as people danced around me. I hiked up the skirts of my dress and stormed away. Father has told me it is impolite to storm away. Even though he isn't here to see it, I still consider it a personal rebellion. I passed Amara, dancing with the Prince of Spain. Her eyes flicked to where my Father had retreated to talk to the Queen of Spain. She frowned and raised an eyebrow. I shook my head. I was fine. This wasn't the first time and it would certainly not be the last.

I returned to my corner where my glass of wine was. Even though I had been nursing the same glass all night, it was still practically full. I didn't care for wine. I also couldn't couldn't fit much in my stomach with this dress on. I set the wine down and headed for the door to the ballroom. I think I need some air and the garden was down the hall.

Once outside, I took a deep breathe. My dress squeezed me tight and I sighed. You never get used to not being able to take a deep breathe. I headed down the stone trail and into the luscious gardens of the palace. My father never came out here. He said that the gardens were for guests to look at, not us, and that I shouldn't waste my time out here. I know that when I come out here, he won't.

This path was my favorite. It led through the roses. Deep in the gardens is a large patch of rose bushes. The florists and gardeners had done years of work to make the bushes grow with each rose being a different color. The rose bushes were grown in honor of me. It took my mom years to get pregnant and when she finally did, the staff of the palace celebrated by planting these roses in the gardens. As a thanks you to the staff, my mom named me America Rose Schreave.

The path entered the rose gardens and I smiled. The roses, and the whole garden in fact, never died. They were in full bloom all year long. I don't know how the gardeners do it but they do. I ran a finger across the bright green leaves and picked a pale blue rose, the same color as my dress. I tucked it behind my ear and ended up knocking my tiara off my head, causing it to tumble to the ground and roll a few feet away. I bent down to pick it up and examined it, noticing a jewel chipped off. I set it next to the rose bush, continuing down the path.

It continued on through the fresh fruit trees and then curved around past the gazebo and up to the front of the palace. It led right next to the gates of the palace and if you looked, you could see all of Angeles.

This was also the one part of the palace where photographers could see in.

"Princess America! Princess over here!"

I plastered on a smile and posed a little bit as cameras flashed. Tomorrow this picture would be on the front of every magazine.

"Hello," I waved angelically

"Your Highness! Your highness, who are you wearing?"

I did a little spin, my dress fanning around me. Cameras flashed. "It's an original dress by my maids."

"They're very talented," The reporter replied. "Where did that rose come from? Did a lucky guy give it to you?"

I did my practiced, fake laugh and did what I was taught to do. Give them something but not enough. "That's for me to know."

Tomorrow it'll be all over the news that I have a secret suitor. If only. Than maybe my dad would get off my back.

"Well I should really get inside," I sighed, as if I just really wanted to talk to them all night.

"But Princess, we have to know—."

CHAPTER 2

M axon

A snow flake fell, gently, on to the window sill, peacefulness against the chaos inside the school.

I turned the camera ever so slightly so that it was sitting at a 30 degree angle and the flake was able to be seen in full detail. Zooming in a bit, I could see the light reflect off its icy form and the little beads of water forming as it began to melt. I blurred the area around it and then.....Snap!

I got the photo.

I changed up the filters a bit, trying to give myself options. Black and white. Cool tone. Dramatic. Warm tone. Vivid.

And then the tardy bell rang, shaking me from my haze and bringing me back into the real world. High School. A series of classrooms filled with twos who thought they were better than you and sevens who wished they could be you. Except none of them were in the halls now. Because they were all in class and I was late.

I dropped my camera and it caught on the band around my neck, and then I sprinted faster than I ever have to science. Well that's not true. I'm pretty used to sprinting to my classes. Usually I was able to barely slide into my seat by the time the late bell rang, but I was distracted today.

Mr. Sanchez was gonna be so mad.

Which is why it was no surprise when I received a not so friendly look when I skidded to a stop in the doorway to his classroom. I caught my breath, smiling guiltily. He gave me the evil eye.

"Mr. Singer, what do I have to do to get you to class on time?"

I pursed my lips. "Move the buildings closer together?"

"Very funny," He said, but he wasn't laughing. A few students were but he definitely was not. "It's a warning today, but a detention tomorrow. Learn to walk faster."

"Yes sir," I nodded quickly. "It will not happen again. Scouts honor."

He gave me a look that clearly told me to hurry up and go to my seat and then turned around to begin writing on the board. I grinned to myself. It was always a warning today, detention tomorrow with Mr.

Sanchez. Tomorrow has never come. I plopped down into my seat and slung my backpack onto my chair. Aspen rolled his eyes at me.

"Dude, where were you?" He whispered, his yes flicking between me, his paper, and the notes he was copying off the board.

I cringed, quickly pulling out my notebook and a pencil. "I saw a snowflake."

"We live in Carolina. We see snowflakes all the time."

"Yeah. But this one was on the window sill and it was starting to melt...."

"Maxon," He groaned. "That camera is going to be the end of you."

"That camera is going to support my family one day," I disagreed.

"Maybe you should break up with old Cam and go find yourself a real girlfriend," He laughed.

"My cameras name is not Cam. And I have a better chance with my camera than you have with your crush."

"Hey," he deadpanned. "Not nice. Princess America and I will happen."

I rolled my eyes. "Mhmmm..."

"Boys!" Mr. Sanchez yelled. We both turned our eyes forward and were met with dirty looks from most of the class. The five and the six, causing trouble as usual. Such a stereotype. "Some of your classmates are trying to pay attention, you should try it."

The upper castes have never been too keen on the lower castes attending school with them. It has always been that if sixes and under want an education then they get it from a public school, but barely any teachers wanted to work at those. Fives could go to the private schools but they barely ever got into them and most of them time they ended up going to the public schools or being homeschooled. So fives and under usually just look for more work and don't bother with school. But Princess America has created an education system that is open for all castes and it has opened doors for children all over the country. Sort of.

"Yes sir," We chorused.

We dutifully took our notes down for a few minutes. Well, I dutifully took my notes down. He was just using colorful hi-liters to make every word a different color. I think the notes were on different blood types or something like that. A, B, AB and O positive and Negative, plus the ISR bloodline.

Aspen turned back to face me, eyes excited. "Just think. I get drafted into the army and wind up at the palace as a guard. It's a win-win.

I get top honors and become a two, my family gets lots and lots of money, and she will be there. We will meet and she will fall madly in love with me and everyone would be happy."

"Except for the country when you become King."

"I would make a great King," He said defensively.

"There is a lot of things wrong with that fictional scenario," I disagreed. "First of all, that it will never happen."

"A man can dream," He said wistfully. He gave me a look that clearly told me that I was crazy for not also sharing this dream with him.

"Every man can dream. And they all do. I do not. It's unrealistic."

"Alright class," Mr. Sanchez spoke. "Now that we have learned a bit about blood types, you are going to find out your own blood type. Because technology is so great nowadays, this does not require you to extract any blood. All you gotta do is prick your finger and hold it against the pad that is connected to the computer on the desks. The computer will take down your blood type and I'll get your results back to you tomorrow."

There was rustling around the class as notebooks were closed and put away and people started chattering. Aspen quickly pricked his finger and held it against the pad and I did the same.

"She could have a selection," He pointed out, continuing our earlier conversation.

I laughed. "Princess America? Having a selection? The same Princess who yelled at Gavril Fadaye on live television about how quote 'sexist it is to think that a women can't rule without a King by her side'. The same Princess who has publicly talked about how the caste system works against women—."

"The caste system works against everyone," He interrupted.

I nodded my agreement. "The point is, it's unrealistic for you to save yourself for Princess America when chances are that she will just windup marrying some foreign Prince. You should just get a girlfriend."

"Girls get upset when they see you checking out other girls. Princess America is on tv everyday and she is hot. Not a good combo."

"Your a pig," I muttered. He laughed it off.

I hated that hormonal teenagers just went around calling Princess America hot. I couldn't deny the beauty of the princess, but the word hot is...degrading. She is not a piece of meat. She is a person. The word hot just makes its seem like she's not.

Aspen was genuinely a good guy. He was extremely respectful to women, always. He liked to mess around though and make jokes, especially about his nonexistent relationship with the Princess, but he was a good guy. He takes great care of his 6 siblings and has been known to have had a few conversations with guys interested in his sisters. I haven't quite had to do that with May yet, but I know it's not far away.

The girl who sat at the table in front of ours turned around and smiled at Aspen. She had small, cute features and brown hair that barely brushed her shoulders. She had sat at the table in front of us forever and never talked to us. It wasn't a higher caste thing. I knew she was a Six. I think she's just quiet.

"Hey," She greeted shyly. It was a small nervous mumble. She was looking at both of us, but I noticed the small, subtle glances that she was giving Aspen. "I was wondering if you, um....wrote down uh—number 7 in the notes?"

"Um....There isn't a number seven," Aspen replied.

The girls face went bright red. "Oh.....um, my bad. Uh, I'm sorry."

She turned back to her table but I could see the blush on the tips of her ears.

I elbowed Aspen in the ribs.

"Hey!" He yelped.

I cocked my head towards the girl.

"What?" He asked in confusion. "Oh...oh!"

He reached forward and tapped her gently on the shoulder. Her head whipped around, her face still a blush pink.

"Brenna, is it?" Aspen asked. She nodded nervously. "I'm Aspen."

I smiled and went back to my work. He was actually talking to a girl that wasn't a photograph of the princess. A girl who seemed nice. I had always pegged Aspen to go for more of the tiny and shy type. He couldn't handle someone as fiery as Princess America. I wasn't sure anyone could.

The bell rang and chairs scraped against the floor as students rushed out of the classroom. I flung my bag over my shoulder and left along with them, heading into the halls. I looked around for things to take pictures of but with all the students everywhere, I couldn't really see much.

A hand was suddenly on my shoulder and red whipped past me. She crossed around me and stood next to my other side.

"Hey brother," May chirped.

"Hey sister," I replied.

The sunlight caught on her hair, making the red burst with vibrant shades of orange and gold. It was like a subset all in a second. I wanted to take a picture of it but I had already taken thousands of pictures of Mays hair.

We began our walk home in a comfortable quiet, which I knew would not last long.

"Did you see those photos of Princess America from the ball last night?" May burst out a few minutes later.

"The ones in the gardens that have been on the front of every magazine and paper?" I confirmed.

"Yes!" She squealed. "What do you think?"

"I think the photos need work. The lighting was too harsh on her hair and while we're on the topic of lighting, there wasn't any. The angle was not flattering and the filter they used made her look washed out. Don't even get me started on—."

"No. I meant the dress. Wasn't it beautiful?" She sighed dreamily. "The blue is such a gorgeous color and it looks so good with her hair. Oh my gosh, it would look great with my hair!"

I nodded along as she went into great detail of the dress and every single way that it complimented Princess America.

"Hey May!" Someone called out from across the street. It was a boy who was walking in the opposite direction.

"Hi Brett!" May yelled back, her face turning a light pink. The boy smiled at her and then kept walking in the other direction.

She turned to me. "He is so cute."

"Hey!" I yelped, covering my ears. "Too much information! No, no. Too young. Not happening."

"Come on Maxon," She whined.

"I do not want to hear about how cute boys are until your at least 17. Scratch that. I don't ever want to hear about how cute boys are."

"Please Maxon. Kenna is gone and I have no one to talk to. Can't you just be that really cool older brother who does girl talk with me?"

"That really cool older brother does not exist," I informed her.

"Please," She begged.

"Can't you talk to Ryanne and Jaime about boys? They are your best friends," I pointed out.

She rolled her eyes. She had this look on her face that clearly told me that she didn't understand how I wasn't getting this. "They like him too. So we vowed to not talk about him in order to preserve our friendship."

"But that's—."

"Please Maxon. For me."

"Fine. One minute."

She squealed. "Okay, so that was Brett. He's a four and he wants to be a chef. Isn't that so fun? And he has these really pretty, blue eyes and he's basically perfect." I nodded along. Perfect. Right. "So obviously every girl likes him."

"Obviously," I agreed sarcastically.

She sent me a dirty look but didn't let me ruin her fun.

"But you saw him say hi to me. He always says hi to me. He doesn't say hi to all the other girls. I think he likes me and I think we're going to fall madly in love and be together forever."

"Not on my watch," I muttered.

May is really beautiful. It is more than her face, though, more than her winning smile and bright eyes. May radiated energy, an enthusiasm that made you want to be wherever she was. May was magnetic. I could understand why boys would be interested in her. That doesn't mean I have to like it.

"Maxon," She groaned, extending my name with 5 more syllables than it actually has. "Stop."

"It's my responsibility as your older brother," I said defensively.

"But were having girl talk," She argued.

"Your one minute ended."

She sighed. "Gerad would be better at girl talk than you are. You know what, I'm going to go talk to Gerad."

She ran down the street and left me behind. At first I was concerned, but I quickly realized that we were on our street and that she was already home. I walked up the stones that led up to our house. They were painted with beautiful landscapes, the victim of one of Dad and May's 'art experiments'.

I opened the door to the house and was immediately met with loud noise. The house was small and the family was big. The kitchen, living room, and dining room were all in the same small space and the majority of the family could be found in that room at most times of the day. A hallway was connected to that room that split off into 6 rooms. 3 bedrooms, one master, a garage, and a shared family bathroom. Bedroom number 1 once occupied Kota and I, but when Kota left, I got it to myself. Bedroom 2 used to be Kenna and May's, but Kenna is married now and living with her husband and May gets a room all to herself. Gerad's never had to share, but May and I stopped complaining about that as soon as the oldest were out of the house and we knew what it was like.

Today the house was extra busy. I immediately noticed that Kenna was visiting with her husband James when I spotted them sitting on the couch, watching the report. I also could see Gerad, playing ball in the house while Mom yelled at him from where she was cooking at the stove. May had apparently decided that Kenna would be much better at girl talk than either of her brothers and was now sitting on the couch next to her and chattering animatedly. Dad was no where to be seen though, probably in the garage trying to create the next masterpiece that would pay for Christmas presents in a few months.

"Maxon!" Mom chirped, turning her head around to smile at me. "Welcome home. How was school, honey?"

She was yelling slightly, trying to talk over the commotion.

"It was good mom. I—."

"That great, Max!" I don't think she heard me. "Can you come stir this sauce for me?"

I nodded, giving her a kiss on the cheek as I passed and taking the spoon from her. I looked around.

"Salad, pasta, and bread?" I asked.

"Your sister brought it with her. She's so sweet," Mom smiled. "There may even be enough for seconds."

"That's great," I agreed.

She was beaming. "Go clean up for dinner and tell your father that it's almost ready. Oh! And say hello to your sister."

"Of course."

I snuck up behind her on the couch and tapped her shoulder. She jumped, her head whipping around.

"Maxie! My baby brother!" She laughed, reaching up to hug me. Once she let go, I shook James hand.

"Not really a baby."

"Of course you are," She said, teasingly pinching my cheek. "Just look at you all grown up and legally an adult. You look like you're working too hard and not eating enough."

I shook my head. "I'm fine. I am eating as well as I can as a five and getting just the right amount of exercise."

"Are you sleeping enough?"

"Of course."

"Well you'll have a nice meal tonight and we will get you in bed at a suitable time," She smiled. "Go get Dad."

"I'll do it," May chirped. "Catch up with Kenna."

I smiled at her and took her place on the couch. Kenna muted the report and the image of the royal family and Gavril fadaye played across the screen in silence.

"So how are you?" She asked. "It's been a few months since we saw each other. How's the photography going?"

"I just booked a wedding and there's a few loyal families willing to do some school pictures. I'm hoping that'll bring in a little bit of money for the family."

"Just make sure you keep a little bit for yourself," She advised. "Your going to need money to support a wife one day."

I nodded. Mom and Kenna had always told me this, but every month I gave every cent to them.

"It smells great in here, Maggie," My Dad boomed, entering the house.

"Thank you Shalom. Kenna brought us extra food," Mom replied.

"Kenna?" He turned around to face the living room and a smile burst across his face. "Ken! It's so great to see you."

He crossed over to give Kenna a hug and greeted James. There was rustling around the house as everyone got up and chattered, slowly gravitating towards the kitchen table. May skipped around the kitchen helping mom bring over the food. Everyone was talking excitedly, catching up.

That's what was great about family. You didn't always have everything. There was always going to be times where there wasn't enough food. There was always going to be times where we couldn't afford the electrical bill or the heating costs. But if one Singer was hungry, we were all hungry. If one Singer was cold, than you could cuddle with another.

When you have nothing....

You always have each other.

CHAPTER 3

America

I like meetings.

Well I should rephrase, I like some meetings.

There are meetings about issues in Illea and I love solving issues. Disputes among castes, law making, consequences of actions. It all sounds really boring, but that's when I feel closest to my people. When I am at a meeting that will fully effect the citizens of Illea, I am at my full attention. I care about the glamorous twos and the working sevens, the wealthy and the destitute. I want to be involved in what will help or hurt them. Sometimes it feels like I'm the only one who is sticking my head out for the people. A lot of the time, advisors only care about the twos and threes. I feel that I have to speak for the sixes and sevens.

On the other hand, I loathe meetings about budgets and events and things such as that. In those meetings, I usually sit politely and nod along. I've always been told to a least look like I'm interested, which is a lesson I have learned the difficult way. Because I am most definitely not interested when I am in meetings about budgets. They are boring and no one really cares what I have to say about Illean funds. I was once interested in budget meetings, when I was young. But my father never liked what I had to say so I learned to stop saying anything. Or a least, I'm learning.

"What about a tax?" I suggested.

"There already is a tax, Princess," An advisor spoke from the end of the table.

"Yes," I agreed. My eyes ran over the papers in front of me. "But the tax is the same for all Illean citizens, two through seven."

"We care about having equality among our citizens, America," My father said gruffly. "Everyone pays the same."

"Our citizens are not equal," I disagreed.

"I—."

"Clarkson, let her speak," Mother cut in, nodding at me. Father gave me a warning look.

I ignored it. "Obviously twos and sevens do not make the same amount. So they shouldn't pay the same."

"That's interesting," An advisor I recognized as Markus inquired. His job was basically to think of how different things may effect the citizens. In my opinion, he tends to only think of how it effects his caste. "Two's wouldn't be happy about paying more than everyone else."

"I'm sure sevens are not happy about making less than twos. We can't all be happy," I said. Of course I said this happily. When I don't say things happily, people think I actually mean what I say. And my dad doesn't like it when I mean what I say.

He doesn't like a lot of things.

"All I'm trying to say," I continued. "Is that the taxes a citizen pays should be based on how much they work and how much they make."

"That's a good idea, America," My mom said.

My father made a gruff noise of disagreement. I smiled tightly. With that noise alone, I knew that my idea would never actually be taken into consideration.

The door burst open and a maid rushed into the room, stopping next to the table. It was Jada.

"King Clarkson," She mumbled. "There is a phone call for you in your study."

"Who is it from?" He asked, uninterested. Father normally doesn't care when people call him. There are few people in this world that are more important than him, therefore there is few people who call him that are worth interrupting a meeting for. Or even answering the phone for.

"A school in Carolina," Jada replied. Her voice didn't shake as her tone wasn't muted. She wasn't nervous, which is a rare trait to find in maids when their talking to their superior. It's one of the reasons I like Jada so much.

"Why do I care about some school in Carolina?" He asked, anger shrouding his features

"It is urgent, sir," She said.

Father gave her a look that would make most drop in fear. Jada was unaffected. It saddened me that my father would see this as a fault rather than a strength.

"If this is not good than you are loosing your job," He muttered before pushing out of his chair and exiting the room. Jada followed after him. My mother was quick to continue the meeting, but I didn't speak again. I would be lucky if whatever this phone call was about would be enough to keep my father from yelling at me for my comments during the meeting thus far. My thoughts wandered off to what the phone call could be about. What could a school in Carolina have to say that could be classified as urgent? Urgent is not a word you use lightly in the palace. A rebel attack is urgent. Schools in Carolina are not urgent.

The door opens again and I expected to see Jada, back to tell us that my Father had to deal with something. Instead it was my father.

"Amberley, America. I need to talk to you."

Me and mother share a look. What could possibly be causing this much commotion and how was it going to effect us? What did this school in Carolina know that we did not?

"Of course," My Mother nodded. "I suppose....meeting adjourned."

There was a mumbling around the room of the advisors varied responses and the rustling of papers being collected. None of them seemed to care but this seemed bigger to me.

"Mom.....?" I trailed off.

"Don't freak out Amy," My Mother said crossing over to me. She stroked the back of my head, smoothing my hair down. This was how she always comforted me and sometimes it was the only thing that worked. "We don't know what this is about and we have no need to worry."

I nodded, and she offered me her hand. I squeezed it once and let go.

Father watched as all the advisors left the room and then shut the door behind him. It was just the three of us, a family. We were rarely ever together as a family. Too bad it wasn't under normal circumstances.

"What is going on Clarkson?" Amberley asked. "This is causing quite a commotion. You're giving me a headache."

"I don't mean to, Amberley. But a matter has been brought to me and we just need to take some cautionary measures. I'm sure it's nothing."

"What is it Father?" I asked.

"I think we all should sit down," He advised. My mom sat back in her chair and father did as well.

"Clarkson, you're worrying us."

"I just got off the phone with a high school in Carolina that has recently been practicing blood typing. They're was a male at the school that's blood tested positive for Illean heritage."

I chuckled. "That's what this is about? Some malfunction in the technological system?"

"That's what they thought. They ran the blood sample through the test 10 times. Each time it came back 100% positive."

I think I could feel the blood drain from my face. My mother went pale.

"Do I have some secret sibling I don't know about?" I scoffed in disgust.

"No."

"I don't understand," My mother mumbled.

My father gritted his teeth, his hands clenching into fists. "He was born on the same day as you, America. In the same hospital. They think there was some sort of mix up."

"Oh my goodness," My mom gasped.

"I promise you that I will shut the hospital down and I won't stop unto everyone there has lost their medical degrees—."

"I don't understand what this means," I interrupted.

"They think their was a mix up. That you and this other child were ...switched."

~oOo~

Sometimes you can hear words, but not understand what they mean. That is what happens when someone tells you that everything you have ever known is a lie.

You grow up with a certain type of education. For normal kids, you learn your abc's and your123's. I learned the entire history of The United States Of America, Canada, and Mexico individually and then I learned the history of how they became Illea. I learned to dance and make speeches, not how to draw shapes.

You grow up in a home. If your a six, it is small and packed full of people. If your a two, it is big and lush and you have to call to figure out where your mother is. If your me, it's in a palace. My knees were bruised by age one from crawling on marble and I still don't believe I have seen the whole entirety of my home.

You grow up with a family. You have a mom, who loves and nurtures you from the second you're born, and who would do anything for you. You love her with all your heart and there's nothing in the world that she loves more than you. You have a dad, who is proud of your every move from day one. You look up to him and he can do no wrong. He is your superman. She is your best friend. You are their everything.

In life, these things can be your only constant. Your home, your family, your friends, your teachers, and the things you've learned from them. These things are all always changing, but your relationship with them never does.

Or so I thought.

This moment. The moment when all those constants became a lie. My mother was not my own. My father was someone else's. My home was never meant to be mine. My friends, or lack there of, was never supposed to happen. The things I've learned, I was never meant to. Everything. Every single thing that I've ever known, isn't true.

How do you comprehend something like this?

"America?"

The world shifted and then clicked back into place as I became aware of my surroundings. I was sitting on a hospital bed. No, I didn't faint. I was about to have my blood drawn and tested on so that we could be 100% sure that I was an imposter to the throne. Or at least that's how I'm thinking of it.

It was dangerous to leave me alone with my thoughts. My parents had gone into another room to inform Dr. Ashylar of the situation and that he was to be at his up most discretion. I sat in here and waited for them to return. But it felt as if my thoughts would drown me before I was ever able to come to terms with the situation.

I don't know anything about this family. I don't know their caste or how many of them their are. I don't know what they do to earn a living or what they do for fun. The only thing I do know in fact, is that they live in Carolina. I heard it snows there and rains endlessly.

I've never touched snow.

I've gone to Carolina before of course. I've been their on tours of the country and things such as that. I've made appearances there at schools and important events. Who knows, I may have seen my family and I would of never known.

No matter how I look at this situation, it's a travesty. I'm not really the heir to Illea. I may have been tuned and polished to rule this country, but one simple blood test is all it takes to wash that all away. I want to change this country. I want to help stop hunger and injustice. I can't do much from under his thumb but when I'm queen, I'm going to do big things. Or at least I was. Who knows if I'll have the chance now.

I am the Princess of Illea, no matter what, but I may be the only one who sees it that way.

On the flip side, there are a million experiences I missed out on because I'm a princess. Those are experiences that I should have had. Holidays spent singing and giving gifts with loved ones. Family diners laced with laughter and loving banter. Going to school and flirting with cute guys and making new friends. Snow days. First Kisses. Siblings. Slumber Party's. Summers at the beach and winters by the fire.

My holidays were spent making appearances in the provinces. My school experience was me, alone in a room with Silvia and a stack of text books. My first crush was on a foreign prince that I see once every two years. My snow days were spent watching the snowflakes from a bulletproof window. It's snowing in Carolina. It's 70 degrees in Angeles.

So did I loose a childhood experience or am I going to loose my future? Either way, I think my life as I know it is ending.

The doors burst open and my three maids rushed into the room, all talking over one another.

"We got what you asked for!" Lucy squeaked.

"You'll never believe—."

"Their fiv—."

They all stopped, stumbling into a line in front of me. I stared blankly at them.

"America...?" Lucy asked hesitantly. "Are you alright?"

"I don't like needles," I whispered.

"You've never been afraid of needles before," Mary said matter-of-factly. Anne smacked her arm and sent her a look.

"Yeah," I agreed, my voice shaking. I don't know why my voice was shaky and my hands were trembling, but I couldn't seem to make them stop. "But I am now. I never want to see a needle again. And I certainly don't want one to stick into my skin and take my blood."

Lucy shuffled to my side. Her hand rested on my arm. "It's ok. I'm afraid of needles too."

"America isn't afraid of needles," Mary repeated.

"I am," I said. My voice was so tiny that I'm not sure they heard it. I think it was a manifestation of how I felt. Small. Frail. Tiny. Gone.

"You're not afraid of needles. The America that I know isn't afraid of anything," Anne cut in. "Stop pretending like your okay when you're not. You can't hold this inside and you can't make it go away. So you have to face it, plain and simple."

"The Princess I know is never afraid to face things. You'll tell anyone how you feel," Lucy piped in.

"I don't know how I feel," I admitted.

"Lie," Mary dinged.

I looked up at her.

"You have all types of scary thoughts running amuck in your brain,"
She elaborated. "Share with the class."

Mary sat down next to me, her hands resting on my arms. Anne and
Lucy stood politely next to me. Mary wasn't afraid of loosing her job
or being sent to the kitchen. She never took anything seriously. Lucy
values her job too much and Anne always has to be the mature one.
But Mary cares too much about me to care about the consequences
of being informal.

"I don't know how I'm supposed to take this. Who am I and what
does this all mean?"

"You're Princess America!" Lucy spoke out. "Fiery and unstoppable."

Anne nodded. "It doesn't matter where you come from or we're
supposed to come from. You know who you are."

"But this will change everything. It doesn't matter how I feel. This is
bigger than me. This is about the real heir. This is about the royal
bloodline. There are logistics and laws. It doesn't matter who I am if
I'm not a Schreave."

"Singer," Mary said.

"What?" I asked.

"Singer. That's their last name." Anne filled in. "They're a family
of fives who live in a small town in Carolina. The mothers name is

Magda Singer and she is a musician. The fathers name is Shalom and he is an artist. There are 5 children. 3 elder and 2 younger. Their names are Kenna, Kota, Maxon, May, and Gerad. Maxon is....."

She trailed off. I nodded. He is supposed to be me.

"Fives?" I asked.

Anne nodded.

It was oddly fitting. I play piano, violin, and countless other instruments. It's one of the hobbies that I took up during my endless loneliness. Entertainers. Fives are entertainers. I would fit in perfectly.

"We did our research like you asked," Lucy said. "We printed out everything we could find on them and left it in your room."

"Oh," I mumbled. Suddenly I was numb again.

"Did Miss Silvia teach you nothing," Anne reprimanded suddenly. "You can feel as many things as you want but you do not show it. Lift up your chin, cross your ankles, and put on a smile. Wear a brave face. You're world can not end in less you let it."

I took a deep breathe and crossed my ankles. I straightened my back, lifted my ankles, and smiled.

"I am a princess," I said. "Blood or not."

Mary smiled. "And everyone knows it."

"King!" Lucy squeaked. My eyes flicked to the door and I could see my parents and the doctor approaching through the glass. Mary scrambled off the table and back into line and Anne checked that they were fine. When my parents entered the room, we were the picture of perfection. Anne, Mary, and Lucy were bent in identical curtsies and I wore my best dazzling smile.

My mom rushed to my side. "Baby, how are you?"

"I'm okay Mom," I assured her.

"Ladies, you are excused," My father said to my maids.

"I want my friends here, Father," I cut in.

"They are staff America. They have no business here."

"I have no business here either," I muttered. "That's what this blood test is going to tell us. That I don't belong and that you should get rid of me."

My mother gasped. "Please, not now you two. Ladies, I world rather not cause a fight. America will see you afterwards."

"Of course, your majesty," They chorused. They dropped into curtsies again and shuffled out of the room.

My mother's hands were on me, first rubbing my arms and then holding my face. "We are not getting rid of you."

Her voice showed her disgust at my choice of words. They disgusted me too. The truth is disgusting.

"We don't even know what this is America. These are precautions. This is probably some fluke in the blood testing system and we are being worried for nothing."

"A fluke that occurred 10 times?" I asked in disbelief

"Yes," She said firmly, finality dropping from her lips. She was in denial, one of the 5 stages of grief. She was grieving me when I was not lost. Or maybe I was.

I don't know anymore.

"Wouldn't it explain a lot?"

My mother's face twisted in confusion but I could see it all over my fathers face. This made sense to him. This was the reason why he never liked me. This is the reason that he has treated me the way that he always has. It's my fault. It's my fault that he is a horrid father. Mine, never his.

"I don't understand," Mother replied.

"Your skin verses mine," I prompted, placing my pale hand over her tanned one. "My untraceable red hair." I could see the orange and red reflected back at me through the gleam of her eyes. "The Schreave's haven't had blue eyes for generations." Her brown pupils met my blue ones. "I am inches shorter than the rest of our family. My personality is not like either of yours. I am an anomaly and I always have been. Well the case is closed because now the mystery is solved, no blood test necessary. I am not your—."

"Stop," She spit, struggling to take deep breathes. "You are my child. You are. I would know my own child. You are mine. Mine."

I wrapped my arms around her, already regretting having said those things. She didn't deserve to hear that. She is struggling with this as much as I am.

"I'm sorry," I murmured. "Let's just hear what they have to say."

"You're mine," She mumbled. She kept on mumbling it.

"Of course, I'm yours. I am your daughter no matter what my blood type is. This means nothing," I assured her.

I squeezed her tighter and my eyes met my fathers over her shoulder. Who knew that the one thing he and I would ever agree on is that this most definitely did not mean nothing.

"Okay," Mother said, patting away nonexistent imperfections caused by her break down. She didn't cry though. She rarely ever cries if she is not alone, but Father and I have both heard sobs through the doors of her room during particularly bad bouts of sickness. That's why I assure her this will all be okay. Because I can't worry about her breakdowns during my own.

"This is usually quite simple, Princess America," Dr. Ashylar addressed me. "You prick your finger and wipe the blood on this pad, and then the computer analyzes it. It is so simple that you wouldn't even need me. But because we think there may be a malfunction in those systems we're going to do a bit more advanced approach."

He crossed over to my left side and showed me the machine that was there. He then proceeds to explain it to me. It looked like any IV or tube that you might use except for two differences. The IV was a loop and after the blood was extracted, it was then quickly injected back inside. Also there was a little piece of technology inside the wire that the blood passed through and that is what analyzed it. It didn't look like more than a wire with a little gadget on it but apparently it was very state of the art. Whatever this machine told us, was guaranteed to be true.

"So after a minute," Dr. Ashylar continued. "The results will load onto this screen as a color." He handed me a sheet with colors on it. "These colors represent the different blood types. Purple represents the Illean bloodline. If it doesn't show purple than..."

He trailed off. I nodded. Not purple, not royal.

"Are you ready?" He asked.

I nodded. My mother looked close to tears and I needed something to distract her.

"Can we, uh....talk about what happens if this shows what we think it might?"

My Father and Mother shared a look.

My father spoke up. "I would want to meet...."

"You're real child," I supplied.

"America!" My mom reprimanded.

Dr. Ashylar began prepping my arm.

"Of course not," My father said. I didn't believe it. "America will always be my little girl, but you can't tell me your not slightly interested in meeting him."

I knew exactly why he was interested. Maybe this boy was a suitable replacement for me. Maybe he would listen more than I was. I had news for my father. I was bred to be a Princess and this is how I turned out. There is no one better than me.

"I care more for America's emotions than whoever this other child is," Mother argued.

I felt the needle enter my arm. I didn't look though, keeping my eyes trained on my parents.

"You should meet him," I said emotionlessly. Stone. I feel nothing. I show nothing.

"America...."

"I want you to meet him," I amended. "I want to meet them."

I didn't. I wanted everything to go back to the way it was.

I could feel the wire pull against my skin.

"I'm finished," Dr. Ashylar whispered. "It'll take a minute."

"You don't have to do this America," My mother reasoned. "We can forget about this..."

"Amberley, we can not. There are laws and rules," My dad tried to argue.

"There are things that are more important than laws and rules," My mom yelled.

I could see it all happening. I could see everything ripping apart. This was already causing arguments between my parents. My dad was a piece of work but he loved my mother. They never argued. But the threads of this perfect tv family were unraveling. It's as if we were all underwater. No, it was as if they were underwater. They were fish in a tank. I was watching from the outside as they fell apart. And yet somehow I was the one who was drowning.

I could see the look in my mother's eyes as she saw the screen behind me before I did. I saw the look in my Fathers eyes too. I slowly turned around, my eyes adjusting to the screen, trying to make sense of what it said. I wanted to look at the sheet so that I could see what the colors meant, but I didn't need to.

The only thing that mattered was the purple. Not purple, not royal. And there was no purple in my blood.

I walked out of the room.

And so again I ask myself, how do you comprehend something like this?

CHAPTER 4

M^{axon}

Sometimes you wake up in the morning and you just smile. You know it's going to be a good day. All the colors seems to be a bit more vivid. The sun is shining a little bit brighter. Every scent is stronger than usual and every sound is happier than normal. Everything is just right, so you smile. You know today was is going to be a good day.

Somedays you wake up and the world kinda just sucks. You don't feel like getting out of bed. Your breakfast doesn't taste as good as usual. You can't figure out what to wear and everything seems too bright, too happy. Today will not be a good day.

For me, I didn't wake up with the day feeling like much of anything. I had no trouble getting out of bed but it wasn't like I was racing off to school. The sun was shining just the normal amount. My breakfast tasted like it always did. The colors were the same shade they always have been. It wasn't a good morning, nor was it a bad morning. It was just....a morning.

School went fine. May and I walked to school, making small talk and messing around as usual. And when we got there, she went off to do whatever freshman's do and I met up with Aspen to walk to first period. All my classes went off as usual. I had homework, but not too much homework. I got to all my classes on time and completed all my class work in an orderly manner. Aspen and I only talked a little bit and I only got the side eye from a teacher once. Nothing phenomenal happened but the day was average.

May and I walked home from school and each went are separate ways when we got there. I walked the neighborhood in search of something interesting to photograph and she went into the garage to paint with my dad. Everything was going as it always did.

It wasn't until we sat down for dinner, that my day began to curve in one direction, good or bad.

"Dinner!" My mom called, her voice drifting through the open kitchen window to where I was outside in the backyard. I squinted my eye and zoomed in on my camera, a fraction of an inch. Get the angle just right and......snap! Perfect!

My mom stuck her head out the window. "Maxon! Dinner is ready."

"I'm coming, mom," I replied, heading inside the house. I set my camera on the console table and looked around the kitchen. Mom was reaching up on her tippy toes to get the coffee cups off the top shelf of the cabinets and my family members were still no where to be seen, each slowly making their way from their respective hiding places. I reached around her and plucked a few cups off the top shelf, and she slid aside so I could grab the rest. I looked over at the stove and saw a boiling pot of soup which made sense. We used coffee cups for bowls because it was cheaper than buying a set of both, and as a working mother of 5, Magda Singer could not live without coffee. Neither could May, when my mom would actually let her drink some.

"Thank you, honey," My mom smiled and began ladling soup into a coffee mug. She handed it to me but it was quickly snatched out of my hands by May, who had snuck up behind me.

"May," My mom warned.

May shrugged. "He can wait for the next cup. Oh and dad said he will be inside in a minute. He's finished up a section of his painting."

Mom nodded, used to this, and handed me another coffee mug full of soup. I grabbed a spoon out of the drawer and headed for the table, sitting next to May who had just burnt her mouth on a spoonful of not fully cooled soup. I blew on my spoonful a few times and ate it smugly. She just rolled her eyes.

Mom ladled up another two mugs of soup before she realized that she was missing a child.

"Where is Gerad?" Mom asked, her hip jutting out to the side.

May and I shared a look and we were about to answer when something thudded against the house. My moms eyes turned dark and she stormed to the front door, throwing it open.

"Gerad Singer, you better get your butt inside and eat dinner or I will pop that soccer ball with a paint brush," Mom yelled, sticking her head out the door.

May giggled and I stifled a laugh with a bite of my soup, afraid that my mom might hear. A moment later, Gerad came sulking through the door. It's not that my mom didn't want Gerad to have fun and be a little boy. It's just that all Gerad ever wants to do is play soccer and and mess with bugs. I think my mom just worries about him not being able to find something in our caste range that he is good at. Trying to caste climb never really works out and we wouldn't want him to go down a caste either.

"Oooo soup," Gerad exclaimed, already forgetting about being scolded. He grabbed his cup off the counter and proceeded to drink it like it was water. My mom rounded around the counter to grab her mug of soup, seeing what she would presume a horrid sight, and slapped Gerad upside the head. He yelped and made a pouty face, a soup mustache lining his upper lip.

"Grab a spoon and eat at the dinner table, young man," My mom scolded, directing him in the direction of the table. He wandered over to the table, forgetting a spoon and my mom followed after him with her dinner and two spoons.

"Shalom!" My mother bellowed and the door to the garage flew open a moment later.

"Sorry Maggie," My dad said guiltily. He entered the kitchen, rubbing his hands together which were coated in bright colors of paint. My mom gave a pointed look towards the sink and my dad quickly washed the paint off his hands before joining us at the dinner table.

"Is this tomato?" My dad asked, rubbing his together hands in excitement.

"Yes," My mom confirmed. "From the can but I added our own spices so it should be good."

"Delicious," May and I confirmed because that was the only answer when Mom was cooking. My dad mumbled his agreement, his mouth full of soup with another spoonful on the way.

My mom smiled proudly. "Thank you. How was school?"

"Good," We said simultaneously.

My mom stared at us, waiting for more. "And..."

"It was good," We repeated.

Agitation shot across my moms face.

"My day at school was great!" Gerad said, shooting off into what would be a long story. "I played soccer with my friends and then I......."

May and I smiled at each other. Our plan never failed.

There was a knock at the door.

"I'll get it!" May yelled, popping out of her chair and running for the door. She pulled it open without checking for who it was. I could see from where I sat that it was a women. She had brown hair that was pulled back in a tight bun and her face was set in a stoic manner. She wore a work skirt and a blouse that were made of nicer fabrics than I'd ever seen around here in Carolina. She wore heels too and held a clipboard and files in her hands. She had to be a 3, most likely a 2.

My mom immediately took notice of this too and rushed over to the door.

"Hello, I'm Magda," My mom cut in, pushing May aside.

"Silvia," The women said, her eyes scanning the files she held. "Is this the Singer Residence?"

"Yes it is," My mother said, her eyes scanning the women judgmentally.

"May I come inside?" Silvia asked.

"We're is the middle of eating dinner..." My mom tried to say.

"Magda? Is it?" Silvia cut in. My mother nodded. "I'm a representative of the palace."

Mays ears practically perked up and my mother's mouth dropped open.

"Uh, come inside."

The women stepped into the house, her heel making a deafening click against the tile. she approached the table, her eyes scanning the room. There were things that she lingered on. May, moms violin.... me.

"Hello. My name is Silvia and I am an advisor at the Illean Palace."

"The palace?" My dad repeated.

My mom returned to the table and Silvia pulled out a chair, sitting down with us.

"I'm not sure that everyone in your family should be present for this meeting. It may be sensitive to younger ears."

My mom nodded. "May and Gerad, maybe it would be best if you ate the rest of your dinners in your room."

Gerad was up and out of his seat, not needing and excuse to eat in in his room nor did he care much about the palace. He wasn't old enough yet to understand the weight that having a palace executive over at the house could hold. Good or bad.

My mom looked over at May.

"I am 14! I'm old enough to be here," May said firmly.

My mom let it go. "I don't understand....what does the palace need with us?" My mom asked.

"There has been a recent development," She said slowly. "And it concerns your family." Her eyes flicked to me and then back forward. "Your son recently took a blood test in his science class."

This has to do with me? How could that stupid blood test have anything to do with the palace.

I realized that they were waiting for me to confirm. I cleared my throat. "Uh...yes."

The women sighed as if this wasn't what she wanted to hear. She the pulled out 4 forms from her folder.

"These are the results from the blood test that you took," Silvia began, pointing to one of the forms. This just worsened my confusion. Why does she have that? Why does the palace have that? She pointed to the form next to it. "These are the results from a blood test taken by Princess America."

I looked at the papers calculatingly as did the rest of my family. We were all trying to piece together what these two blood tests had to do with each other but each of us fell short. None of this made sense. By the look on Silvia's face, she also wanted us to figure it out on our own. Probably so she didn't have to say it.

She pushed the paper with my name on it forward. "Your sons blood report shows that he has 50% Illean blood."

I watched the blood drain from my moms face slowly and a look of disbelief cross over my Dads, but I was still confused. What was she trying to say?

"I'm going to repeat myself so that I make myself 100% clear."

Silvia looked at each of us in the eyes.

"Maxon is not your son. Maxon is the true Prince of Illea."

~oOo~

Family's are supposed to be the ones who are always there for you. No matter what is going on in your life, your family will be there for you and help you through it. Through bad break ups and broken arms, they are there. They're your built in best friends and they are bound to you through blood.

I'm not sure that my family can help me through this though because they aren't by family, at least not biologically.

I...am a Prince. The words feel fuzzy in my mind and I mull them over. What does that even mean? I was supposed to grow up in a palace and wear a crown. I was supposed to rule Illea with a Queen by my side. How does any of that translate into who I am now? What does any of this mean?

Silvia probably could answer these questions, but she left. She said that we should take the night to think about this as a family and that she would return in the morning. As soon as she left, I had sat on the couch and stared at the wall. May had sat down and wrapped her arms around me and squeezed. She's been there since. It's only been a few moments but it seems like a lifetime. My parents were standing off to the side and talking quietly about what to do next. I don't know what to do next. Everything I know kinda just went down the drain.

"Maybe this is some kind of mix up? That blood sample could be someone else's," My mom tried to reason. "He is our son. I know he is."

My dad hugged my mom, stroking her hair. "Shhhh Magda. It'll be okay."

"I'm just worried. What if it's real?"

Was my mom actually worried? Is this really happening? Could I actually be a Schreave?

"Why are we doubting it?" May whispered.

My moms blue eyes pierced into May. "What?"

"I said," May spoke louder this time. "Why are we doubting? You can be in denial or whatever, but look at the facts." May let go of me and stood up fiercely. She crossed around the couch and over to the table, grabbing the papers that Silvia left their. "His name is on the paper with the blood test that should belong to Princess America, but it doesn't! Mix ups like that don't just happen. And if it did happen then the palace would of caught the mistake before the news made its way to us. This is real. And as much it's sucks, that's the truth."

My mom sniffled and hid her face in my dads shoulder as these words pelted her.

May stormed down the hall and then returned to the family room with a magazine in her hand. She waved it fiercely in the air. It was a magazine with an image of Princess America in an elaborate gown on the front.

"Look at her!" May shook the magazine, the sound of pages ruffling filling the room. "She has red hair, blue eyes, and pale skin. You can't deny that she is your daughter because she looks just like us." May took a calming breath and sat down on the couch. She grabbed my hand. "Maxon is my big brother and I don't want it to be true that he is biologically otherwise.....but we can't just sit here and convince ourselves that it isn't true. Cause it is." May took a huge racking breath that sounded so heartbroken and out of place from her mouth. "This is real."

My mom raised her chin as if she rose above this than it would all fade away. She sighed and then wiped the tears from her eyes, stepping away from my dad. "What are we going to do?"

No one said anything.

"Maxon, what do you want to do?" My mom elaborated.

"I don't know," I spoke, my voice sounding foreign. "How do we even look at this? Did you gain a son or loose a daughter?"

"Maxon—."

"No. You have a child that isn't me, mom. She plays music like you. She looks like May. Your blood runs through her veins and she had lived her whole life without you. I was supposed to be a Prince. I'm a freakin Schreave."

My mom choked on a sob.

"A Prince," I repeated. "A Schreave."

"You are a Singer," My dad said. "Blood or not."

"But so is she," I argued, running a hand through my hair. I steadied myself. "Look—I'm.........I'm just gonna go to my room. You should call Kenna. She'll want to know."

My mom nodded and walked slowly over to phone on the wall. She picked up the phone to dial Kenna's house but the phone began to ring. Mom pressed the speaker button as if she was too exhausted to even hold the phone to her ear.

"Magda Singer," She murmured in greeting, leaning against the wall.

"Hello," A melodic voice emitted from the speakers. The voice was familiar. "This is Queen Amberley."

My mom straightened up immediately as if the Queen was here in the room with us. The queen. My....mother.

"Your Majesty," She stuttered. May rushed over to my moms side, jumping up and down.

"Hello," Another voice said. King Clarkson.

Another voice responded too, smooth like velvet and musical like it was singing a song. "Good Evening."

"I am here with King Clarkson and Princess America," The queen said. "We see it only fit that we talk to you."

"Ohmigod, hi," May blurted, she covered her mouth and bounced on the balls of her feet nervously.

"That is my daughter," My mother apologized. "I apologize for her behavior."

"It is alright," King Clarkson said. "Would your...son happen to be around?"

"Maxon," My mother called. "Come over here."

I did as I was asked.

"Maxon?" Queen Amberley repeated.

"That is his name," My mother confirmed. "Queen Amberley, King Clarkson.....if you don't mind me asking, what is going on? We don't understand. Is it true?"

"We would never bother you with something as serious as this if it weren't true. I'm not sure how it happened but it appears that are children have been...switched."

Switched. A word so plain and simple that it almost didn't seem fitting for this situation. How could two people just be mixed up. How can you mixed up the royal heir of Illea with someone else. Oh god. Im supposed to be the royal heir of Illea and I was switched with Princess America. I suppose she was just America then or not even that. Just a nameless baby who counted on other people and those people failed her.

I swear my mom almost fainted but luckily my dad appeared at her side to support her.

"We took test after test and there is no denying it," Queen Amberley added.

"So Princess America is......our daughter?" My dad asked slowly. Hearing it put so plainly was like a slap to the face.

There was a long sigh on the other end of the line. "Biologically, yes."

"Oh my god," May whispered. May threaded her fingers through mine and rested her head on my shoulder. "Maxon...."

I wrapped an arm around her shoulder and pulled her close to me.

"He's my big brother," May said. I don't think she meant to say it to all of us but she did. "He's our family."

"Of course," Queen Amberley said quickly. "We would never want to take Maxon from you or give Amy—Princess America to you. But we are at least interested in meeting Maxon and we would want you to be able to meet America. We would like to invite you to the palace."

May's mouth dropped open. The palace, that world, was her dream. It was unfortunate that it had to occur under these circumstances.

My mom and dad shared a look.

"You said Maxon is there with you?" Princess America said suddenly. It was the first time she had said anything since the introductions.

I looked at the phone and spoke for my first time. "I am."

"Do you despise how they talk about us as if we are not here?" She asked.

I chuckled lightly. "It is pretty annoying."

It was kind of reassuring to talk to her. I'm sure this was as world destroying for my whole family as it was for me, but I don't think they understand what it likes to learn that you are an imposter in your own life. But she understood. She is an imposter in her own life too and on such a bigger scale. I wonder which one of us was lucky to have been switched. Is it easier to be a five or a one?

She also had a voice that made me want to talk to her. The way she spoke was just slightly more proper than the rest of us and her words were ordered a little bit differently. Her vowels were pronounced a small degree rounder and she used full words instead of combining them. It intrigued me. She was saying normal things but how she as saying was intriguing.

"I am sorry to rush you but things here at the palace are always on a time crunch," King Clarkson said. "Will you be joining us at the palace?"

"We will be," May said quickly. She turned her head to my mom. "Right?"

Mom glanced over to the couch where the magazine still lay with Princess America's smiling face staring at us. When that picture was taken, she was just a Princess. What is she now?

"Of course," My mom said. "Of course."

"Lovely. We will have Silvia arrange the rest of the details but we hope you can fly back with her. We look forward to meeting you all."

The line died out without a goodbye. There was no time for a goodbye when you're a royal I guess.

I met eyes with May and then my parents.

"Oh Maxon..." My mom choked. She rushed forward and gathered me in her arms. It wasn't long before May and my father joined the hug too.

And this was it. Whether I was meant to be some sort of Prince or not. Whether I lost a kingdom or a few family members. This was my family. These were the people that I grew up and that shaped my personality into who I am today. I had no idea where this news was going to take my life but I did know one thing.

This was my family.

These are my people.

CHAPTER 5

America

When I was born and as I grew up, there were lots of rumors. Many people thought that my father had an affair and that I was another women's child. Others thought that my mother was the one who had an affair. It was a small part of the population that came up with these conspiracies. I had bright red hair that couldn't be traced back to any of my relatives. My mother was Hispanic and had olive skin, and yet my skin was pale as snow. My eyes were blue, but both my parents have chocolate eyes. None of it made sense. I was the Princess though. And you didn't question royalty.

None of them were right. Neither my mother nor my father had an affair. As it turns out, my mother and my father are not actually mine. I belong to another family. I am not a princess. I was switched with another child by accident on the day of my birth.

I bet none of the conspiracy theorists came up with that.

How does something like that even happen? You would presume that if the heir of Illea was born at the hospital you worked at, than you would want to take extra care to not mix them up with another child. Genuinely, I think you wouldn't want to mix up any persons child! Are there not regulations and systems in place so such a thing wouldn't occur?

"America," Amara spoke, interrupting my thoughts. "Amy, get your head out of the clouds."

I shook my thoughts away. "My apologies."

She rolled her eyes. "Your tea is cold and you've been staring at that tree for like 5 minutes." Amara absentmindedly pulled out a mirror and checked her makeup as she talked. "The gardens are beautiful, but that tree is not that interesting." She closes her compact mirror with a satisfying click and gave me a level look. "What's on your mind?"

I breathed in deeply and then sighed. "This dress feels like it's chocking me and my tea is cold."

"A maid brought us a warm pot of tea a moment ago and your dress is always too tight. Tell me something new."

"I'm fine, Amara."

"You're always fine." The way she said fine, like the word didn't even belong in her mouth, made me cringe. "Because that's all you think you're allowed to be. Fine. Heavens forbid you feel angry or sad. But you can't keep all those big emotions locked in that pretty head of yours. Or else I'm going to be cleaning up your broken pieces and you know how I loathe cleaning."

She grabbed my hand, squeezing it tightly. Her voice was lower when she spoke next and it didn't have as much edge.

"Amy, you know I love you. I just want you to be okay. This is not something that you can just be fine after. You must have so many questions and so many thoughts and I need you to know that you can say them to me."

"Thank you Amara, but at this moment in time...I really am fine. It weirdly makes sense."

She raised her eyebrow. "Girl, you're insane."

"I'm serious! I've never been good at being a princess so it makes sense that I was never supposed to be. Think about it, I'm rash and impulsive. I never stop talking and when I am talking I'm saying the wrong things. I'm not bred to be a Princess. I'm a nobody!"

"Now you even sound crazy," She drawled. "America, who cares if the advisors aren't you're biggest fans. This country loves you. You are literally Illea's sweetheart. You represent them and they know that. You may not be a Royal by blood or whatever, but you are a Princess. This is your country."

Her words soaked into me. This is my country. I am it's Princess and I will be it's queen. The only question is where do my mom and dad and this new family fall into that equation.

I grabbed my tea cup and raised it to my lips, sipping quietly. "Well cheers to that."

She clinked her cup against mine. "Are you ready to meet them?"

"God no. They'll give me one of two looks. One, the sad look. The look that's all 'your my daughter and we're not meeting till now and it's so sad'. Or they'll give me number two. The 'who are you because you're certainly not my daughter' look."

Amara shrugged. "Which one is better?"

"I don't even know what my parents expect to come from this," I said instead of answering this. "We are definitely not going to become some big happy messed up family. Nothing can change. The people can never know that this happened so I'll continue as Princess and live my life, and they'll return to Carolina in live there's."

"They're giving you a chance to meet you're family in case you do want to," Amara reasoned.

"They're my family."

"Your mom and dad want you to be happy. They are opening all doors so that you can be."

I'm sure that's what my Mom was doing but I couldn't explain to Amara why my dad was doing this. For him, this was about more than giving me what I wanted. This was about him being hopeful that maybe he could find a way to replace me with his real child.

I nodded. "You're right," I lied. "They're looking out for me."

Amara's eyes stared through me as if she knew there was something I wasn't saying. Amara and I have alway been open to one another, but we understand when there is something the other isn't saying. Amara never talks about the future and I know not to ask. I never talk about my father. I don't know if she knows not to ask but I'm very good at avoiding her questions. I came to her one time after my father yelled at me but no one else knows my father like I do and she didn't understand. So now I just tell her that everything is fine.

He's a great King.

He just wants what's best for me.

He's a busy man.

He's looking out for me.

She doesn't ask. I wonder what life I would have lived with my birth father. Would I have a good relationship with him? Or maybe I'm just paternally unloveable.

"America!"

I looked over at Amara and she shook her head, her eyes flicking towards the palace. My mom was running, well walking swiftly, down the front steps of the palace. Even when she was in a rush she looked gorgeous. She carried the skirts of her gown in one hand and they swished along her legs as she descended the stairs. I'd seen her walking towards me and down these steps many times. I was always in the gardens and she always had to come find me. It still struck me each time I saw my mother. She is so gorgeous and I don't know how anyone has ever believed I'm her daughter. Not that I'm not pretty. My hair and face and body have been sculpted to perfection for years. But we were beautiful in two totally different ways.

"America!" My mother called again, approaching our table in the gardens.

"Mom," I greeted, smiling at her.

"You need to get ready," She said.

I laughed. "I am ready mom. Dress, check. Tiara, check. Makeup, check."

"You're wearing a day dress, America. And normally that's fine but we are having guests. Important guests."

"Mother, they are fives. They are not going to know the difference between my day dress and my evening gown."

"We have appearances to uphold. Don't you wanna look you're best when we meet them?" She asked.

"Why?"

She was taken aback. "Excuse me?"

"Why are we doing this? I'm gonna meet them and then I'll spend a day with them. It will be super awkward and they'll realize that my blood doesn't matter because I'm not their daughter. They'll go home and everything will go back to normal."

My moms face sunk. She pursed her lips. "Amara, would you mind stepping away?"

"Of course not, your majesty," Amara said quickly and basically ran from the table.

My mom grabbed my hand. "America, a family is not something that you can just wash away."

"They're not my family!" I said. "You're my family! And if you want, you can have a relationship with Maxon. He's your son and I understand. But I don't know them. One visit will not make up for 17 years of my life."

I couldn't explain to you why I wasn't excited. I was gaining all these people into my life but it doesn't even matter. I just have a bad feeling in my bones about this.

My mom sighed. She pulled me closer and into her arms. She did this thing that she had been doing my whole life where she put her chin on top of my head and tucks my hair behind my ears. Sometimes it was the only thing that could help me remember that she wasn't just a queen, but my mom. But when she pulled me into her arms, like now, and placed her chin on my head......it's all okay.

"You're my little girl, Amy. Whether or not I birthed you, you are still the child they put in my arms and I have never let go since, and I never will. I raised you. I taught you to talk and I taught you to walk. I watched you grow up and become a wonderful young women and an amazing Princess. These people can come into our lives and they may or may not stay in them. But I am your family and you are mine."

I threw my arms around her and she held me, never letting go.

"Now," She said, pulling away. "Go change."

I shook my head and sighed in exaggeration. She rolled her eyes at me and ushered me inside.

~oOo~

My maids were all lounging around my room as I basically got myself ready. There wasn't much that I couldn't do myself even though they usually do it for me. But after they did more gossiping than actually doing anything, I started getting myself ready. Now they were just laying around in the one place where they can be informal. They've seen me at my worst and they are so much more than my maids now.

"Do you think they'll have red hair?" Mary asked, speaking more to Anne and Lucy than to me. She was laying on her stomach across my large bed and flipping through one of my magazines.

"Don't you think they would have suspected something if they had the same hair as America?" Lucy argued, sitting on the edge of the bed politely. She was examining two shades of neutral pink nail polish and attempting to decide which one to paint my nails later on tonight.

Anne scoffed from her place in one of my armchairs. She was sewing me a new dress for some event I apparently have coming up. "Do you think they ever would have even considered their son wasn't their own? They never would have thought twice."

"Do you think he looks like my parents?" I pitched in. I hooked a pair of earrings through my ears and immediately took them out. I can't wear rubies with my hair. I switched them out for diamonds that were custom made to be the same shade of blue as my eyes.

"Do you think he's hot?" Mary countered.

"That's a good question," Lucy agreed. "Do we have any photographs?"

"What color is my dress?" I asked, interrupting this casual conversation about something that was not at all casual and probably confidential.

"Blue. It's in the closet," Anne said. She picked up the papers they'd printed out on the Singers off of my piano where I left them. "Hm mmm....no photos on here."

Lucy and Mary mumbled there opinion on this as I walked into the closet to get my dress.

"Can one of you help me into my dress instead of a debating the hotness of Maxon?" I called.

"Maxon is a hot name," Mary said instead of getting up. I shook my head at her. Lucy hopped off the bed and met me at the door to the closet.

"Names can hold beauty?" I asked, shedding my robe as Lucy helped me step into my dress.

"Of course," Mary replied. "Everyone knows that someone with a name like Maxon is much cuter than someone with a name like... Harold. Simple facts."

"Well of course," I said sarcastically, rolling my eyes. "So there's.....4 siblings."

"2 younger and 2 older," Anne read off the paper.

"My god," I sighed.

"You've always wanted siblings," Lucy said quietly, beginning to tie the back of my dress.

"And I've always had them and I didn't even know," I whispered. "Only two of them are coming to the palace today. The older siblings names are Kenna and Kota."

"Kota Singer?" Anne asked, mulling this over. "I've heard of him. He's a five but one of his sculptures sold for a large sum of money a few years back. I'm pretty sure that the palace is the one who bought it."

I recognized the name slightly. If I'm correct, I picked out the sculpture.

"I get the feeling that he's not as close with the rest of the family. They haven't mentioned him at all," I said.

"All family's have their issues," Anne commented.

"Done," Lucy announced, stepping back. I had been so busy talking that I hadn't even noticed her squeezing me into the tiny dress. I picked up my tiara and handed it to her. She placed it carefully on my head and nestled it into my hair. I smiled and whispered my thanks before sitting at the vanity so she could do my makeup.

"You look like you're going to a ball," Mary said.

"I know! This dress is so overtop and these are fives not the royals of Italy!"

"Nicoletta would hate that dress," Lucy observed.

I nodded my agreement.

"I wonder what you would have been like as a five," Mary said, appearing behind me with the necklace that matched my earrings. She placed it against my chest and clasped it.

"I would be a musician," I decided. "I play music now so I would most likely do the same in that life."

"I couldn't imagine not knowing you," Lucy sighed.

"We would meet each other, I'm sure of it. No one else could handle you three as their maids. They might expect you to actually work," I laughed.

Mary swatted at my arm. "We work! We are just comfortable."

I shook my head. Lucy held my head still and tsked me for moving it. She then appeared in front of me and begin to line my lips with light pink. My feet were suddenly grabbed and I peeked down to see Anne slipping heels onto my feet. I was going to make a witty sarcastic comment but Lucy was applying lipstick and I've learned from experience that lipstick stains.

"I think your done Miss," Lucy said.

I smiled and stood up, turning around gracefully so I could see myself in the mirror. I always checked even though I always looked similar. It was great work

"I look gorgeous," I said thankfully. "Beautiful work as always."

Lucy clasped her hands together and gave me a little bow. Anne repeated the action but Mary, never one for protocol, scampered over to the door and pulled it open for me.

"You have to tell us everything when you get back," Mary said enthusiastically. I scooped up the skirts of my dress and followed her to the door.

"Who else would I tell?" I agreed. "We will get Amara up here and we can make a party out of my problems."

"Sounds like a plan," Mary laughed ignoring my sarcasm. "Have a good evening! Don't be rude to them and try to smile a little!"

She shut the door behind her and I shook my head at her antics. If it weren't for me, Mary would have been fired multiple times for her complete lack of protocol and her informal ways.

"Good day, Princess," The guard on this floors rounds greeted me as I approached him.

"Hello to you too Officer Tanner. I hope your day is treating you well," I replied. He bowed deeply as I passed. But than he became less formal. "Did you hear about the draft?"

"A whole new round of officers," I nodded. "I'm sure you'll show them the ropes."

He grinned. " I like to watch them flounder a bit before I teach them to swim."

I laughed lightly. "Go easy on them. Good day Officer."

I continued on down the hallway, nodding at guards and maids as I passed. The Princess sweet resides on the more remote third floor where only royals and special individuals have access to. I turned around the corner that opened towards the staircase that led to the second floor. I descended them and continued through the corridors that led to the grand staircase that opened straight into the foyer. My parents would be waiting at the staircase and we would descend them as one. The singers would be waiting in the foyer as is customary. The royal family should always be the last to enter the room. We would make awkward introductions and have them have dinner together before eventually deciding that it would be best if we all just returned to our respective lives without one another, and maybe send a holiday card each year.

I reached the landing and stared down the smooth marble stairs to the foyer below. The Singers were down there but they were out of my view. In a matter of minutes we would all be standing there. How do you greet your long lost family? Hey so we're related but I'm actually the Princess of Illea and my life is pretty complicated so maybe we just part ways? Yeah. That would go off swell.

"Amy," My moms voice called from behind me. She and my father approached from down the opposite hallway, her arm looped around his. He was wearing a nicer suit with a few of his medals pinned to it. My mom was wearing a dress similar to mine and her tiara. They looked like a picturesque, perfect couple.

"Mother, Father," I greeted.

"Are you ready?" My mother asked, slipping away from my father. She grabbed my hand.

I tentatively smiled and nodded my head, afraid that if I spoke than my words might contradict my actions.

She squeezed my hand and placed a motherly kiss on my forehead before returning to my father.

My father offered me his other arm and I took it, placing a kiss on his cheek. We descended the stairs in perfect time, our feet were the only thing you could hear as they tapped against the marble in synchronization. I closed my eyes and listened. It was this sound that I always thought about when I thought about myself as a princess. The noise that my heel makes when it connects with marble. The way it echoes off the silent palace walls and alerts everyone of my presence. The sound is important.

The sound makes me important.

I keep my eyes closed for a moment longer. I know that when I open them I will see my family. I wish a for a second that they would go away and that I wouldn't have to deal with this. When I open my eyes, this becomes real.

Three.

Two.

One.

Open.

I have been told my whole life that I capture a rooms attention as soon as I enter it. My mom has always told me that my fiery red hair made me unique and that it was my most defining feature. When I entered a room, she said, everyone notices. 'You can't ignore a fire' she would whisper to me comfortingly.

It wasn't until this moment that I fully understood what she meant.

The first thing I saw was fire. Two females with blazing red hair that was unmistakable. One had long wavy hair that was bounced with her every move. Light beamed through the palace glass windows and her hair shimmered into a million shades. The other women was older. Her hair was still strikingly red but it was streaked with brilliant silver strands.

They both looked just like me.

I staggered back, my shoulder clashing with my mothers. I covered my mouth with my hands to keep a sob from escaping. But I couldn't stop the single tear as it rolled down my cheek and splashed onto the marble below.

"Oh my god," I gasped.

I may have been able to deny my relation to this family up to this point.....but not now. Standing here, with these people that looked just like me, there was no denying it.

"America," My mom tried to say, placing a hand on my shoulder.

"I can't," I choked out. I pushed my mothers hand off my shoulder and ran past all these strangers and out to the gardens.

CHAPTER 6

I choked in a large gulp of fresh air as soon as I heard the palace doors boom shut behind me, and sprinted into the opposite side of the garden. I am familiar with both sides of the garden but I never really go here. Maybe it will be more difficult to find me. As soon as I saw a stone bench, surrounded my flowers, I collapsed on to it.

My mind ran wild with thoughts, each trying to be at the center of my head but being fought down by another. I ran through all the people I saw. The women, with silver streaked red hair, must be my mother. And the man who was holding her hand must be my father. And the younger girl......She looked just like me. Her features hadn't matured as much as mine but she looks like I did when I was her age. And then there was the little boy. Who had curly reddish-brown hair and who was looking at me with big eyes. He doesn't know what's really going on.

I don't know what's going on.

Inside I had let a single tear fall, but now they were rolling down my cheeks. I didn't want this to be their first impression of me. I am a mature, graceful, and polite young women. I am a Princess. I don't run away from things that I'm afraid of. But here I am, sitting on a bench, while my complicated mix of families chat inside. My blood family. They had seen and learned everything about me from tv screens and magazine covers. They had watched me grow up from the lens of a camera and I didn't even know they existed.

"I know how you feel," A voice called out.

I looked up to see Maxon. He was standing there awkwardly, looking out of place. He wore street clothes and I wore a gown.

I hastily wiped away the tears from my eyes. "No, you do not."

He hesitantly walked up to me and silently asked to sit down. I nodded my head. At least he was a gentleman. Maybe he was just following protocol. Then again, he doesn't really know the protocol.

"But I do," He said, sitting. "We're in the same boat. You are not the only one who found out your life has been a lie."

"Why did you come out here?" I said indignantly, looking up at him.

"Same reason as you. Both of our parents kind of broke when you ran out the room. It was like my parents already care about you and it made me kind of sick," He admitted.

"Well I don't want them, so there is no need to share," I sniped.

"I have no problem with sharing. I have 4 siblings, I am used to sharing. It's just weird," He sighed.

We sat in silence for a second, just thinking. We were in the same boat but my side is sinking and his is still a float. He can't fully grasp the weight of this conversation because he doesn't understand how matters of the state work. It isn't like we can just announce this to the country and then have him go home. There are things that have to happen. We have to cover this up and then smooth the whole story under the rug. Sure, our families are meeting for personal reasons but the Singers are here for more then just a family reunion. My parents have told me nothing but I know how this works.

Our lives will never be the same.

"So I'm sitting next to the Princess of Illea?" He finally said.

I raised my chin. "Indeed, you are. I'm not sure what that even means anymore."

"Am I supposed to kiss your hand or something?" He asked. I think it was supposed to be a joke but he genuinely sounded like he wasn't sure.

"A bow would suffice because I am your superior. If we were on equal levels than you would kiss my hand," I explained

"Is there a rule book for all of this?" He wondered.

"There is....but I don't recommend reading it. Many of the protocols are outdated and don't even apply anymore."

"What's the protocol for being switched with the princess?"

"Technically I was switched with the prince."

That was the first time I had really said it. He's the prince. At least by blood. But being a royal is about more than that and that was what I had to tell myself. He is a prince by blood but I am the princess of Illea.

"Maybe we should—."

"Can you tell me about them?" I said quickly, interrupting him.

He looked up.

"Please," I reiterated.

"About....my family?"

I took in a shaky breath and nodded. "I'm going to have a lot of trouble opening up to them. It would help if I knew more."

"Well there is my mom."

"Magda," I said

"Yeah. She's an amazing mom. She can be a bit hard on us but she wants what's best. She is like a superhero. She works during the days as a musical entertainer and still always has dinner on the table for us. Then there's my dad. He's an artist. He likes to sit in his studio, well the garage, all day long and just paint. Every memory I have of him, he has paint on his hands."

I smiled.

"Then there is May. She has always had enough energy for all of us. She is sweet, and funny, and boy-crazed, and she is kind of amazing. She does art and she's good, really good. The youngest is Gerad. He doesn't really know what he wants to do, but he likes sports and he's decent at them. He's just a little boy who is trying his best. My two older siblings are Kenna and Kota. I don't see them much, but Kenna visits when she can. She's a four now and is married. She is a really good sister."

"You really love your family," I stated.

"I do."

I stared down at my hands. His words surrounded me. He is so close with these people in a completely different way than I am with my mother. My mom is my everything but we will never have the stories they have.

"Speaking of our families..." I glanced towards the house where I knew they were awkwardly conversing, without the two reasons that they were brought together. I imagine them examining each other and noticing the similarities between their child and the birth parents.

"May has probably already broke some sort of royal protocol. She kinda just does what she wants and doesn't care much for what she should do," He sighed.

"Well if she didn't curtsy than she has that in common with her brother," I laughed. "We should probably go back before the rest of your family breaks protocol."

"Or before dinner gets cold," He smiled before standing up and offering me his hand. I slipped my small hand into his and he helped me to my feet. "How does one escort a princess?"

"You are supposed to offer me your arm," I advised. He did so and I accepted it, wrapping my arm around his and placing my other hand on top.

He looked down at his arm. "And this is just how you travel? Always on the arm of a man?"

"No," I laughed lightly, shaking my head. "I usually travel by myself. But when I am walking with a man, then yes, I do take their arm."

We approached the doors and the guard on duty, Officer Markson, widened his eyes at me.

"Way to make a dramatic exit," Markson teased.

I shrugged. "I am working on adding a bit more flair next time."

"No more flair needed," He said, nodding his head at me and pulling the door open.

I stepped away from Maxon just as I spotted my family and his standing in the foyer. My parents eyes immediately met mine, reflecting different emotions. My mothers conveyed concern and were silently asking if I was alright. My fathers reflected his disapproval of my actions. I bowed my head to them.

"I apologize for my actions," I spoke, though it sounded like more of an announcement than an apology. "I was overwhelmed and it was very improper of me to behave in that way."

The older man, Shalom, my father, smiled at me. "It's okay. We're all overwhelmed in this situation."

"Thank you for understanding," I said.

The silence that ensued was deafening. It was comforting to me because it assured me that this would all go away. We've met now, but we're meant to be with our respective families and we can return to how it was a week ago.

The silence, however, was pierced with a high-pitched shriek.

"Oh my god, It's like I'm meeting my celebrity idol except she's my biological sister. I can't believe this is happening," The younger red-head, May, squealed.

She stepped forward and hugged me. I mean a full-force, death-grip, both arms, squeeze. She stepped back, not even seeming to notice my shocked look.

"Your makeup is so gorgeous, I can't even," She continued. "I love to play with my mom's makeup but she gets mad at me when I do." She unleashed a full force eye roll. "Moms, you know? But the thing is, I can never find a foundation shade in my color. I'm too pale or something which I didn't even know was a thing. How do you get your foundation shade?"

It took me a second to realize that this question wasn't rhetorical and that I should respond. I composed myself. "I have them custom made."

"That's so awesome," She rambled. "I'm an artist and I've tried to explain to my mother that makeup is an art. But no. She says that I'm wasting her makeup."

"You cannot sell your makeup looks, May. Even if it is art," Magda said, coming up behind May and wrapping an arm around her shoulder. "If it doesn't pay the bills than it isn't worth your time."

May sighed and shook her head.

"I'm May by the way," She said, realizing that a name probably should have been given along with the life story. "And this is my brother Gerad, my dad Shalom, and my mom."

"Magda," Her mom added.

I nodded as if I hadn't done background checks prior to meeting them.

"It is very nice to meet you all," I said, addressing them as a whole. The formality of this whole situation did dawn on me, but I preferred it this way. I wanted there to be an obvious separation between I and them. Blood doesn't make them my family. I have a family.

My mother and father glided over to where we stood, with Maxon hesitantly joining his family.

"We would love if you would join us in the dining room for dinner," My mom said. Her hand inconspicuously slipped into mine and squeezed, then disappeared as if it was never really there.

"Of course, Queen Amberley," Magda agreed.

The formal dining room was centered between two ballrooms, parallel to the door to the palace, and at the end of the foyer. This is where we would be eating today. The informal dining room is where my family and I usually eat when all of us are miraculously free at the same time. Which never happens. Usually I take my dinner in my room, where at least I have my maids to keep me company, or sometimes in my study. When we have visitors though, we like to keep up the image that we all eat dinner as a happy family. I am one hundred percent sure The Singers eat together as a family every night, no image to be kept. Two guards stand outside the dining room when the royal family is inside, but I didn't recognize the ones that waited there as we approached. I assume they're part of the draft.

They bowed deeply as we approached before opening the door to the dining room. Behind the scenes, the amazing palace maids had set the table for a feast. My parents and I headed for the front of the table as usual, with my father at the head and my mother and I to his left and right. My father approached my chair and pulled it out for me politely. I smoothed my dress down while I sat and he pushed me in towards the table before doing the same for my mother. While we were doing this, the singers had also sat down though less formally. May had sat next to me and Maxon, across from her

"This china is gorgeous," Magda commented.

"Thank you," My mom replied. "It was a gift from the Italian Royal Family. America is great friends with the Princess."

I confirmed this with a nod of my head. The smaller doors, that were discreetly hidden on the side's of the dining room, swung open and a group of maids entered with our dinner. Heat radiated on to me as a steaming plate was sat in front of me. We went for one course today. Contrary to common belief, we only have multiple courses when there are prestigious guests in attendance. Normally we opt for just one plate of hot, delicious food.

"Wine?" Veda asked, appearing at my side with a bottle of red. I nodded my head and moved my hand out of the way of my glass as she poured a small amount. Veda has worked at the palace for a long time and is fully aware that I don't care for wine and only tolerate it in small amounts.

"Wine?" She asked turning towards May.

Mays eyes lit up. "Yes!"

"No!" Magda interrupted. "She will have water."

Then Mays eyes basically popped out of there sockets as she saw Maxon receive a wine glass of his own.

"Mom," May sputtered.

"May," Magda whispered angrily, but quietly so that she wouldn't alert anyone else at the table. I'm positive I'm the only one who heard this exchange. "Maxon is old enough to make his own decisions. You are 14 and live under my roof, so I'll be deciding for you."

I kept my eyes on my plate, trying to seem like I couldn't hear them. It seemed too intimate. I looked up and locked eyes with Maxon. His eyes flicked to his Mom and sister to my left and then back to me. There was an obvious question there. I inconspicuously lifted my hand towards my wine glass and tapped my nail twice against it. The sound vibrated over to him and after a second his eyes showed understanding. He pointed at himself and then his wine glass and I nodded my confirmation that, yes, he had indeed caused a family argument.

However he was only amused by this.

Cockily, he lifted his wine to his lips and dramatically took a sip. His whole face instantly squeezed together and he stuck his tongue out in disdain. I had to purse my lips together to avoid laughing, but I couldn't help but giggle slightly. I raised my own glass to my lips and took a sip of the disgusting liquid, but my face remained neutral. I even went as far as to smile.

My mother was in conversation with my father and the singers with each other, so nobody else heard when Maxon said. "You actually like this stuff?"

I swirled the wine around in the glass and took another sip. "No."

"Than why do you drink it?" He asked.

I looked from my moms glass of wine to my fathers glass. I frowned but shook it off.

"I meant that it's not my favorite wine," I lied. "I prefer white."

Maxon tilted his head at me but said nothing.

"Hey mom—."

"Your majesties! Your majesties!" The doors to the dining room were thrown open as the two guards, that are supposed to be on duty at the palace door, ran into the room.

My family and I were immediately on our feet.

"Markson?" I asked.

Markson and the other guard slammed the monstrous doors to the dining room shut and to my surprise, bolted and barred them. I understood immediately.

"They're inside the walls, your majesties, but we're holding them back as best we can. We would like to get you to the safe room but we're too close to the door—."

"Understood Markson," My dad cut him off.

I pushed my chair back so quickly that it fell over, and I ran to the closest window to pull down the medal shade. It only took me a moment to get it down but I've never been too good at latching them. I had just gotten it clicked into place when something rammed into the window from outside, sending me screaming back and toppling to the floor.

"Are you alright?" Maxon asked, appearing at my side.

"I am fine," I said, brushing him off. "Don't worry about me. Hurry up and help me get the rest of these."

We headed to the next 2 windows and secured them into place and luckily the rest of the Singers realized what to do. All except May and Gerad. Gerad was following his mom but unable to help and May, well she was still sitting down.

"Get away from the windows once there latched!" My mom remind-ed us. "Crawl under the table!"

I headed for May. She was sitting in her chair still, watching with wide eyes at the commotion as it happened.

"What's going on?" She asked.

"It's an attack," I explained. "But it will be okay. I promise you. We are safe in here."

"But their right out there," She said, her voice quivering.

I placed a calming hand on her shoulder. "It's safer under the table, just in case. Come on."

I tugged on her arm encouragingly as she climbed past her chair and under the table. I made sure she didn't bonk her head or snag her outfit before I climbed under myself and settled down.

"Princess," May whispered, her voice faint amongst the crashes and yelling coming from outside the dining room.

"Just call me America. We are sisters," I took her hand comfortingly.

"Really? I didn't think you thought that because you've been kinda cold. I know your more like proper but there is a difference."

My mouth dropped open. And here I was thinking that I was being secretive about drawing a line.

"May, it's not you—."

There was another loud crash that sounded like it came from right outside. May clung to me suddenly, making a little squeak of fear. It shocked me and for a second I stood frozen, but a second later I wrapped an arm around her. I didn't whisper to her that it would be okay or rub her back or anything, but I held her to me. And I think that was enough.

It wasn't for a while that a guard contacted Markson with the okay for him to open the door.

I slowly slid out from under the table. I attempted to do this gracefully and without any crawling involved, but I'm not sure I was one hundred percent successful. I reached up and griped the edge of the table, pulling myself to a stand. After running my hand across my dress to make sure it was clean and with minimal wrinkles, I tried to quickly adjust my tiara in the reflection of a wine glass. I saw my own eyes stare back at me through a deep red haze.

They were blank.

My father was helping my mother up and the singers were slowly standing up one by one. I helped May to her feet.

"Well this is definitely a welcome to the palace," May murmured as she gathered her footing.

"It's not too common," I said glancing at the metal covered windows. "But it comes with the palace.

"Doesn't that scare you?" She asked.

I didn't know what to say for a second because no one had ever asked me. My whole life, this has always been how it was and no one cared to ask me if I was afraid. I was a little girl once, who was still enthralled by the beauty of being a princess. But I had my home constantly invaded by people who wanted to hurt me. I was only 9 when I began asking after each attack for a list of which guards and maids made it. So that I could know which of my friends I would see again. I still do it to this day. It's sad to think that these people have tormented me for so long and in the end they've one, because they truly took something from me.

I wasn't afraid right now.

There isn't much that I'm afraid of anymore.

"Yeah," I whispered instead. "It does."

"It scared me," She said. I nodded my head and slipped my hand into hers and squeezed, like my mom always had.

"Than I hope you never have to experience it again."

CHAPTER 7

My room was trashed once I got back. They had really done a number on it, I think it may even be some of their best work. Every book on my bookshelf was thrown across the floor, my bed sheets were crumpled in a pile on my carpet and I found a pillow in my bathroom. One of my nightstand drawers was open so wide it was close to falling out and the other was on the floor completely. My bathroom had been ransacked and they ripped a dress or two in my closet.

"Northern," I murmured. I knelt down in front of my bookshelf and sighed, slowly stacking my books into neat piles. One of my Illean history books was gone and my childhood favorite, Diaries of a Witch, wasn't here either. After I'd put my bookshelf together, I retrieved my pillows and made my bed. I know Anne was just going to take it apart to wash them but I put it back together anyways. My maids always wiped down and freshened every inch of my room after rebels had been in it.

If they make it through the attack.

I shook my head unconsciously and ordered the thoughts away, moving on to the bathroom. I knelt on to the floor to clean up a glass bottle of shampoo which was now broken, it's shards scattered across the tiles. I tried to settle my own beating heart and reason that this was a northern attack. They had never killed anyone before so why would they start now. But I would need a list to be sure. You can never be sure of what kind of an attack it is until you have a body count.

The door to my room was pushed open.

"America! America!"

"I'm in here!" I called back. Anne immediately appeared in the bathroom doorway and took a breath of relief.

"I'm alright," I assured her. "I was in the dining room but we locked down in time. There is not a single scratch on me and no reason to worry at all."

"No bruises or broken bones either, I hope," Anne replied, scanning me with her own eyes as if she couldn't trust my word. I reached my hand out and though she didn't take it, she did examine it for imperfections before nodding.

"This place is a pigsty," I heard Mary exclaim from the other room.

"She made the bed! She made the bed!" Lucy yelled, appearing next to Anne.

Anne rolled her eyes. "You should not be touching anything in here until I've disinfected everything."

"How do you know that I made the bed? Maybe they didn't touch the bed."

"That is definitely not my bed making work. I'd be fired from my job if it was," Anne said, already tidying up the bathroom.

Lucy rushed over to me and ushered me to my feet. "Up, up. You are only in the way."

"I'm trying to help," I argued. Lucy pushed me out of the bathroom and into the main room where Mary was stripping the bed.

"Well your doing a bad job," Lucy responded. "Princesses are meant to look pretty and be smart so that they can lead the country. The only one who ever cleaned was Cinderella and even she stopped that eventually."

I frowned. "Well what am I supposed to do?"

Mary dropped the sheets and stepped over to the door, pulling it open. "Get out of our way."

"But the rest of the palace is still being cleaned and there are fives who I'm apparently related to roaming around."

Lucy pushed me towards the door. "Than go to the gardens. Or better yet, actually speak to the Singers. They are your blood and you may find you actually like them."

"Doubtful."

"I don't care as long as your out of our way," Lucy directed, pushing me into the hall.

"You know I could fire you for laying a hand on me and speaking to me like that," I reminded her.

"But you won't." And then the door shut in my face.

I exhaled loudly and looked around the hall. The third floor was usually empty besides the guards on rotation. The King and Queens suites were usually empty until my parents retired to bed. The prince suite was always empty for I had no brother nor a lover. And the rest of the floor held bedrooms only for royals, of which we had none visiting.

I tried to rock onto the heels of my feet but was quickly reminded of the heels on my feet. Probably not good to break those.

"Are you lost?"

I turned around to see a maid and a guard, hand and hand. It was Shea and Officer Hector who are both fairly young and new staff members. The only reason I know them is because I found them kissing in an empty hallway. That situation ended in them begging me to let them keep there jobs, and me laughing at their expense and assuring them that it was fine, but that the next person who caught them may not be as lenient.

I rolled my eyes, smiling. "Yes, Shea. I am lost in my own home, outside the door to my bedroom."

"It happens," She bubbled, shrugging.

I looked pointedly at there hands. "Didn't I tell you two to be careful? If someone catches you, you could loose your jobs."

"She just can't keep her hands off me," Officer Hector said, pinching her side. It was adorable.

"It's true," Shea giggled, wrapping her arms around his waste.

"I don't believe your really trying," I laughed. "Get back to work, please."

"Of course, your majesty," Officer Hector said, but they just continued down the hallway holding hands. I'm beginning to think that I'm enabling my staff to misbehave. Oh well.

I found myself walking down the hallway and then I found myself on the second floor. I guess I could go to gardens, look at the stars or something and try to identify there colors. I walked by door after door after door. The second floor is where advisors that stay in the palace sleep and also guest rooms used to host less distinguished guests. And it's just bedroom after bedroom. It's usually quiet. The whole palace is usually quiet. But there was noise on the second floor tonight, and idiotic me walked right into the hub of it.

4 adjacent doors were wide open and facing each other and noise and people were streaming out of them.

"Mom!" I heard Mays voice call from one of them. "I can't find my good shirt!"

"The green one with the flowers?" Magda called from across the hall.

"Yeah!"

"I haven't seen it either!"

Gerad suddenly stuck his head out the door next to Mays. "Mom?"

"Your supposed to be asleep Gerad!" Shalom called from the same room as Magda.

"You told me to wait for you to tuck me in!" Gerad yelled back.

"Maxon! Tuck your brother in!"

"Yes Dad," Maxon's voice came from the last room. He exited the room a few moments later and crossed the hall to his brothers room, not noticing me. The door closed behind him.

"Mom I—."

May suddenly appeared in the doorway of her room, wearing grey flannel pants and a t-shirt. Unlike Maxon, she saw me and her eyes widened.

"Princess America!" She squealed.

"Princess America?" Magda and Shalom chorused from their room.

"Uh.....hello," I said, looking around at their foreign family set up. Magda and Shalom appeared into the hall a moment later.

"Dear God," Magda said, mortified. "I am so sorry that you had to hear our inappropriate yelling."

"It's fine," I said. Magda shuffled awkwardly from side to side.

"Whatcha doing?" May sang, bouncing over to me.

"I was just going to the gardens," I said, glancing over her in the direction that I would have to go to get to the gardens. There was a blockade in front of me, however, with fiery red hair and bouncing feet.

"That is so cool. I only saw the gardens for a second but it was awesome," May said.

Lucy's words echoed in my head.

You may find you actually like them.

I hated to admit that she was right. I wasn't giving them a chance. We didn't have to instantly become best friends or whatever, but I could at least stop being so cold. Well I hadn't been too cold to May but I've been pretty icy with the rest of them.

I mentally rolled my eyes. Stupid Lucy, making me feel guilty. Well here goes nothing. "Would you guys care to join me in a walk around the gardens?"

You know that saying "their eyes lit up"? Well that doesn't apply to May because her whole face lit up.

"Oh my goodness, yes! That sounds like so much fun. Yes, yes, yes. Let me go put on my shoes!"

She was already retreating into her room and closing the door before I could say anything. I looked over at Magda and Shalom. "Are you two going to be joining us?"

Magda glanced at Shalom. "I don't see why not..."

"Perfect," I smiled, clasping my hands together. "Why don't you put on some shoes and a coat as then we can walk down there?"

"Of course," Shalom agreed and led Magda back into their room.

I watched the door to their room close behind them. The only one of the four rooms still open was the door to what I was assuming was Maxon's room. He had been in Gerad's room during this exchange. The door to said room creeped open.

"Mom," Maxon whispered, closing the door behind him. "He's asle ep.....oh! America."

"Hi," I said quietly.

"What...." His eyes flitted around the hall as he gently shut the door to Gerads room behind him. "What are you doing here?"

"I live here," I smiled.

"No, uh, I meant—."

"I know what you meant," I laughed. "I was making a joke. I'm on my way down to the gardens and I ran into your family. I offered for them to come along."

"Oh that's—."

"You're welcome to come," I added.

"I—."

"If you want."

He laughed and shook his head. "Do you always interrupt people this much?"

I gasped slightly, realizing that I had indeed interrupted him 3 times. "I am so sorry. That is so improper of me—."

"Hey," He interrupted. "Now we're even. And sure. The gardens sound cool."

"Cool," I repeated.

The door behind me opened and May came bouncing out. She held two pairs of shoes in her hands. "Red or blue converse?"

"Um....red?"

"Nice," She said approvingly, and plopped onto the hallway floor to slip them onto her feet.

The other door opened and Magda and Shalom exited the room.

"May, put on a jacket," Magda said immediately.

"Kk. Be back in a sec," May said. She retreated and returned in a matter of seconds wearing a bright red hoodie. It matched her shoes.

"Let's go, lets go, let's go," May chanted beginning to head down the hallway. The rest of us just followed her. Magda looked about ready to reprimand her but when she saw I was smiling, she calmed slightly.

"So do you walk the gardens often, your maj—America?" Shalom asked.

I grinned, nodding my head slightly. "It is my favorite part of the palace. The gardeners do beautiful work."

"I used to look at photographs of the palace gardens in magazines," Magda said. "They grow fresh fruits and veggies for the palace correct?"

"We used to. The crops can be an eye sore so they're hidden in the center of the gardens, covered by trees. Accessible but more difficult for guests who may be wandering to find."

"It doesn't seem like that would be enough to sustain the palace," She commented.

"Oh it's not," I agreed. "Hardly enough. That's why I said used to. We used to get extra crops delivered by a big supplier, but when I was 14, you may remember, but I created a program that supported local farmers by using their crops."

"I remember that!" Maxon chimed in. "I had come home from school and my mom was watching the report and cooking dinner. She had turned to me and said something along the lines of 'she would be proud of me, if I did something half as amazing'."

We approached the palace entrance. I nodded at Officer Avery, the officer who was always on night shift at the palace entrance. He pulled the door open.

"So wait," May said, turning to walk backwards so she could face me and talk at the same time. "You were my age, and already creating programs and like, changing the world."

"It was pretty simple, but yes. They start us off young at the palace"

"That is so awesome!" May yelled. Her voice echoed into the quiet night and she looked up at the stars as if she could see her voice reaching up there. I wondered what it was like in her head and how her imagination worked.

"Do you have a favorite part of the gardens?" Magda asked.

"It's hard to choose but I think I like the rose bushes best."

"I've heard that story," Shalom said. Magda nodded along.

"What story? What story?" May asked, clearly upset that she was out of the loop.

"I'm sure you know it better than we do," Shalom said.

"Well, to put it simply," I began. "My mother had a lot of issues with getting pregnant. It had to do with how she grew up and also just her genetics in general. It was really difficult for her. It was difficult for the palace staff as well. They never liked to see my mother upset over it. So when it finally happened, the place staff planted multicolored roses in honor of her being pregnant with—." My voice shook and I trailed off. My god. My mom wasn't pregnant with me. She was pregnant with...Maxon. Those roses. My favorite part of the whole palace. Where I like to sit and just think. Those weren't for me. My chest ached and I think this must be what heartache is. "Maxon."

His name rolled off my tongue and floated away into the night and it startled us all. Tears welled up in my eye but I blinked them away. I feel so stupid. Here I am, telling them this heartwarming story about my moms struggles to conceive me and how I'm some miracle child, when I'm not. I'm not even her daughter. I feel so embarrassed.

"I'm so sorry," I whispered. I shook it off and regained my composure. I made a sharp left and led them away from the path that led to the roses, hopping we could forget that happened. I walked slightly faster so that I was just ahead of them, putting as much distance as I could without completely running away. "Let's just move on."

"America—."

"Please just forget it," I said a little harsher than I meant to. This wasn't their fault. I felt like I didn't even know how to act anymore. Years of etiquette and lessons and in an instant I couldn't remember how to function.

"I had no trouble getting pregnant with you," Magda said so quietly that I almost missed it. I lifted my head towards her and stopped walking. She took a step closer.

"Shalom and I spoke about having another kid after Kota and it must of only been a week later that I was pregnant with you. It was so easy. It was at the same time as the queen announced that she was pregnant after trying for years. I remember actually turning to Shalom and asking him why it was so easy when she was struggling so much. Seems kinda ironic now"

I laughed breathily. I knew what she was doing. She was trying to make me feel better by telling me a story that was actually my own. And I was upset that it was sort of working.

"Well you may have been easy to conceive but you were not an easy pregnancy. In fact, I think you must have been the most difficult out of the 5." She looked to Shalom for conformation and he nodded his head. She smiled sweetly at me. "You were always fighting with me. Punching and kicking 24/7. I was about ready to start punching you back. You were such a fighter that.....ok, I know this is going to sound crazy. But if Shalom and I had a girl, we said that we were going to name her America after our country that fought so hard. I know that sounds insane because you're name is America but it's true."

"I believe you," I whispered, staring down at my hands. "My mom said that she heard the name mentioned in the hospital and she thought it was beautiful. That's how I was named."

I breathed in sharply and took a shaky step forward. The heel on my shoe caught in the crack of the side walk and snapped off my foot completely, sending me hurdling to the ground with a yelp.

"Oh my gosh, Princess!" May yelled, rushing towards me.

I groaned. "I'm okay."

"If it makes you feel better that was one of the most graceful falls I've ever seen," She said, kneeling down next to me. "It was like ballet and you didn't even rip your dress."

"I broke my heel," I replied.

Her eyes glanced down to my feet and then widened. "Those are so beautiful."

"And now they're broken," I agreed.

"Only one of them," May said lightly, grinning.

"Well I can't exactly walk with one heel, now can I?"

"Do you need help up?" A new voice asked, breaking into the conversation. It was Maxon and he had his extended out towards me.

"Oh uh," I blushed. "Yes please."

I slipped my hand into his and he pulled me to a lopsided stand, with one heel and another one broken. May popped up besides us.

"You can wear my converse," May burst out.

"Oh no," I denied. "I couldn't do that and anyways you need to wear them."

But May didn't drop it. "No really. I don't need them. And I have socks on so my feet will be fine but you have nothing."

This was shaping up to be a really weird night.

"If you insi—."

"I insist!" She interrupted. She had already used her her other foot to take her shoes off and was now kicking them towards me. She was wearing baby pink socks.

I looked down at them questionably. Hesitantly, I lifted my foot and slipped it into the bright red shoe. It was no Cinderella moment but we were definitely the same size shoe. I did the same with the other and stared down at them. You could barely see them peak out from my dress. They were actually quite comfy.

"They look so cute with your dress!" May complimented.

I lifted up the skirts of my cream dress and peaked down at the red converse.

"Yeah," I smiled. "Yeah, they do."

CHAPTER 8

I heard the three of them before I saw them. They were whispering, quite loudly I might add, right outside my door, but they did not wake me up. I was already wide awake.

"It's time to wake her up," I heard Anne whisper.

"But she gets grumpy in the mornings and after a day like yesterday, I can only imagine the mood she will be in," Mary argued.

"Mhmm," Lucy agreed.

I rolled my eyes.

"She gets kinda yell-y after a bad day," Mary sighed.

"Yell-y is not a word," Anne responded harshly.

"Well, it's the only word to describe her!" Mary replied.

"Why don't we just go in..." I heard Lucy say quietly, her whisper even smaller than their whispers. They didn't hear her.

"It's kind of our job to wake her up in the morning," Anne said.

"Yes but—."

I closed my book and tossed it onto the bed, throwing the covers off me and heading for the door.

"I can hear you," I said, pulling it open.

Mary froze. "Oh," She murmured, blinking twice. "You're up."

"I am," I smiled. I turned back into my room and floated over to the vanity, taking a seat. I began to run a brush through my hair.

"No, no, no," Anne trailed off, her eyes flitting around the room. "She's up. And she's dressed and she's showered. She is also smiling before 10:00 in the morning."

"You're all so dramatic," I said.

"Something must be wrong," Mary said. She walked up behind me. "America, drop the weapon."

"It's a hairbrush."

"You can't be too safe."

I sighed and shook my head. "I'm allowed to be happy you know."

"But you had a terrible day yesterday," She said, taking the hairbrush from my had and beginning to smooth it through the tangles.

"Yes but now it's over so I can celebrate."

"Can you elaborate, please? I'm really lost," Lucy mumbled, balancing on the edge of my bed.

"I will admit that yesterday was pretty bad. It was confusing, awkward, and I'd really like to forget about it. But it happened and now it's over," I twirled in my seat so I could face them. "Everyone's met and now everyone can leave. We will keep in touch and maybe make an awkward phone call every few years, but for the most part...It's over and done with. I'm going to get some work done today and attend my 1' o clock meeting, just like I would do on an average day."

"That sounds like a mix of denial and pushing your feelings down," Anne said.

"It's not," I assured her. "I'm really just relieved."

"America, you're being naive. You know this isn't over," Lucy spoke.

Mary nodded her head in agreement. "You of all people should know that there are things that have to happen. This is anything but over."

I sighed, wishing they would stop raining down on my parade.

"Yes, but now I can tell them that I have to work so that I don't have to spend time with them."

"You said that you had a nice night."

I tilted my head to where May's red converse was lined up neatly against the wall. "It was nice, but only after a whole bunch of awkwardness. They mess with my mind and throw me off my game. I try so hard to be composed and proper, a perfect princess all the time. But when I'm around them, they look at me with their sad curious eyes, and they mess everything up. They're not my family. They're just the people who are responsible for my birth."

"It's about your blood, America. The royal bloodline is important and it has to be preserved," Anne tried to explain.

"Well let's think this through," Mary decided, waltzing over to the bed and lying down. "Worst-case scenario, you're thrown onto the streets as an eight and Maxon becomes king."

"Doubtful," Anne said.

I nodded my head. They can't explain to a whole country why the princess is suddenly gone.

"Best case scenario, you stay queen and Maxon just becomes your baby daddy." She snapped her fingers. "Impregnated and then done."

My mouth dropped open. "That is so crude."

Mary shrugged.

"That is not the best-case scenario," I said in disgust.

"I fear," Anne sighed. "That there may not be a best-case scenario."

I stared at my hands as I unconsciously played with the hem of my pencil skirt. I shook my head. I stood up from the chair and was heading for the closet when Lucy caught my hand. I stopped and looked over at her.

"America, it will work out," She said softly.

"I'm just worried," I mumbled.

Mary rounded around me, placing a soothing hand on my shoulder. "Just remember who you are. You are this country's ruler. You give all of us faith that maybe one day this can all be better. You are so strong and so kind. Fight for your place and don't let anyone else decide it for you."

I turned and wrapped my arms around her, squeezing tight. "Thank you, Mary."

I felt 2 other pairs of arms circle me.

"Thank you all."

We stood together for a few moments before Mary pulled away. "Now, I believe you have work to do."

"I'll grab your shoes." Lucy headed for my closet. She returned moments later with, bless her soul, a pair of flats. "For the long day ahead," She explained. "I have a feeling that you're meeting today is not going to be an easy one."

I frowned and nodded. "Well, luckily I have time to prepare. The meeting isn't until one. I'm going to at least try and get some work done beforehand."

"Alright. We are going to do your laundry and get started on some new dresses," Anne explained.

"I'll call if I need anything."

I left the room and caught my mom as she left the queens suite.

"America, darling," My mom greeted. She pulled me close and kissed my head sweetly. "You're up early."

"I'm trying to get some work done before the meeting later."

Her face went dark. "Yes, that's probably for the best. I'm heading for my study also."

We walked the corner together, arriving at our studies in a short few steps.

"I'll see you later than mom. At the meeting."

"Yes dear," She said, distracted. Her hand reached for the door handle but it took her a second to get it. "I'll see you then."

~oOo~

I grumbled angrily and set the file down on my desk. I loved my work but it always ended up making me upset. This particular file sparked a fire in me that would need to be doused with water. A three in Waverly had tried to give some food to a family of sevens who were on the street. But a two witnessed it and assumed that the sevens were stealing, so they called the police. Now the sevens are being prosecuted and there is nothing I can do. The three refuses to testify because they want to stay out of trouble, which only leaves testimonies from the two and the seven. Two vs. seven.

It doesn't matter who I believe in this situation. It is such an easy case that any other person wouldn't even think twice about their situation. Sevens have a history of stealing so why would I believe the seven. Except I do. But there isn't enough evidence. My dad has an advisor who checks all my work. If he saw that I ruled in favor of the sevens, I would be in big trouble

I have no choice.

I took my pen and scribbled my signature in favor of the two. I cast the file away and fought the urge to shriek in anger. I don't know if I can do another one.

Luckily I didn't have to.

"Oh god, this place looks like a dungeon." Anne entered the room as she said this and scrunched up her nose. "Why don't you pull back the blinds?"

"These reports are depressing so the room must be depressing," I said gesturing to the stack of files.

"We've brought you lunch," Mary told me as she followed Anne into the room. Lucy followed behind her with said food on a tray.

"I brought her food," Lucy huffed, setting the tray with soup, bread, and a glass of water in front of me.

"Ooh a reason to avoid my work," I exclaimed and took a polite sip of my soup.

"You shouldn't avoid your work," Anne said disapprovingly.

I handed her the file wordlessly. I don't think I'm supposed to show them confidential reports but whatever.

Her eyes scanned over the words and you could tell when she got upset because the edges of her eyes squinted together. "B–b-but the three gave them food. Why are they being fined for stealing?"

"The three won't speak up—."

"America," Anne interrupted. "Why did you sign this? This is unfair. There is no proof that the seven is lying."

"But there is no proof that he isn't."

"You can't let this happen, Ames—."

"Anne, I did all I can. It's only a fine. At least it's not a caning or jail time. I don't know what else I can do."

"Those sevens can't afford a fine. The system is broken."

"I know that—."

"Shut up, you two," Mary sniped. "Listen."

I snapped my mouth closed and tried to listen, but I didn't hear anything.

"I don't hear anything," Anne echoed.

Lucy was creeping towards the door and she slowly opened it.

"What is it?" I asked.

"I think it's your parents," Mary explained. "There talking....in your mom's study."

"So?"

"I heard your name," Lucy said.

I scrambled out of my chair and towards the door. I would never usually do this, but with this whole Maxon thing going on, I needed to be as informed as possible. People love to keep things from me and this is one thing that I needed to know.

"You shouldn't listen in on their conversation," Anne tried to say. I shushed her. I approached my mom's study door and gently put my ear up against it.

"—Don't say that Clarkson," My mother was saying. I could only imagine her sitting at her desk, reading glasses still on, as she gave my dad a disapproving look.

"We need to address it, Amberley. I've tried to talk to you but you won't even let me mention it," He replied harshly.

"Fine Clarkson. Let's talk then. What do you have to say?" The slight sharpness in my mother's voice startled me.

"America."

I stepped back from the door quickly, as if they could see me on the other side. But this wasn't my father catching me snooping, it was him broaching my name as the topic of conversation. I realized that I didn't even need to stand close to hear their words. Mary came and stood by me, her hand resting on my arm.

"What about her?"

"Don't be short with me, Amberley. I'm just trying to get us on the same page."

"And what page would that be?" Mom asked. She wasn't exactly angry, Queen Amberley hardly ever got angry, but there was something off.

"She isn't our child."

And those are the words that had me looking for something to hold on to. I was at a loss and all I could do was brace myself against the wall. Those words, I had expected, but the thing I dreaded was hearing my mom say them back.

"Remove those words from you're vocabulary because I don't want to ever hear them again," My mom hissed, her words dripping with acid. And even though the tone of her voice sent shivers down my spine, I couldn't help but sigh in relief.

"Amberley-."

"How can you say that about our daughter? The little girl that we raised, taught to walk and speak, instilled morals into and watched grow up to become a fantastic young woman."

"Her hair is bright red where as ours are not. She has sickly pale skin and weirdly clear eyes. She can't keep her temper in check and she is constantly challenging us. I've always thought it was our fault but it makes sense now. She doesn't belong here. She isn't our flesh and blood."

My fingertips touched the skin on my face and dragged a path from my hairline to under my eyes and came to rest on my lips, futilely trying to silence the whimper that wanted to be free. Mary's eyes met mine and she silently removed my hand from my face and linked my fingers with hers.

"Her red hair is beautiful as is her skin tone," My mom spoke, not missing a beat. "Her eyes are my favorite part of her. Their clear blue and even when her face is stone-cold, you can see how she really feels if you just read her eyes. I'm sorry that she doesn't fall in line and do everything you want, but maybe at least one person shouldn't. Flesh and blood does not make her our daughter, Clarkson, love does. I don't give a damn if our skin tones are the same. She is my daughter."

I could practically see my dad retreating like a scared mouse from a cat. Not often does someone put him in his place, but I suppose my mom has been wielding this secret power and keeping it for a rainy day.

"No, no, of course not my dear. I didn't mean that she wasn't my daughter, per se. Obviously, I love America. I just meant that this is a difficult situation and we have to figure out what to do with her," My father backtracked.

"What to do with her," My mom seethed. "She is not an object that we can cast away when we are done with her. She is staying exactly where she belongs. Here. As for Maxon...you already know what we are doing about that. Not that America will be happy about it."

I looked over at the door. Huh? They already know what they are doing about what with Maxon? And why won't I be happy with it?

"Amberley, I didn't mean-."

"Yeah I'm sure you didn't mean any of this," She interrupted."This conversation is over."

I heard my mom's chair scratch across the floor and I rushed back into my study as quickly as I can, barely giving Mary a second to realize what was happening, none the less getaway. Anne and Lucy sent me worried looks but I just raised my chin. I'm fine. Better than fine even.

The door opened and luckily Mary was able to make it look like she was just passing by.

"Your majesty," Mary mumbled, dropping into a curtsy.

"Mary," I heard my mom say. "You didn't...hear any of that, right?"

"Of course not," She replied. No maid would say otherwise even if they had.

"Good." Mom didn't sound like she believed her. "I have a favor to ask, between you and I. Can you prepare a guest bedroom for the king? He won't be sleeping in the king's suite tonight."

I grinned. Go, mom!

"Of course, your majesty," Mary said. She walked away and flashed me an inconspicuous grin as she passed. Were in the clear.

"We will go help," Anne decided, her and Lucy exiting as my mom stepped into the doorframe.

"Amy," She said wearily. Her eyes roamed the room as if the conversation that I definitely didn't hear would be showcased across the walls, and her shoulders already sagged with the weight of the day. There was a reason my mom didn't yell much. It seems that she is built for kindness.

"Hey mom," I said coolly, casually moving a file aside as if I had been reading it. I checked the clock on my wall. "Oh! Is it time for that meeting already? Sometimes I just get lost in the work and tune out everything else."

She smiled weakly. "That's what is so great about you, darling."

"I get it from my Mom," I replied and pushed away from my desk. "Shall we walk to the meeting then?"

Her smile faltered.

"Look America...the meeting is about you and-."

"I know Mom," I said, grabbing her hand. She didn't need to worry about this. She had done enough today. "I'm ready for whatever."

She nodded thankfully and rested her head on my shoulder as we began walking towards the meeting room.

No matter what lies I told my mom, I knew that I couldn't prepare for this meeting. You never think that your life will change in a single room at what is usually an everyday event, but if my suspicions were right, mine would never be the same.

CHAPTER 9

As soon as mom and I had walked into the meeting room, the mood shifted. I was familiar with these people. I had grown up with them being my parent's right-hand man's and I had been sitting with them in these chairs since I was allowed to. But right now they were treating me as if I was an imposter that they had never seen before and not their future Queen. It's like that situation where the group of girls is talking bad about someone behind their backs and then that someone walks into the room.

I am someone.

And these people are about to talk about me in front of me.

I tilted my chin up and glanced over their heads in the way I'd seen my dad do, like he doesn't even see them, and then I took my seat. My dad wasn't here yet, still sulking from his fight with my mom I assume, and taking his sweet time to get here. I watched my mother discreetly take notice of his empty chair and tip her head in recognition.

"Good morning, ladies and gents," She announced, taking her own seat across from me. There was a chorus of good mornings and your majesties before the room went silent.

The mood of the meeting room was different. And I knew it was because I'm out of the know. I don't know when, but sometime in the last 48 hours, there was a meeting that I was not present at. And the only reason that I wouldn't be there is because the meeting was about me. This conference was supposed to be the addressing of the situation in which we would try and talk out the situation. My idea is to send them home, but I'm not naive enough to think that is happening. But if my suspicions are correct then they have already decided the solution to the situation and I'm just going to have to take it.

This meeting is a setup. My fate has been decided for me and I don't even get a say. The thought made me go cold.

I took a deep breath. Calm down, America, I told myself. I've worked on this. I cannot get angry about situations that I cannot control. I just have to wait. One day I will be in charge and then I will decide my own life and make sure everyone else can decide their own.

Unless they take my throne away

I shoved the thought away so deep into my head that it would need a tour guide to find it's way back.

"Err...uh, Princess America, how is your day going?" A brave soul asked from the other side of the table.

"It depends on how this meeting goes," I said innocently, tapping my nails against the surface of the table in a completely non-menacing manner.

My mom shot me a look and I just shrugged. What? For all I know these people are planing to kick me off the throne. I hope their scared.

The door was pushed open. "My apologies for being late. I got caught up."

I smiled behind my hand as my father sulked by my mom and slumped into his seat. There was another chorus of 'no problems your majesty' and 'we didn't even notice'. I mentally rolled my eyes. Kiss ups.

My mother cleared her throat. "Well why don't we just get straight to it."

"Yes," I agreed. "Why don't you go ahead and tell me what all of you decided about me."

"America," My father warned.

"I'm just stating a fact," I replied.

My father ignored me.

"So obviously we are trying to figure out what to do about this reversal that occurred," Stravos began. I frowned. I like Stravos but now I suppose he's the enemy. "You out of any body, Princess, should understand the importance of the royal bloodline."

I nodded.

"Which makes sense as to why we can't just let Maxon Singer and his family go home."

I begrudgingly nodded my head again. As little as I liked to admit it, I understood.

"But you are the princess and that means something. Obviously we can't just switch you back."

I audibly sighed in relief. I was going to stay Princess. What left is there to discuss?

"But the royal bloodline needs to be preserved," My father said.

"Is there a document or something I can read?" I asked. "To make this a little easier so that you don't have to explain it."

"I'm afraid we couldn't put this into writing. The contents of this conversation can not leave this room," Another advisor spoke.

My blood ran cold.

Stravos stood up, immediately capturing the attention of everyone at the conference table.

"In order to preserve the Illean bloodline in future monarchs to come and to ensure that you keep your rightful place as Princess of Illea, we have arranged for you to marry Maxon Singer."

This, I had not expected.

My mother instantly saw my face drop and she looked like she wanted to cry. I didn't start screaming and calling people names. I didn't freak out and throw my chair across the room. I didn't even gasp. It just hit me like a brick and then my heart sunk.

It kinda hurt.

My mother and I have always been close. I've confided in her with things that I hadn't even told my maids or Amara. I had squashed many dreams while living here in the palace, but finding love wasn't one of them. I refused my selection. I didn't allow foreign suitors. I wanted it to happen naturally and on my terms. I had told my mother this and she had always held my hand and told me of course. And now she was taking it all away.

I'm being forced to marry a person that I do not love. I barely even know the man.

"Amy," My mom pleaded.

"Okay."

"Okay?" Stravos repeated in disbelief. He has seen me loose my temper on many an occasion, I understand why it was such a shock for me to agree.

"Yes," I whispered numbly. "I understand the logic behind it."

"Oh," Stravos stuttered, dumbfounded.

"Then I suppose we go over the logistics," Another advisor piped in.

Stravos nodded his head. "Oh, um—yes. Yes we should. Well obviously it is a matter that needs to be discussed with Maxon's family."

"They're both 18," Someone else said. "The decision is up to him alone."

It didn't fly past me how the advisor said him instead of them. I have no choice even if I am an adult.

"Correct. But assuming that he is on board with the situation..."

This was the problem with the people in this room. It never occurred to them that Maxon might have a problem with this. They're Ones, the people in charge. There are no obstacles in their head. Anyone else would stop and think that Maxon is probably not going to want to marry the Princess or become a royal. But that doesn't matter to them. That is merely a technicality that they can make go away with the snap of a finger. Maxon and I are just chess pieces for them to move around. I don't have a say or else I would be fighting this with every fiber in my being.

I only pray that he has the sense to get us both out of this.

"We will have to figure out a cover story to tell the country..." Someone was saying.

I zoned out again. It was like my mind was going black and white. I couldn't focus. I wanted to stand up and scream but it was like I was frozen in place.

"Princess!"

I snapped my head towards the voice. It was Silvia. I hadn't even realized she was in this meeting.

"You spaced out," Silvia said.

"Oh—uh, I'm sorry," I mumbled.

"I think we should end the meeting early," My mom suddenly said.

"But there is still much to discuss—."

"And it can be discussed later," She agreed. "But this is going to be a lot for Princess America to think about and it would only be courteous for us to give her the night."

"Your majesty, this is pretty emergent—."

"Meeting dismissed."

I was out of my seat in an instant and I could barely contain myself enough to allow my mom and dad to stand. We would walk out together. That was protocol. I was counting my steps, one foot in front of the other, as we left the room and silently began to walk down the hallway. I waited until we were out of earshot of the advisors before I finally exploded.

"What the hell was that!" I yelled.

"Amy—."

"You didn't think to warn me that you were going to change the whole course of my life in there. I would think that would be something you might mention," I hissed.

"Don't speak to us that way," My dad said.

"I don't understand, no, I will never understand this decision. An arranged marriage. When are we, the 1800's? What ever happened to love and choice?"

"The world works differently for royals America," My father said calmly. "Sometimes you make certain decisions because it is what is best for Illea."

"What about what's best for me! I'm your daughter! Don't you care?"

"We understand that your young and love is a big deal to you but—."

I continued without letting them talk. "This isn't about love! This is about me being left out of the decision. Since when do I not get a say in my own future? When did we start keeping secrets from one another?"

When I said this last part, I said it right to my Mother. There was no way that I would get through to my dad. That was never even my intention. But my mom had some way with my dad that I would never understand. Maybe she could reason with him. I just had to reason with her, pull on her heart strings and get her to do something.

She immediately entered damage control mode. "You have to understand that this is the best solution. Obviously there are still kinks to work out but this was the only way we could preserve the ill—."

"I don't care about the Illean bloodline!" I yelled. "No one will know that I'm not of royal blood. Why can't everything just stay the same!"

"Amy—," My mom tried to say.

"No Amberley," My dad interrupted. "Stop trying to justify our decision because we don't owe her that. America, you should understand. This is your duty as a Princess. This will not be the last time you have to make a personal sacrifice for the good of the country. This is not the end of the world so stop acting like it is. You are marrying Maxon Singer, end of discussion."

I fumed silently as he glared into my eyes. Every nerve in my body told me to back down, but I couldn't. I can't. I only hope that he wouldn't make me regret this later.

"Come on, Amberley."

His arm snaked around Mom's waist and he forcefully began to pull her away. She looked back at me sadly but said nothing.

She stayed silent.

But I can't.

"I won't," I said.

Father stopped in his tracks, turning around silently.

"Excuse me?"

"You heard me."

"You have no choice," He said, enunciating every syllable.

"Your right," I agreed. "I don't have a choice. But I'm not the only variable in this equation. You can't legally force Maxon to do any-thing. He does have a choice."

My dad just grinned. "And I'm sure that he will make the right one."

CHAPTER 10

I smoothed my hand down my figure, tracing a trail from my waist to my hips. In the mirror, I could see my maids grinning wide.

I spun around. They waited expectantly for the compliments to start pouring in.

"This is the tightest thing I've worn since the Prince of England visited when I was 14," I finally said.

Mary's face fell. "Alright...I could see why your mind might go there, but it's doing wonders for your figure."

"I can't feel my figure," I replied.

"You wear too many loose dresses anyways," Anne said, ushering me away from the mirror. I tried to look back but Lucy casually stepped in front of the mirror. I knew whatI looked like though. The dress clung to my body until it reached my waist where it flowed into the skirts.

"That's because there is no need to rearrange my insides when I am just working today."

"But the dress is sleek and It'll look great when you're spying," Lucy said, bouncing in excitement.

I sat down on the bed and I think I felt a button come loose.

"Let's get one thing straight. I'm not spying. I simply believe that my dad will most likely speak to Maxon today. And I need to figure out how my dad is going to manipulate him so I can try and fix it."

"Are you sure about this, Ames?" Lucy asked. "Is this really the hill you want to die on? We talked about the arranged marriage situation and it is one of the better options."

Anne nodded her head in agreement.

"You're right. It isn't the worst option. But where is my choice in the matter? This is my life and I'm not going to stand by while someone else makes the decisions for me. That's not who I am and that's not who I'll ever be."

"But did you ever think," Anne spoke. "That maybe this is just a gateway. This is all you need to do to achieve all the things you've always talked about."

"All I need to do? This is marriage. I'll be spending the rest of my life with this man. We will be planning all of our future decisions together. He will be the father of my children. This is not something that I can just give in to. I have to do something or at least try."

"I second that notion," Mary said. "Fight for it! Though he would make pretty babies..."

I rolled my eyes and hoped off the bed. "And with that, I'm heading to work."

The girls waved at me as I headed out the door. This is where it got tricky. The main meeting rooms are on the first floor in the conference wing, but those are for bigger meetings where the advisory board will be present. There are smaller meeting rooms down there, but there is always advisors going in and out of those rooms and I have a feeling my dad doesn't want to be heard. His office is on the third floor where our bedrooms are but my Mom's and my offices are right there too, so he probably wouldn't do it there. My best guest would be one of the extra study's that we have for when royals are staying for a few days and need a place to do their work. They are on the third floor but the opposite side of the King and Queens suite. They're hardly used when we don't have company's.

It's worth a shot.

I headed down the hallway, keeping my ears open. I would know my dads voice anywhere. I just had to find it. There was an obvious change where the guards became fewer apart because there was less protection needed in a part of the palace that was rarely inhabited. I tried to be fast but this stupid dress that I had on was clinging to every part of my upperbody it could. I was going to have a very serious conversation with my maids about this.

It wasn't long before I became unsure of where I was. I wanted to think that this meant that I might be getting closer but honestly I wasn't sure what floor I was even on.

"—Singer."

I froze.

"I'm not really sure what you're trying to say sir."

I almost leaped up and down with joy. I had found them and now I just had to get the information I needed and then make myself scarce. I slid my shoe against the carpet my heel getting caught slightly. The door wasn't quite closed and I was able to slink over and peek in.

"You and you're family are fives correct?" Maxon nodded. The scene was exactly as you may expect. My dad sat at a desk and Maxon sat in a chair across. You could visibly see the intimidation. "Thats not exactly the easiest caste."

"We make due, your majesty," Maxon responded.

"Well of course you do. I'm sure you all work very hard."

"We do."

My dad pushed away from his desk and stood up casually. He strolled around. Nervously, I flattened myself against the wall between the doorframe and the console table.

"Do you know how old the Illean bloodline is, son?" My father asked. The way he said son was in that casual way that adults do but it still made my face go red.

"A few 100 years, sir," Maxon replied. I cautiously approached the door frame again and peeked into the room. Maxon's eyes followed my dad warily as he walked slowly around the room. It was like a dog cornering it's pray.

"It is sacred and it must be preserved. But because of this turn of events, you have the royal bloodline and not the future queen. But we have a solution and all we need is for you to agree."

I think Maxon had realized that this was not a two sided conversation and was now just waiting patiently.

"An arranged marriage between you and Princess America."

I don't know why I hadn't expected him to be so blunt about it but he just came out and said it. And Maxon definitely did not expect him to say this either. Maxon chocked on air and his face went red.

"I don't really understand," Maxon stuttered.

"It's exactly as it sounds. You marry her."

"Sir—."

"Just think about what it could do for your family." Maxon's expression shifted. "You and your family would never have to worry about food, or shelter, or money, or anything again. You and you're whole family will be taken care of. You're mother will never have to skip dinner so that you can eat. Your father will never have to spend all night painting instead of getting a good nights rest. You're younger brother and sister can live their childhoods like they should instead of having to worry about working. Anything and everything you have ever wanted can be yours."

"That all sounds great. But I'm sorry, I'm not interested. My family and I are doing fine." He tried to stand up but my father placed a hand on his shoulder. Maxon sat back down under his force and my dad crossed back around to the desk.

He smiled as if his proposal hadn't just been rejected. "I'm not trying to insult your family. I've always respected the entertainer caste. You guys work so hard. But sometimes the work can be so unreliable. I mean, you rely entirely on other people hiring you for your work. What if no ones hiring? It would be a shame if you guys were to loose money. Nowadays it is so easy to drop down a caste. Or even a few. I would hate for you and your family to wind up as eights."

"Are you—."

"I'm just saying that you never know what's going to happen. Why don't you.......think about it," Dad said smiling. "Take your time."

He stood up from the table, turning around in that kingly way he does, and heading for the door. I gasped, scurrying away from the door. My heel snagged on the end of the side table next to me and I crashed into the wall as the door opened.

"Dad," I squeaked. I stood up straight and smoothed down my dress looking up at him. I smiled brightly, the same smile he taught me to use when facing advisors.

His eyes went dark as he slowly shut the door behind him.

"I didn't hear anything," I burst. "I was just passing by!"

He grinned. "Oh it doesn't matter what you did or did not hear. The only thing you would've heard was the sound of me securing your marriage."

"You're manipulating him and that poor family," I hissed.

"I'm doing what I have to, to get what I want. What we want."

"I don't want this!"

"You want to be queen. You want to continue your cushy, privileged life in my palace. In my country. This is how it's going to be."

"You can't just scare people into doing what you want."

"That is the only way you do it! That's how this country runs America."

"It shouldn't! Everything is wrong about this! Why don't you get that?"

I was fuming. I should have known that Maxon wouldn't be able to stop this. He was just a five from Carolina. How could he even know about this? Him and his family are all about protecting one another. Every cent they make is for each other. He's going to say yes. For his family.

I had to something.

"I'm not marrying him," I said firmly.

"Well too bad. This marriage is as good as done."

"I. Am not. Marrying. Him," I repeated.

"Watch your mouth," He growled, grabbing my wrist tightly.

I tried tearing my wrist from his grasp but he held firm. I glared angrily at him.

"You don't want to make me angry," He said maliciously, twisting my wrist tightly. "You know what happens when I'm angry."

A warning tingled down my spine and I ignored it.

"Does manipulating people make you happy?" I asked. It was a jab at him, but at the same time I wanted to know.

"Oh, honey," He sighed, almost pitifully. "Your a Princess. This is what what Princesses do."

"If that's so then I don't want to be a Princess," I spit.

"That can be arranged," He hissed, throwing my wrist down.

I grabbed it in my hand, examining the damage. There would be a bruise tomorrow but my maids were no strangers to covering up bruises.

"Watch yourself, America. It'd do you good to remember you have a replacement now."

He walked away with authority, his shoulder colliding with mine. I slammed into the wall. He always ended the conversation. There was no other way. I gasped for breathe, holding back tears. Why can't I breathe? Why is it so hard to breathe?

I took off down the halls. I needed to get to my room. I needed someone to help me. Why can't I breathe? I kicked my heels off, leaving them in the hall and ran faster. It felt like my dress was getting tighter. Or maybe it was getting heavier making it impossible to move. I couldn't breathe. I couldn't take in air. What was wrong with me? My lungs were filling up with water and it felt like I was drowning. I wiped away my tears as they fell. I ignored the guards and maids asking if I was alright. They couldn't help. I needed help. Why can't I breathe?

I burst through the door to my room, collapsing on the floor. I was hyperventilating and yet I couldn't breathe at the same time. Why can't I breathe!

"America!" Lucy called.

"Ames, are you alright?" Mary asked.

"C-ccc-ccccant," I gasped. "I can't breathe."

Anne was at my side in seconds, her hand on my shoulder. "Speak America. Tell us what's wrong."

"This dress," I stuttered. "The dress is too tight! I can't breathe! Please help me, I can't breathe."

"America, your not making any sense," Anne said. She was trying to wipe my tears away, but they were falling too fast for her to catch. "You need to calm down."

"I can't breathe," I gasped, clutching my stomach. Why is this dress so tight? It wasn't this tight earlier. Now it feels like it's slowly sucking the life out of me. Along with my hopes and dreams.

"Take deep breaths," Mary encouraged.

"I can't breathe," I cried. "This dress is too tight. Get it off me! Get the dress off me!"

Anne and Mary helped me to my feet while Lucy tried to coach me into taking deep breaths. I couldn't hear them. I couldn't hear anything. My lungs were slowly shrinking and the walls were crashing down on each other.

"Get it off!" I sobbed, stumbling. Anne and Mary supported my weight completely, keeping me from falling. "Please! I can't breathe! Get it off!"

"You need to calm down," Lucy said. "I'm going to undo the laces. Take deep breathes."

"I can't," I wept. "I can't. I can't breathe. Get the dress off. Get it off. Please."

"I'm trying, America!" Lucy squeaked. "There's a lot of ties here. I'm going as fast as I can."

"Get the scissors!" Anne ordered. "She needs the dress off!"

I cried while Mary fetched scissors from the table and came back over. She than held me as Anne and Lucy cut the beautiful dress off my body in jagged motions. They snipped from the neckline to the very bottom of the long skirts until the dress fell off my body and onto the floor around my feet, leaving me in just my slip. I took in a long, ragged breathe, my lungs finally filling with air. And yet nothing felt better.

I fell to my knees, huge sobs racking through my chest. The girls knelt down next to me, their arms circling my body, holding me together.

"I don't want to be a princess anymore," I whimpered. "I can't do this anymore."

"Shhh," Anne consoled, stroking my hair. "We're here."

"I don't want to. I don't want to do this anymore," I wept.

And I mumbled that into the late hours of the night while they held me. There are times when you crack under the pressure and everything just becomes too much. If my father was what I had to he like as a Princess than I didn't want to be one anymore.

Tonight, I cracked.

"I don't want to be a princess anymore," I repeated. "I can't."

CHAPTER 11

Amara set her tea down on the table and leveled me with a look. She gestured around to our surroundings. "Not that I don't enjoy the view of the gardens...but why are we drinking tea and looking at the gardens instead of drinking our tea in the gardens."

I sighed. I definitely wasn't thrilled about moving the location of our biweekly tea to my balcony. The gardens are my favorite. But the gardens aren't private enough.

"Ooo, is it confidential?" Amara asked, her eyes lighting up.

"Isn't it always in the palace?" I asked rhetorically.

"Yes, but there is palace confidential and then there is royals only confidential," She explained. "The real gossip comes from the stuff I'm not supposed to know."

"It's not really confidential, actually. It'll be public knowledge come this Friday."

Amara leaned forward, her eyes sparking. "Do tell."

I moved my hand from behind my tea cup where I had been hiding it. Sitting on my ring finger was a giant rock that my father had delivered to me yesterday. This was happening too fast.

"I'm engaged," I said monotone, showing her my ring.

Amara laughed. I always loved Amara's laugh. It was a quirky mix between a cackle and static that was kinda ugly sounding. But she had never been ashamed of it once. She was laughing so hard that she snorted.

"Girl, you're playing. What have you been doing, hiding a man in your closet or something?"

She thought this was so funny that she cracked herself up, going into another fit of giggles.

"I'm hilarious," She mumbled after she had settled down enough.

"It would be if I were joking," I responded.

Her face fell. "Mer...?"

I just shook my head.

"Wait, you're not kidding with me?"

"I really wish that I could say I am, but I can't. I've been arranged in a marriage."

Her mouth dropped open.

"No...." She could hardly even fathom it. "You? An arranged marriage? You'd never agree to that. That doesn't even make sense. I applaud your commitment to this joke but I've got you."

"I didn't agree to it. I'm being forced into it."

"I don't understand. What? Why? This is so sudden. It's only been 4 days since our last tea party and gossip session, how much could have possibly happened?"

"A lot," I said, my mouth dry.

"This news is so unbelievable, I need a fresh cup of tea for it." Amara proceeded to take her cup of tea and pour it over the ledge of my balcony. The tea splattered onto the plants below."

"Mar! You could of had a maid get you a new cup instead of killing those plants!" I gasped.

She rolled her eyes. "That would of taken too long and I need details now. Besides, it's herbal tea. I'm just returning it too it's natural roots. Now tell me everything."

"I wish there was more to tell but I'm having trouble even figuring it out myself." I retracted my hand from where it still lay in front of me. I twisted the ring around my finger, it's weight feeling like it was chaining me to the floor.

"Well I'm assuming you know who," She said, pouring a new cup of tea.

"It's Maxon."

"OMG Maxon!" She yelped, almost knocking something off the table. "Wait...Maxon. That makes sense. I don't know why I didn't predict that one. It really is a simple way to keep an eye on the Singers while also preserving the Illean bloodline."

"Why is everybody so obsessed with the stupid bloodline! It's all I seem to hear about these days!"

"It's kind of the only reason you were born. So that you could create future heirs to the throne and also keep the monarchy under the Illean-Schreave name."

"A stupid bloodline doesn't seem like reason enough to ruin my life," I muttered.

"Ruin your life?"

"If you can't tell already, I am not happy about marrying him. In fact, I strongly do not want to."

"I'm sure you'll be happy with Maxon. He's a good man," Amara said, putting another scoop of sugar in her tea.

"It's not that I haven't enjoyed the limited time I've spent with him. I could see myself one day...dating him. But now I don't have a choice."

"You know this is how it works, Mer. It's your duty as princess. Your not stupid. Your not an ordinary girl and you don't get to choose who you love."

"I could have had a selection!" I argued. "I could of had the decision be my own."

"You fought against your selection. And even if you had a selection America, the choice wouldn't be yours. It would be the advisors and your fathers decision down to the very last second," Amara sighed. "Your no stranger to how being a princess works. This decision isn't about you. It's about him being the one with Illean blood running through his veins."

"I'm the Princess of Illea," I said angrily. "Royal blood or not, this is my country."

"And now it is his," Amara said, saying the truth that I've been too afraid to admit to myself.

My fathers words echoed in my head.

She's not our daughter.

What are we going to do with her?

She doesn't belong here.

"America, you are a princess. Don't act like you didn't know this was going to happen. There was never going to be a choice in who you married. Why are you so upset now?"

"This feels different. I feel replaced," I admitted.

"Your not. Maxon's just an addition."

I looked down at my dress, feeling the material between my fingers. I grew up in silk and satin. I learned to sit and look pretty before I learned my abc's. I learned how to eat properly at a dinner table before I learned to eat solid foods. I was dancing before I knew to count and and I was wearing heels before I could walk. I was raised a princess and I'm perfect at it.

How can someone who was raised as a five replace me? Somebody who never took an etiquette lesson and never knew there was more than one type of fork. He never took a dance lesson or sat in meetings. He was a five. A lower caste. A worker. My father makes fun of fives. He thinks them as nobody's. In his opinion fives contribute nothing to society. And now he is replacing me with one.

"You like Maxon," She pointed out.

"I like you too but no one is arranging our marriage," I muttered.

"Oh Mer," She laughed. "You couldn't handle me..."

And just like that, the conversation had changed topics.

"...But he could."

"What? Who? Maxon?"

She shooed the thought away with a flick of her wrist. "No, not him. Him."

She pointed off into the distance. I followed her finger over the railing of my balcony and down into the gardens. By the door, where Officer Avery usually is stationed, was a admittedly good looking guard.

"Dang is he spicy. Look at that hair and that body in that uniform. I've never seen him before," Amara whistled.

I studied him.

"Yeah," I agreed calculatedly. "He must be apart of the new draft. Are you interested?"

She smiled dreamily at him. "No."

"No?"

She shook her head.

"No. I've got myself the number of a Spanish prince. But maybe for you."

"I'm engaged," I deadpanned.

"Technicalities," She sang, grabbing my hand and pulling us away from the table and back inside.

A few moments later, we were approaching the grand palace doors. Avery and some other new recruit were on duty.

"Avery!" Amara called.

"Lady Amara," Officer Avery greeted, nodding politely at her.

Amara approached him excitedly. "How are the new recruits?"

"Normally you don't care about the new recruits. You haven't bothered to learn the last batches names," Avery said.

"I learned their names," I added in.

Avery bowed his head at me, smiling. "You always do. Though you did call me Officer Adams for a few weeks."

"It doesn't matter who's names I've learned," Amara interrupted. "The only name I care about is the dashing young man outside."

"Markson?"

"No. The new one."

Avery nodded his head. "That would be Officer Legar. New recruit from...Carolina I believe."

"Carolina," I repeated. "Maxon's from Carolina."

"Maybe they know each other. Plot twist!" Amara gasped. She jumped around excitedly.

"Why the curiosity, if I may ask?" Avery spoke.

"Wouldn't you like to know," She quipped. Her eyes met mine and she whispered. "Tanner."

I nodded.

Amara grabbed my hand and began to pull open the palace door. A "tanner" was a move that had been created when I was 16 and she was 14. She had wanted to talk to the son of General Tanner, who is now an officer just like his father, and we had created a plan to do it. It didn't work but it was now our go to for when we wanted to talk to someone. Usually it was to get her a date but now I suppose it was just to get his attention.

As she was stepping out the door, I hooked the heel of my stiletto around the heel of hers, sending her tripping out the door.

And into the arms of a handsome young guard.

He luckily did his role perfectly and caught her around the waist as she came tumbling by. Sending me a wink, Amara pretended to be shocked.

"Oh my, I am so sorry Officer," Amara gasped, placing a hand on his chest. "I can be such a klutz sometimes. I'm so lucky to have strong young men like you around to catch me when I fall."

Wow. She was really laying it on thick.

"Anytime, Lady..."

"Amara," She smiled, straightening herself up and stepping away from him. "And this is—."

"Princess America," He finished, dropping into a clumsy bow.

I loved new recruits. It was fun to mess with them until they finally realized that they could tease me back. That was one of the reasons I favored Officer Avery so much. It took him a few years to finally make a jab at me but it was a good one. And it only took 2 years to come up with.

"That was the clumsiest bow I've seen in a while," I commented once he had straightened. His eyes went wide and Amara basically smacked her forehead in disapproval.

"I'm sorry, your highness. I'm new at this and I was just trying him be respectful. I'll try harder," He stuttered.

"Legar."

"Yes?"

"I was joking."

He sagged in relief and I actually laughed out loud.

"She's mean to the guards," Amara sighed. "The only way to survive it is to be mean back."

"I'm not mean. I'm just really funny," I said defensively.

"At others expense. So Officer Legar, from...?" She trailed off as if she hadn't been told 5 minutes earlier where he was from.

"Carolina," He filled in.

I mock gasped. "Carolina! Any relation to Maxon Singer?"

"He is my best friend."

"Best friend," Amara and I repeated together as if this was the coolest thing in the world.

"It's gorgeous there. My favorite province to visit," I said.

"And what a coincidence it is that you two know each other," Amara agreed.

His eyes flicked from Amara to I in complete confusion. It was hard to follow our conversations but I'd say he was doing alright. He seemed polite enough but also like he would have some pretty good comebacks in the future. I think Avery and him would be good friends.

"America! America!" A voice called from in the gardens. I glanced over my shoulder and saw Lucy approaching from a side passageway that I think led to the sub floor.

"Lucy! Lucy!" I mimicked as she walked up the steps to stand beside us. Her eyes glanced over at Officer Legar nervously and she didn't say anything else. She gets nervous around new people.

"Officer Legar this is my personal maid Lucy. Lucy this is Legar," I introduced.

"We ran into each other in the sub floor," Officer Legar informed me.

"Really my fault," Lucy mumbled. "I was carrying towels and I couldn't see where I was going."

Oh. They literally ran into each other.

"It was no big deal," He assured her. "I had my face stuck in a map and should have been paying better attention."

They both just went silent, which I suppose was there way of agreeing that it was both of their faults.

"Well isn't that adorable," Amara cooed. "Very very meet cute. But I'm assuming you're here Lucy to tell us that our tea is getting cold."

"Actually—."

"And I hate cold tea. We really should be going Officer Legar but it was nice meeting you. We should do it again sometime."

Amara was already pulling open the palace doors, which was supposed to be the guards job, and pushing me back inside. Her control freak levels are rivaling her mothers.

"I'm sorry America but I'm afraid Lucy is going to steal your man," Amara said sadly.

"I'm engaged," I repeated.

"Simply a formality," She brushed off and began to head back for the stairs.

I smiled. This is what I loved about Amara. I was ready to mope today. After my minor freak out that occurred last night, I was all for laying in bed all day. But Amara broke into my room followed by a maid carrying a tray of tea, and forced me to get up. She is always there when I need a friend and she always distracts me me from letting my mind get the best of me. She is definitely insane but she kept me from thinking too hard about everything else in my life.

If only for a day.

I appreciate it when you comment :)

CHAPTER 12

I usually enjoy the day of the report. Every Friday at exactly 6' o clock, the person behind the camera counts down from 5 and the report begins. Gavril Fadaye hosts it and I usually just sit down and smile. The report is when I get to talk to the people. I get to tell them the new program that I've created and how it's going to improve their lives. I get to explain to them the new law that has been put in place that's going to help them out. I get to put together a presentation and show the country who I really am, and how I want to help them.

I'm the one who is standing up for them and this is how I show it to them.

However, as I walked into the stage for the Report, I couldn't help but think that I will not enjoy the report today. Not at all.

"Princess," A women called, stopping me. She was part of the makeup crew. "We want to try a new lipgloss shade on you."

"What color?" I asked.

"It's a pink that we think will compliment your skin tone," She explained, presenting the tube to me.

"I don't see why not," I agreed and stood still as she lined my lips with the pretty pale pink. I rubbed my lips together and smiled at her.

"And your blush is a little light. You know how the lights wash you out," She said. She pulled out a compact and a brush and proceeded to put blush on my face until I'm sure I looked like a strawberry. "Alright, that's good."

Than she just walked away. I sighed and walked over to my mother.

"Do I have to do this?" I greeted her.

She was having makeup applied to her eyes so she just grabbed my hand. "Baby, you have to understand..."

"I don't, but I'm going to do it anyways," I replied.

She took a deep breath and shoed the makeup artist away. One of her eyes was framed by gold and burgundy, while the other was blank.

"Please don't be cross with me, Amy," My mom pleaded.

"I'm not mad at you. I'm just...hurt but I'll get over it."

My mom pulled me close and did the one thing that I really needed in that moment. She placed her chin on my head, and tucked my hair behind my ear and just hugged me.

"I'm sorry," She whispered.

"I know."

"5 minutes!" Gavril Fadaye yelled.

"I have to go get my makeup done," She said and pulled away. I nodded. Out of the corner of my eye, I saw Maxon enter with my fathers hand on his shoulder. My father was speaking lowly to him and Maxon's face was stone cold. I'll give him props, at least he already has that down. My father found me with his eyes and he motioned me over. I hesitantly went.

"You two should get your stories straight before you screw up while we're live," My dad muttered harshly and walked away.

Maxon and I both watched him go. Than we looked at each other. Than we looked at the floor. He was wearing a brand new pair of nice dress shoes and a tuxedo.

"Oh, um...." I shoved my hand into the hidden pocket of my dress and pulled out the shiny piece of metal. "I should probably put this on."

I opened my hand and we both stared at the metal encrusted with glittering jewels.

He mumbled. "This is weird."

"Yeah. It is."

It was quiet for a moment except the hum of the room of people preparing for our downfall.

"Look—," We both tried to say.

"You go first," He said.

I had to be careful of what I said in such a public place. "I'm sorry for..." I glanced around. "For the choices you had to make because of people."

"I'm a five. I've seen what can happen when you get on people's bad side."

"Still, I'm sorry. We're not all like that."

He nodded and was going to speak but he was interrupted by Gavril yelling 20 seconds.

"Just act like your in love with me," I murmured and left him backstage to take my seat.

My moms eyes met mine and she looked like she wanted to say something, but the red light on the camera started blinking and the camera man counted down from 5.

5...

4...

3...

2...

1...

I smiled brightly at the camera that I knew focused specifically on me as Gavril Fadaye began his introduction.

"Good evening, Illea. I'm Gavril Fadaye and this is your Illean report. We have some big announcements today but I'll start us off with a few news updates. Yesterday in Clermont..."

Though I was still looking at the cameras, my eyes glanced over at Maxon. He was having his suit fixed by a maid and a makeup artist was giving him some powder. His eyes met mine and he frowned. He made an exaggerated fake sneeze at the powder and I couldn't help but giggle. He smiled wide and I smiled back.

"Well Princess America, don't you look happy," Gavril commented, waltzing over to my throne. "Rumor has it that you have some big news. Would you care to sit with me and tell us?"

I smiled giddily and fluttered my eyes. "I'm so excited."

I did my best teenage girl in love impression while I walked over to the chairs. I think I was laying it on a tad thick but hey, I'm just a girl in love right?

Gavril took my hand and helped me sit in the comfy chair. As planned, he took my left hand and gasped. Gavril knew about the engagement ahead of time, however he was unaware that it was fake.

"Princess...this simply cannot be what I think it is."

"I'm afraid I can't deny it," I laughed. I stuck my hand out forwards as all the cameras in the room zoomed in on the shiny rock. "I'm engaged!"

There was no live audience at this taping, but there was a whole crew of people who all basically fell over as I sang out that I was to be married.

"Well congratulations to you, your highness. But I can't be the only one here who is a little shocked by this information. You haven't been dating anyone."

"Publicly," I finished for him. "It's been my own little secret. And I'd love to tell you all about it, but I think you should meet him first."

"He's here?" Gavril asked, looking around.

I smiled brightly. "Gavril, I'd like you to meet my fiancé, Maxon Singer."

Maxon was pushed onto the stage by a crew member who followed him with a chair. He played it off naturally, and strolled over to me.

This is where the acting really played in. I stood up to greet him with a kiss to the cheek. Without me even having to tell him to, he grabbed my hand and we sat down together.

"I must say, I am shocked by this news. You've never had any public relationships before but most of us just believed it was because you were waiting for your selection. How did you two meet?"

"Well Maxon is actually from Carolina," I explained.

"That's a long ways away," Gavril commented.

"Well we met on a tour of the provinces," I said. "My family and I were attending a ceremony in his town on our tour. We were staying with the mayors family and I had wanted to go out, but my parents wouldn't let me go without a disguise. So I had changed into a hoodie and some jeans and I was taking a walk. It snows in Carolina, did you know that? I'd never been in snow. I had stopped in the middle of the sidewalk to look at the snowflakes and Maxon had accidentally walked into me. When I fell in the snow, my hoodie slipped off my head and Maxon recognized me instantly."

"You're hair is pretty memorable," Maxon piped in, the timing was perfect and he said it with just the right amount of teasing. It was a cherry on top and just like that we had the whole crew, and all of Illea swooning with our story of first love. This story actually was true. It just hadn't been Maxon, but some other person instead.

"Like I said, I hadn't been in the snow before and I definitely wasn't wearing enough layers. But Maxon gave me his snow jacket and then just walked away."

"How did you guys get in contact?"

"I got back to where I was staying and saw his name and number on the tag of the jacket."

"And you called? Just like that?" Gavril pondered.

"Just like that."

"Now Maxon, what was it like to have the Princess call you?"

"I swore that I was being messed with but it didn't take long to realize that it had to be her. The kindness that she shows is completely real and I felt it right through the phone. I was in love from the very first word."

We both looked at each other at the same time, completely un-planned. He was looking at me to play his part as the madly in love boy but I was looking at him because he was playing this role so well. He had Gavril melting at his every word and he was doing it so naturally. I guess that's where the genes come in. I was trying to play the young girl in love. I only hoped that I was doing a good enough job.

"You two are adorable. So how long has it been than?"

I smiled cheerily and leaned towards Maxon. "Two years."

"Wow. That's a long time to keep a secret," Gavril said. "Why did you choose to make that decision?"

"It's just...I'm a princess. And that complicates so many parts of my life. I wanted Maxon and I to be normal. I just wanted to keep him for myself."

"But than he proposed," Gavril said.

"Than he proposed," I agreed, aiming my hand so the ring was visible again.

"And how did he do it? It must of been a grand gesture to impress a lady such as yourself."

My eyes went wide. I hadn't even thought about that part.

"Well uh..." I stuttered. "It was simple and—."

"I think it was the simplicity that made it so special, wouldn't you agree my dear? Can I tell him the story?" Maxon cut in.

I just nodded.

"Well I had come from Carolina to visit America for the week. It had been a while since we saw one another and I was overjoyed to see her. I hated spending time away from her and I knew that I didn't ever want to again. It was time to put a ring on it as the saying goes."

"So on the second night I was there, I took her out to our favorite spot in the gardens. It's this quaint stone bench that we like to sit on and watch the stars." That's the bench where we met. "We sat, I told her how much I love her, got down on one knee and the rest is history."

Gavril smiled. "That's wonderful. And you're ready for it? As you know, marrying the Princess comes with more than just love. You'll be the future king."

Maxon's grin faltered but only for a moment. "I'm ready."

"Well than, with confidence like that, we should be asking when the wedding date is?"

Maxon and I both turned to each other in fright.

"I'd like to pitch in on that!" My dad yelled jovially from where he sat to the side. His smile was that of a proud papa, but his eyes were calculated.

Gavril, Maxon, and I both were at high alert.

"Do you have a date in mind, your majesty?" Gavril asked.

Maxon and I were still holding hands from earlier but now we were squeezing the others in fear of what my dad might say.

"Quite the contrary Gavril. The kids were thinking a long engagement. They're both so young and it just seems too early for marriage. They should wait a few years," My dad spoke.

For once in my life I was beyond happy with what my dad said.

"Yes," I agreed before he could take it back. "We wanted to make it official but we're not quite ready for the 'walk down the isle' part."

Maxon squeezed my hand and I squeezed it back. We had crossed over one bridge.

"Well we are so glad to have gotten to speak to you two but I'm afraid we're out of time. It has been a joy."

"A pleasure for us too Gavril," I replied.

"Thank you Illea and Goodnight!"

As soon as the light on the camera flickered out, I snatched my hand from Maxon and looked over at my father. He met my eyesight and summoned me with a flick of his wrist.

I rushed over. "Long engagement?"

"Are you having second thoughts about the arrangement, Clarkson?" My mother asked, placing a tentative hand on his arm.

"What? No," My dad said, appalled. "The engagement will be long because America needs to get over herself. I understand that you may be miserable, but you'll get over it. Take a few years but when I say wedding, you better reply with a smile."

He didn't wait for a reply and just walked away. My mother stared after.

"He's—."

"Frustrated. He's always frustrated, Mother."

"Amy, maybe the engagement will be good. Maybe you'll actually fall in love with him."

Yeah. Right.

CHAPTER 13

I leaned back in my chair and sighed loudly. Another boring day of work. Another heartbreaking problem that I can't fix. Wonderful.

"What is if this time?" Anne asked.

"It is nothing in particular. Just complete helplessness as usual."

She skillfully maneuvered a needle through silk at a speed faster than I think I've done anything. Her eyes glanced down to her work to me swiftly as she multitasked. Currently she was a seamstress, therapist, friend, and assistant of sorts. My maids have decided that I don't really function as a human being when one of them isn't around.

Basically they're taking turns babysitting me.

"Why are you being helpless than?" Anne asked, not even bothering to look at me.

"What?" I whispered.

"Look Ames, I've known you for a long time. And it's always hurt me to see how cold you have to be to get through the day. Stone cold. I hate seeing you like that because it's not good for you to be so pretend all the time, emotionless."

"I have to be."

"You did," She agreed. Anne stabbed the needle into the dress and set it down next to her. "But something inside you broke when you found out about Maxon and I've seen you break down countless times since. You need to piece yourself back together."

"I don't understand what you're saying Anne," I stuttered.

"You've alway told me that even if you have to pretend for your whole life, it would be worth it to be queen some day. You need to pretend again. Paint a smile on your face and pretend like you are so in love with Maxon that you can barely stand to be apart form him. Put on a show. Be the Princess I know you can be so one day you can be queen. And then you can achieve all the things you've alway wanted. You're stubborn and you don't want to give in to you're father. But right now, there is no other choice. Make you're Dad happy. Play the role of the lovesick girl. This is just obstacle and it's taking you a little longer to get past it."

"I don't want to give up," I admitted. "I don't want to give in to his control."

"You're not giving up. The America I know, never gives up. You're doing the opposite. You're doing what you have to."

I lifted my chin up and breathed in deeply. She's right. I won't give in. I won't break down. I am going to be the best damn fiancé that there has ever been so that I can be the best damn queen Illea's ever had.

I only cuss in my head, like a true lady.

"Well than I'll get back to work," I said, lifting the next file.

"Nope. That's not in the schedule," Anne said.

"Schedule?"

"Yes. I received you're schedule this morning."

"And you didn't share it with me?"

Anne ignored me. "You have a photoshoot next. With Maxon. Engagement photos."

"Engagement photos?" I yelped.

She nodded.

Oh god. This not giving up thing was going to be harder than I thought.

~oOo~

"I hate this cream dress," I muttered as I shuffled through the halls, switching between covering up my chest and making sure the slit doesn't ride up too much.

"Yes, but this exact type of dress has been worn by the selected for generations when they take photos with the prince. Your parents thought it would be an appropriate dress for engagement photos." Anne was following next to me, reminding me very much of an assistant. Maybe I should get an assistant...

"We both know that those selected photos are only a ploy for the public to see if the selected look good with the prince."

Anne nodded. "Yes, I'm aware. And the public wants to know if Maxon looks good with you."

"I think that they should just mind they're own business," I informed her.

"Quit being dramatic. That's not how being a Princess works," She said. "Now are you ready?"

"I don't know, am I? I wasn't even made aware of this photo shoot none the less what I should look like?"

"Tiara?"

I tapped my head. "Check."

"Sash?"

"Check."

"Than you should be ready," Anne confirmed. She did a double check of my outfit and than ushered me into the room in which they had converted into a studio.

"Princess!" The photographer called as I entered the room.

I smiled fondly. "Hello Rosaria."

"I am still setting up but I shall only be a few more minutes!" She exclaimed and got back to work. Rosaria was a five who became famous for a single photograph and climbed the castes to a two. My mom fell in love with her work and began hiring her for all our photography needs. She was a sweetheart though a bit pushy.

I smoothed out my dress and glanced around. That's when I noticed Maxon standing awkwardly in the corner.

"That's a nice suit," I called.

He practically deflated in relief when he saw me. "Princess."

"Just call me, America, please," I spoke, approaching him slowly. "We are engaged."

"Yeah. I guess we are," He mumbled. "Oh, uh...you look pretty."

"Thank you. And you clean up nicely in a suit," I complimented.

He smiled and reached up to nervously fiddle with his bow tie.

"I wouldn't have pegged you for the bow tie type."

"I'm not. I just don't know how to tie a tie."

I chuckled.

"Alright. I'm ready! Bring me the happy couple!" Said Rosaria.

Maxon and I started walking over and it only took me a few seconds to realize that we looked like strangers. I wrapped my arms around his waist and he practically jumped out of his skin.

"I'm sorry," I murmured. He took a deep breath and wrapped his arm around my waist too.

"Adorable!" Rosaria cooed. "Now I want these photos to be completely natural. So just sit on the couch and have a conversation."

I squinted as she took a test shot. I led Maxon to the loveseat. We sat a foot apart.

"So how are you?" I asked.

"Well my family left this morning so I'm a little down, but I'm alright."

"Your family left? I had no idea or I would have said goodbye," I said. "How are they taking everything?"

"Well...." he lowered his voice. "May is too in love with the idea of us being together to question anything. My mom and dad don't understand why I'm doing this and it's not like I can really tell them why. I think they have an idea of what's going on but they're going along with it."

I nodded. "That's safer for them."

"Oh don't be modest on my account," Rosaria interrupted. "Sit closer, cuddle. I'm not even here."

I scooted right up next to him and grabbed his hand.

Rosaria squealed. "Ah, to be young and in love."

She started clicking away with her camera.

"I really hate them saying that," I sighed.

"What? Really?"

I laughed dryly. I don't know why I was going to tell him this, but why not. "Yes. I suppose, I had planned on finding real love...eventually. It was stupid of me to ever think that I would."

"No. It's not. Everybody deserves it no matter what they're position in the world is."

"How naive," I sighed weakly. I smiled just as light flooded our faces.

"I think it's just hopeful," he replied.

"I'm sorry you've been dragged into this." I froze for a second, posing with my hand on his chest and looking into his eyes. I stopped after a few seconds. "I've kind of always known this is a possibility. You're life has been turned upside down and it's all my fault."

"It's not your fault. But yes...it has been quite a change. I've kinda tried not to dwell on it."

"It's all I can think about," I countered.

It went silent as we both looked at the other. It was uncomfortable to be having this conversation in front of a camera. Obviously the camera couldn't hear, nor could Rosaria at the volume we were speaking, but Maxon and I were strangers. We had talked and obviously we were now bonded by this event, but we had only known each other for a small amount of time. We were strangers. Not only that, but we hadn't even had a chance to get to know one another. We had only spoken during our brief conversation before the report. And here we are in love and engaged.

Rosaria snapped her fingers, capturing our attention. "Princess, sit on his lap and wrap your arms around his neck."

I looked at him with wide eyes. He just shrugged. I hesitantly shifted closer to him. Pursing my lips, I lifted myself so that I sat on his lap. His hands instantly rested on my hips. God, this is embarrassing. Do people really do this? I'm an adult, not a child, why am I sitting on a grown mans lap?

"Gorgeous," Rosaria said approvingly. I wrapped my arms around his neck and smiled brightly.

"What's her name?" Maxon whispered.

"Rosaria," I replied through my teeth.

And then Maxon, out of nowhere, spit out some observation about how if she did this somewhat or other with the camera than it would do this thing and make us look like one or something. I'm not sure, but I was astounded.

"Wha......" I trailed off and cleared my throat, laughing nervously. "That's my fiancé. He knows wonders about photography." I think...

"I believe that I'll take that suggestion. I didn't know we had a photographer on our hands," Rosaria beamed.

Neither did I.

"You do photography?" I muttered as soon as she had started taking pictures again.

"Yes, I do. I am a five, America."

"Well yes I know, I had just never really asked..."

"You haven't really had much of a chance."

"Well I suppose if we are to be married than I should learn some basic information about you."

"Favorite color?" He asked.

"That would be blue. What about you?"

He peeked at me. "Mine's blue too."

"What is your favorite food?"

"Mmmmmm, my mother's potato casserole."

"I love Chef Delilah's strawberry tarts. They are the best in the world."

"I'll have to try them," He said.

"You'll have to eat two in honor of me," I agreed. "What hobbies do you enjoy?"

"I help my mom cook sometimes and I like doing that. But photography is my main hobby that I enjoy most, not just a job, so I'm pretty much snapping photos all the time. You?"

"Music."

"Music?"

I smiled shyly. "Yes. It isn't a well known fact about me but I dabble in music."

"What do you do?"

"I play piano, violin, flute, a few others and I sing a little bit."

"Dabble?" Maxon choked. "I'm pretty sure that's more than 'dabbling'."

"Well when I was younger, I obviously wasn't making important palace decisions yet, so my mom suggested that I take up an instrument. I started with piano and my love grew from there."

"How come nobody knows that?"

I shrugged. "I didn't think anybody would care."

He was about to respond when Rosaria spoke. She was analyzing Maxon with her brows furrowed, when her smile slipped into a frown.

"I hate the bow tie," She finally announced. "Can someone bring me a regular tie?"

A maid who was on standby rushed to go get one. While we waited, she had us change our pose quite a few times. Most of them required me to stand in front of Maxon, which coincidentally or not, covered the bow tie. We stopped once she had ran out of creative ways to pose us, but the maid arrived just in time with a plain black tie. She handed it to Maxon.

He cringed. "So, um...I don't know how to tie a tie."

"For real? I thought you were joking. Do you not dress up for weddings and events when your taking photos?" I whispered.

"I do, but I'm behind the camera so I just leave out the tie."

I exhaled. "Alright, I'll tie it."

"You know how?"

I nodded and took a step towards him, leaving only a foot of space between us. I could feel his breath on me. It smelt like minty toothpaste. I wrapped the tie around his neck and adjusted it carefully to his shirt. Out of the corner of my eye I could see that Rosaria was loving this and I plastered a big smile on as the flash burst across our faces.

"How did you learn how to tie a tie?" Maxon asked, watching me.

"I learned from my secret lover," I deadpanned.

Maxon's chest heaved and he chocked on air.

I grinned and wrapped one end of the tie around the other, creating a loop. I looked up at him from under my eyelashes. "No, actually I learned from my father."

I laughed lightly as his face calmed and he shook his head at me. "Not nice. Wow. I'm very close with my old man and he never taught me how to tie a tie. You and your dad must be really close."

My hands faltered for a second. I shook it off and stuck the tie through the loop, beginning to adjust the height.

"Yes," I said slowly, testing the words on my tongue. "We are very close."

There is no way to explain to Maxon why I actually learned how to tie a tie. My dad said that I would need to be able to tie the future Kings tie because a maid wasn't worthy of it. He followed that by saying that I was hardly even worthy but he had no other options. I bet he didn't know that his other option is the future king of Illea. I stepped back.

"All good?" He asked.

"Perfect."

"Yes, yes. Much better than before," Rosaria decided. "Now can I get one of the two of you holding hands and looking into each other's eyes."

We nodded our heads and turned towards each other. I slipped my fingers into his and looked into his eyes. I've seen the photos of my parents engagement and this pose was the one that was chosen to be plastered on every magazine. Maxon's eyes are brown, I noticed, but not an ugly normal brown. They were like swirling orbs of milk chocolate.

"I remember the first time I looked into your eyes," Maxon stated.

I raised an eyebrow.

"It was our first date."

A grin stretched across my face. "Oh really? And what did we do on our first date, babe?"

"You don't remember? Allow me to jog your memory. After we had been talking for a little bit, you flew out to Carolina to bring me my jacket and I asked if you were going back right away. You said that they had to prep the plane and that you wouldn't be leaving for a few hours. So I asked you if you wanted to go ice skating on a real Carolina lake and you said yes."

"Right, right. And I had a jacket this time?"

"You kept mine."

"Does it pair well with an evening gown?"

"It blends right in, darling."

I couldn't help but laugh. "So what else have we been up to these last 2 years?"

"You're being so forgetful today, but I'll remind you anyways. We had to hire a pilot to be on standby because we would constantly be flying back and forth between Carolina and Angeles."

"Well I couldn't go long away from you, Max."

He cringed. "I hate that nickname."

"Oooooo," I sang, breaking character. "Do tell."

"My two older siblings, Kenna and Kota, would call me that. It was cute until I was about 8, but than I grew out of it."

Rosaria called out to have us switch positions and we followed.

"So than what do you go by? Maxie? Just M?"

"I prefer just Maxon. What about you? Do you go by Princess America all the time?"

"No, actually. I have quite a few nicknames. My best friend calls me Mer. And my mother calls me Amy."

"I'm learning so much," He chuckled.

"Yes, my nicknames are of key importance," I agreed.

"Well obviously, as your fiancé, I have my own nickname for you which is....A-America-Am—Ames. Ames!"

"My maids call me that but I suppose you can too. It's much better than what all of the other suitors I've had have called me."

"What?"

"They all call me 'my dear'. And it's very sweet and endearing until I see them on tv with another girl a day later. We can't all be 'dear'."

"Well now you're tied down to one man so technically I can call you 'my dear'."

"No, I'm afraid it's been ruined for me. It is strictly off limits."

"America, my dear," Maxon said teasingly.

"Ugh!"

"I'm so happy to be taking photos with you, my dear."

I sighed. Wonderful.

"Perfect! I have got all that I need!" Rosaria yelled.

"We're done?" Maxon asked.

"I think we got a lot of great shots. You two are a very photogenic couple," Rosaria complimented.

We nodded our thanks and Maxon turned towards me.

"Well I do believe if has been a pleasure taking engagement photos with you," Maxon paused. He swung his hand down and brought my hand to his lips, kissing it mockingly. "My dear."

Comments always make my day

CHAPTER 14

I ran my fingertips along the keys testingly, listening to the music.

"Lucy?"

My hand froze.

"Yes Miss Amara?"

"Should I take Americas red pumps or her gold stilettos?"

"As her maid, I am not allowed to condone you stealing her things," Lucy said. "But gold."

Amara nodded and threw my shoes by the door in a pile with two of my dresses. I rolled my eyes and continued to pluck notes out on the piano. It must of been a few weeks since I last played and it had always been a good stress reliever for me.

"Anne?" Mary asked. "Is this supposed to be a running stitch or a slip stitch?"

"A running stitch, I believe," Anne replied. "Or was it an overcast? Lucy?"

"Running."

I dropped my hand, sending a disastrous sequence of notes throughout the room.

"That's not a pretty sound America. I thought you were good at piano," Amara quipped.

I grumbled. "I am. If you would just let me have some peace and quiet."

"The piano isn't quiet."

I sighed. "Is there a reason you decided to grace me with your presence Amara? Or are you only here to make noise and steal my things?"

"Hmmmm...there was a reason why I came but I can't seem to rem ember...Oh yes! I have a message from my mother."

"Since when does she send messages through you?"

"Well I was coming this way anyways."

"What's the message, Amara?"

"Mom says that you have to sit in on etiquette lessons with Maxon. To get to know him or whatever."

I groaned.

"I'm already marrying the man. Now they want me to get to know him too?" I complained.

"That would make sense," Anne said.

"My father is just trying to see how far he can push me before I fall over and we are reaching the tipping point. I'm not sure how much more of this I can take."

Mary appeared at my side. "You are indestructible. Once you get through all this than it's smooth sailing. Just you, a crown, and a country to lead."

"And a husband who I don't love."

"Technicalities," Mary brushed off.

"A pretty large technicality. Amara, is that it?"

"Oh, yeah. And um...the etiquette lessons are starting now."

"What!"

~oOo~

I tried to discreetly slip into the room but there isn't really a way to do that when you are being waited for. Especially when it's Silvia who is waiting for you.

"Your majesty, you're late."

I noticed Maxon chuckling and I shot him a look.

"I apologize, Miss Silvia, but I had some miss information and was not aware of this lesson."

She rose an eyebrow. "Do you mean to blame this on my daughter?"

"Yes."

"I'll allow it but please work on your punctuality. I think it's been slipping lately."

I nodded and took a few steps closer to Maxon. "So what exactly am I doing here, Miss Silvia? I've taken etiquette lessons my whole life and simply do not see why I'm sitting in on these."

"Because of the situation," Silvia said. "You two need to become very close, very fast. This is a, killing two birds with one stone, of sorts. You're here to help out and maybe learn a few things about him."

I grinned forcefully. "Oh joy. This is exactly what I want to do with my day."

"I'm glad," Silvia replied, ignoring me. "Let us begin."

"What are we starting with? History? Social issues?"

"No, no. Neither of those are important enough. We don't have as long as we normally would to groom him to be a prince. We need to get the basics down and we need to do it fast. A dignitary or royal could visit any day now and he needs to be able to at least interact with them."

"Um...."Maxon cut in. "You do know I haven't been living under a rock, right? I know how to behave in normal social situations."

"These aren't normal situations though. There are rules that must be followed when you're a royal."

"Is there a rule book?"

"No. Stay on task."

I wondered to the other side of the sitting room we were in and over to the bay window.

And so began the endless drawl of Maxon learning how to greet people. I don't understand why I was present here. There is no time for me to get to know him when he is occupied with learning how to greet different types of people. I had occupied myself with twiddling with the hem of my dress, discreetly though so that Silvia wouldn't become aware and scold me. She seems to think that I'm some robot who can just sit and do nothing for hours on end. I need entertainment just like everyone else. Though it was certainly entertainment enough to see Maxon going through etiquette. In a weird way, it was rewarding. I've spent my whole life learning these things. He gets to experience this torture now too.

I was basically sprawled out across the seat now, trying to keep myself from falling asleep. I was sprawled out like a lady of course, and I wasn't sleeping, but both of those were only because Silvia was a short few feet away.

"You should learn how to greet people in as many languages as possible. It's too late to have you learn the languages, there's simply not enough time. But knowing how to say hello, goodbye, and it's nice to meet you is essential to being a royal."

"Bonjour, Ciao, Hola," I drawled lazily, from where I lay.

"N'interrimoez pas, votre majesté," Silvia sniped in French, basically telling me not to interrupt her. I sighed. I repeat, how am I supposed to get to know him if I'm not even allowed to speak. I noticed Maxon chucking and I gave him a look.

I mouthed the word French to him and he nodded. And then in perfect French he told me that he already speaks French.

Oh. Well I guess I am learning new things about him. I should tell Daphne that all the French she taught me so that we can gossip is going to good use.

There was a knock at the door and Silvia called out for the person to enter. It was a maid.

"Miss Silvia?" She asked.

"Yes, what is it?" Silvia rushed.

"Your presence is being requested by the queen."

"The queen?" Silvia repeated.

"Yes, she understands your busy but says it won't take long."

"Very well," She agreed. "I will be back so please don't get into too much trouble."

"As of February 26th, we are responsible adults," I smiled.

"You're 18, the rest is up to debate," She replied, and headed for the door. I waited for it to boom shut behind her before rolling my eyes.

"You're mother is a life saver," Maxon said, wondering closer to my seat. "I'm not sure how much more of this I can take."

"We are barely scratching the surface, your highness, this is not an easy job to have."

"I'm gathering that," He agreed. "Don't you ever just do normal things?"

I pursued my lips. "Yes. I enjoy reading and I play music."

"But like everyday things. You know...do laundry or cook."

"I'm a future queen not a housewife," I scoffed.

"Those are just examples. I just mean, you know...well I actually don't know what I mean."

"No, I don't do laundry and I don't cook. I have made food before but I don't cook. I prefer to learn boring history and read boring reports."

"Well laundry's not that fun anyways," He said.

The door was pulled open suddenly and I sighed. That wasn't very long. It wasn't Silvia though, but a maid.

"Do I have the wrong room..." She muttered to herself.

"Who are you looking for?" I called out, standing up.

"Oh your majesty!" She jumped. "And Sir Maxon. My apologies, I didn't mean to interrupt your time together. I'm looking for Miss Silvia. I have some food that she requested to this room."

"Silvia has stepped out but this is the correct room."

"Oh, good. Don't mind me, I'm just going to unload some things." She stepped out for a moment and returned with a cart full of delicious smelling foods. I smelt spices and sugar and....I took a sniff of the air. Mmmm. Strawberry tarts. She also had plates and other things for table settings.

"What's the food for? I wasn't aware they're would be appetizers," Maxon asked.

I narrowed my eyes as the maid set out napkins on the table across the room. "I believe it's for dining etiquette."

"Dining etiquette?"

"Yes. It is the easiest of the etiquettes and probably the one you'll use the most."

"So do we just like...eat?"

I smiled. "There's a bit more to it than that but I suppose so."

I stood up and walked swiftly over to the table. I nodded at the maid as she finished up. And she bowed before leaving.

I gasped. "Oh my..."

"What?" Maxon questioned, joining me at the table.

"I love strawberry tarts," I said wistfully, eyeing the plate on the table. Their steamy scent wafted up to my nose, teasing me. "I'm not allowed to eat them though."

"What?" Maxon asked. "Why not?"

"Two reasons. One, there is really no way to eat them politely. It just turns into a gooey, crumbly mess. And two, I have to watch my figure. I'm not supposed to eat too much sugar."

"One strawberry tart isn't going to kill you," Maxon argued.

"I know, but I just try not to. I never need to give my father a reason to be mad at me," I said. I immediately regretted saying this but Maxon just let it slide past him.

He carefully picked up a flaky, buttery tart off the plate and balanced it on his hand. "Take a bite."

"I'm good," I said, pushing his hand away gently.

"You know you really want to. Just take a bite," Maxon urged. He lifted it towards my lips and I stared it down. Layer and layers of flaky crust tempted me and the aroma of sugary strawberry filled my nose. I couldn't resist. I leaned forward and took a small nibble from the end of the tart. I didn't get any strawberry and I barely got any tart, but at least it'll satisfy Maxon so that we can get past this.

I looked up and smiled at Maxon. He did not return it.

"Take an actual bite," He said.

"I did!" I said defensively.

Maxon took the side of the tart that was facing him and took a giant bite of it, consuming a good fourth of it into his mouth. Crumbs scattered across his shirt and jelly spilled onto his lips, while he chewed a big mouthful of it. I watched enviously.

"If Silvia was in here, she would have your head," I said, though I couldn't help but giggle as he licked his lips dramatically.

"Mmmmmm. So good," He said loudly, bringing the tart closer to my face. I pursued my lips and looked up at him. I glanced at the tart and to his eyes which were teasing. My eyes scanned the room. I suppose it was just him and I...

I quickly leaned forward and practically unhinged my jaw in order to take the biggest bite of the tart I could. My mouth filled with warm, buttery crust that was so flaky that it almost melted on my tongue. And that jelly. The flavor of real strawberries and sugar and deliciousness.

It's been so long since I've had this.

It took a moment to realize that there was too much food for me to chew and I kinda choked for a second. The next second I was swallowing and then the next I was laughing. I mean laughing. Full on belly laughs with mixes of giggling in there. I was laughing like it was forbidden and I would never do it again. Nothing funny was said. No joke was made. I just felt good. My laughter was dying out but I couldn't stop giggling. I almost fell out of my chair.

"Woah," Maxon chuckled, steadying me by my arm as my giggles faded into a smile. "No wonder you can't eat those. They send you into fits of giggles! Noted."

"No," I said. "It was just...I haven't taken the big of a bite of...probably anything."

"Well I've never taken an etiquette class before so I guess we're both trying new things," He said

I took what was left of the mangled tart and split it, handing half to him. "Cheers to new things."

We clicked our tarts together, sending crumbs across our laps. We ate them in one bite and we had just finished chewing when Silvia came back into the room.

"I've returned. Oh good, the food is here. So we can begin the next stage of etiquette."

I glanced over at Maxon and his eyes met mine. We shared a single, short gaze before I looked away. I lifted my fingers towards my lips

and checked for any crumbs that may linger there. But all that remained was a smile.

"Now I feel we should start with..."

And the smile remained they're afterwards.

CHAPTER 15

Today, was not going to be a good day.

Nor was it going to be a good evening or night. Tomorrow morning probably isn't going to be that pleasant either. In fact, it may be worse than today.

"Will you please stop pouting, America?" My mom sighed.

"I am not pouting," I replied.

"You're no fun to spend time with when your acting like a child," She reiterated. "More tea?"

"No, actually, I think I'm tired of tea. I drink it far to often."

"And now your taking you're emotions out on your beverage. I could be doing some thing else more productive right now if you would like, America."

I breathed deeply. "I apologize Mother. I am just in a bad mood and you know exactly why."

"As a logical person, you have to understand the reasoning behind it. It's only so much to tell the people that you two are in love. They want to see something, anything that proves it's true."

"So making me go on a date with him is the solution we came up with?" I muttered.

"It is perfect and it doesn't require all that much work on your part. As long as you are in view of the press than it's up to them to do the rest. Just put on a show."

"I am not an object for the press to write a play of my love life about." I resisted the urge to let out a cry of frustration and took a calming breath. "All I'm trying to say, Mom, is that isn't this already challenging enough for me? My whole world has been flipped upside down and now you want me to go act like I'm happy about it in front of the cameras? I am trying to be complaisant in this situation and do what I am told, but where do I draw the line?"

"From here on out, I will try and put it in a word for you—."

"That's another thing. Why am I not being present at these meetings where my fate is being decided?"

"Amy, you know you are sort of biased against these things. Your opinion cannot be held to much meaning and at the end of the day, we already know where on the spectrum you lay in terms of your relationship."

I gritted my teeth and pursed my lips.

My mother reached for my hand. "Just try and have a good time dear. It doesn't have to be something you're forced into. You could go on a genuine date with him and gave a good time."

"I'll go on the date but that's about as much as your going to get."

Her fingers squeezed mine. "I suppose that's all I can ask for. Please wear something nice though. Your face will be everywhere tomor-row."

~oOo~

"So where are you going on the date?" Lucy wondered. She gently picked up my limp arm and rubbed lotion into my skin that smelt like flowers and what I imagine rainbows smelt like. I was sitting on my vanity stool, but backward so that the three of them have better access to me or so they say. It also meant that I couldn't see what they were doing to me.

"In the gardens up by the front gate," I said. Once she let go of my arm, I tinkered with the makeup options in front of me, choosing a pale pink lip gloss. It would be a more youthful and carefree look than I usually went for, but I think the cameras would like that. They'll chalk it up to true love instead of just makeup science. I handed the tube to Anne.

"On the grass patch?" Mary inquired. "Like a little picnic?"

"Yes. There was a leak that I would be going on a date with my fiancé in the gardens. The press should be lined up to get their photos."

"Well look at the bright side," Mary told me. She delicately ran a brush through my hair, the way a mother does a daughter. It was weirdly calming. "Publicity like that should placate the advisors, and your father, for a while. As long as people are still talking about this date, you're a free woman."

Anne nodded in agreement. "Like the engagement photos that you two took. Everyone has been speaking about how good you two looked together for weeks. They were a hit and if I remember correctly, you were left alone for a bit."

"Those pictures were gorgeous! The maids quarters were buzzing about them and still are!" Lucy said.

"Well America, it sounds like all you have to do is give them something to buzz about," Mary advised. She set the brush down next to me and took my hair into her hands. "What do you think, Luc, hair up or down?"

"Down is more youthful," Lucy pitched in.

"That is true, but..." Mary experimentally twisted my hair up at the nape of my neck. "This gives more emphasis to her makeup and dress. And we could maybe pin flowers into a twist..."

"What? Flowers?" I stuttered, spinning my head to face her and sending my hair cascading down my shoulders. "I am a young adult, not a child playing in a meadow!"

"America, we are going for youthful. You have always been so grown up that the country missed out on seeing you be young and carefree. Your father wants to express that now," Anne explained gently.

I bit my lip and sighed.

"I hate flowers," I grumbled.

Mary smiled condescendingly. "I know, sweetie. Going on a date with a hot guy must be so difficult for you."

I rolled my eyes.

"I'm glad you understand," I countered.

"Just try and have fun, America. This doesn't have to be all bad," Mary sighed.

I was forced to be silent as Anne started my makeup. I was acutely aware of what she was doing as she chose different shades of soft pinks and different products with dewy consistencies. She was painting a version of me that did not exist. A girl who has dreams and believes she can fall in love. My dad crushed this version of me because it did not please him and now he wants her to come out and play. This girl still thought her father loved her and still believed that anybody in this place cared for what she had to say. My father took care of her.

But maybe Mary and my mother were right.

It might be fun to play the role of her again.

Anne pulled her hand away from my face as soon as she had finished with my lips, just as Mary was securing my hair to my head with pins.

Anne smiled. "You should really let us do your makeup like this more often."

"Don't get any ideas," I warned.

"You look beautiful," Lucy murmured. "So are you meeting at the gardens?"

"He is coming here."

"We get to meet him?" Lucy gasped. I nodded hesitantly.

Mary called something out about grabbing my dress and retreated to my closet. She returned quickly and my face fell.

"What is that?"

Mary raised a challenging eyebrow. "You're dress."

"It's so....frilly."

"You're judging it for no reason. It is your favorite color. It has a simple lace bodice. And the skirt is like many you've worn before."

I grimaced. "But....together. I'm going to look like an enchanted fairy who sings about flowers and glitter."

"Not a bad look to have," Lucy said. "It'll be a nice change from your daily pencil skirts and the usual long, boring evening gowns."

"You make all those clothes for me!" I argued.

Anne took the dress from Lucy and held it up to my form. "Because it's what you like for us to make. But this is what we need to finish the look. You act like your 40 already, America. This makes you look your age, which if you have forgotten, is 18. You are a young woman, still a teen."

I frowned.

"Fine. But I am only going to wear it because the press will eat it up," I agreed.

"Oh yay! Go put it on! Go put it on!" Lucy squealed, taking the dress and ushering us both into the closet. I distinctly heard a knock resound in the other room which meant that Maxon was here.

"He's here," I whispered to Lucy.

She helped me get into my dress quickly. "I have ears too, Ames."

Her supple fingers clasped my dress, which luckily had buttons instead of ties, and she was done in a snap. I grabbed a pair of heels and went to meet Maxon in my main room.

He was standing awkwardly by the door making polite conversation with Mary, who for some due credit was behaving like a maid should, which was abnormal.

"Hey," I greeted, slipping a nude heel onto my foot.

It was silent for a few seconds before he finally replied. "Oh, um hi."

I stepped into the other heel and turned around to check my reflection in the mirror. I was right. I did look like a Barbie fairy princess but I didn't hate it. It's...different.

"Well I'm ready," I announced turning back towards the group. I observed Maxon. I'm not going to lie, he looked very dashing in his suit. I can only assume that a group of maids helped him get ready but he looked nice. "I see you tied your own tie. Or did a maid do it?"

He smirked. "I did it."

"Good. So are we ready—."

"Wait America!" Mary yelled out. "You're not ready yet!"

"What I—."

"Come with me to the closet," She demanded and pulled me away. Anne and Lucy followed.

"He is so cute," Lucy whispered.

"This is what we're in here for?" I muttered.

"Yes! He was like totally awestruck when you entered the room. Jaw basically on the floor," Mary said.

"You are so dramatic," I sighed.

"Did you see his eyes, Luc? They—."

"And this conversation is over," I interrupted, heading out the door. The poor guy was just looking around, not knowing what to do. "I apologize, I needed....to adjust my dress."

"Is this the part where I offer you my arm?" Maxon questioned.

"Yes, actually, it is."

He held his arm out and I wrapped mine through his. My maids bid us goodbye and I ignored them. I wouldn't be surprised if they spied on us from my balcony.

"So my fiancé, where are we going to?" Maxon asked.

"A romantic picnic in the gardens," I replied.

"Will there be strawberry tarts?"

"I sure hope so" I grinned.

"But it is a crime to consume them," He mock-gasped.

"You're being a bad influence on me. I think I've had three tarts since that etiquette lesson."

"That just sounds like I've made your life better," He chuckled. I noticed us pass by a familiar guard and he nodded at him. It was the friend of his I met.

"Do you know him?" I asked innocently.

"Yeah, I do actually. That's Aspen. He was my best friend from home. I'm really lucky that he winded up here."

We were coming up on the staircase. "That is extremely lucky. Is he aware of this... arrangement?"

"Yes, I mean obviously he knew that I hadn't been secretly dating you for two years. But he has promised his silence."

"Well, it's great that you'll have someone to talk to about things. I mean you can always talk to me, of course, but someone impartial."

We headed out into the gardens and he didn't even ask where we were going, simply following me as I led him down the long pathway.

"So then you guys grew up together?"

"Were family friends turned best friends. He comes from a family of sixes and his mom worked all the time. So my mom would watch them while she worked as a house cleaner. In return, she would clean our house. My mom could do it on her own but Lena Legar would never let my mom watch her kids for nothing. But anyway, since he was always around we became natural friends."

"I have a similar story with my best friend actually. Her name is Amara and she is the daughter of Miss Silvia, who you've met obviously. She lived here and she was the only other kid anywhere near me, so naturally, we interacted often. We played as toddlers and that was easy, but we didn't always get along as children. But along the way we clicked and we still have tea parties to this day."

"What about picnics?"

"Well, this one is actually my first..." I trailed off, presenting to him the picnic in front of us.

It was nothing more than a blanket laid across the grass, but it was one of the most romantic things I'd seen. There was a spread of all types of food, from pasta and salad to brownies and tarts. Two bottles of wine, red and white, and a bottle of champagne were in a small cooler. The spot that whoever set this up had chosen was framed by gorgeous fruit trees and was in perfect view of the palace gates. As planned, a hoard of photographers swarmed the fences but they weren't close enough to speak to us nor hear us. But as we approached, I reached for Maxon's hand, and the cameras began to snap.

"That's a lot of press," Maxon whispered.

I squeezed his hand. "Ignore them."

Like a true gentleman, he helped me sit down politely on the blanket and he followed.

"How does this work?" He mumbled.

"They can't hear you," I told him. "So we can say anything. But to them, it must look like we are a newly engaged couple on a date."

"So like hold hands and stare into each other's eyes?"

"That should suffice," I laughed. "But I'd like to eat first. Strawber-ries!"

"....tarts?"

"No, fruit!" I laughed, pulling strawberries out of the cooler. I opened the Tupperware and took a bite of a juicy strawberry. "Mmmmm. These are so sweet."

Maxon took a strawberry and ate all besides the stem of it in one bite. "These are...delicious!"

"Palace grown," I smiled. "Wonderful in tarts but delectable all on there own, as well."

I set the strawberries between us and rubbed my hands together.

"So what else can you tell me about you?" I asked.

"I've already told you about my family and home town."

"But what else? Tell me about your job."

"Well, I was a photographer. And photography was my favorite thing to do. My camera stayed with me at all times."

"Do you have your camera?"

"Unfortunately I didn't bring it to the palace because I hadn't planned on staying. I haven't really taken a picture in a while," He admitted.

My jaw dropped. "That can't be allowed. It's your thing. If someone took my violin away from me, I wound throw a fit. We will get your camera here."

"Thank you, America. Shall we open this..." his eyes scanned over the wines and landed on the champagne. "Champagne."

I retrieved the flutes and held them in my hands. He topped them off with bubbly champagne.

I took a sip and smiled. "This is so much better than wine."

"Cheers to that," He agreed and we clinked our glasses together.

It was silent after our glasses connected and I could practically feel the eyes of reporters peering into my back.

I slipped my fingers into his own and he hardly even noticed.

"Can we be a tad serious for a second?" I asked.

Maxon raised an eyebrow and set his glass down next to him. "Yes..."

"This whole switched thing...obviously both our lives are changed completely because of it. Which one of us lost more?"

"Well, we both lost a chance at living the lives we were supposed to. But both of us have hardship, in very different ways though."

"You grew up poor. You could've been so much happier if your caste didn't prevent it."

"And your life is so stressful. I've only been living it a few weeks and I feel like pulling my hair out." There was something else he wanted to say and it took him a moment to come up with it. "But you never starved and you've never had to want for anything."

"I suppose you're right," I said.

But I wanted to tell him that he was wrong. Because he has a real, happy family and that is the one thing I have always wanted for.

"On a lighter topic," He said nervously. "Pasta."

"And salad."

The date continued on much lighter topics. The food was delicious. There is something about eating out of the Tupperware that made it 1000 times better than usual. I also learned more about Maxon. He has a lot of stories about growing up in a small town, and also many stories about his siblings and they're many shenanigans. I personally was enjoying myself a lot. Maxon has a great personality and is someone that I would see myself being friends with if the situation was different. If he had been drafted like his friend, I think we would have been instant buddies.

We had been naturally holding hands for a while now and it was actually kinda nice. It knew it was strictly platonic but I can definitely see why couples are always joint by their fingertips.

"Okay..." I laughed, sipping my champagne and setting it next to me. "Stare into each other's eyes in 3...2...1."

We looked deeply into each other's eyes which I had now become familiar with. They were brown, but a lighter brown, with hints of gold. Very unique.

"Staring contest in...3...2...1..." Maxon spoke.

I tried to inconspicuously focus on his nose and do that thing where you zone out so that you don't blink.

"That's cheating," Maxon said, catching me in the act.

I almost blinked as my eyes readjusted but I stayed strong. Out of nowhere, Maxon widened his eyes to a comical size and I couldn't help but burst out laughing, my eyes squeezing shut.

"That's also cheating!" I mumbled between giggles.

"Nope. Completely legal," He denied.

I shook my head. "Cheater."

He was about to respond when something caught his eye. "Is that...a tiara?"

I followed his eyes back down the path we took to get here and to the rose bushes. Nestled into the grass, and almost completely concealed by flowers, was a tiara. I remember knocking it off my head during the night of a ball we hosted a few months back. I had been living my life oblivious then and look where I am now.

"Yes, it is," I smiled to myself.

"Is someone trying to see if a tiara will grow into a tree or..." Maxon joked.

I laughed. "No, actually it was me who left it there. I had knocked it off my head and then was caught by some press and never got a chance to retrieve it."

"Those things are expensive, right? Should you just be leaving that there?"

"Should I...no. Did I, yes."

"I've noticed....." Maxon stopped to think of what to say. "That you're dialect is less formal when you become...more comfortable."

"My dialect?" I repeated.

"Like the way you talk. You talk like a very educated person and you use big words and fancy sentences." I raised an eyebrow. "But you've kind of become more comfortable as the date has progressed."

" I suppo–I guess I have."

Something suddenly occurred to me. In the midst of enjoying myself, I had forgotten to give the camera much of anything at all. I could only hold Maxon's hand so many times.

My heart began to race. I remembered what my maids had said. If I could just give the people something to talk about than I'd be left alone.

I knew what I had to do.

"Trust me, okay?" I whispered. I could see the cameras out of the side of my eyes. They weren't missing anything. They couldn't hear our conversation. None of them would dare get close enough to be able to hear what we were saying, but I still felt I had to whisper.

"What?" He asked, his eyes showing his confusion.

"Shhhhh," I mumbled. "There are at least 10 cameras on us right now. And the strawberries and the smiles have been nice, but that's not what they want."

"I don't understand..."

"I'm going to kiss you."

"Uh....." He stuttered.

"Shut up," I mumbled.

I leaned forward and placed a hand on his cheek. His eyes stared at me, all nervous and wide. It's a shame that his life turned out to be like this. He could have had a normal life with a normal relationship. A nice, sweet girl who he meets and falls in love with. They get married and have kids and live happily ever after.

I always knew this would be my life. I knew from a young age that any relationship I would ever have would be fake and in front of cameras. Young me may have hoped that I would fall in love and it would work itself out. But it didn't take much for that little girl's dreams to be crushed. I moved my hand from his cheek and dug it into his hair. I was giving the cameras everything they wanted. That's what my life has always been about, pleasing everyone else. I looked into his eyes, brown and confused.

I feel sorry for him.

He doesn't deserve this.

I brought his face closer to mine and his eyes closed in anticipation. I ghosted my lips over his in a whisper of a kiss. His lips were soft and smooth and didn't deserve to be used for publicity, but there wasn't much of a choice on either of our parts. I kissed him again but a little more, moving my lips sweetly against his and it took him a second but he realized he was supposed to do the same. But when he did.....I got lost in the way his lips felt and how soft his hair was, and I just got lost in...him. I slid my fingertips away from his hair and down his shoulders until I found his hands, and directed them to my hips. Without any instruction, he pulled me closer. We were so close that I could feel his heart beating rapidly against my own as our lips moved together in synchronization.

I pulled away gently, taking in a deep breath.

That was my first kiss. I wonder if it was his too.

"Wow," He whispered, breathing heavily.

"I bet the cameras loved that," I whispered.

"Right....." He trailed off.

"The cameras," I agreed.

We both realized simultaneously that we were still up close and personal and scrambled away. I played it off as much as I could for the cameras but I could only do so much. Though that kiss was probably enough to smooth it over.

"Sooo..."

"Strawberry tarts?" I filled in.

"Yes please."

I noticed soon after that the photographers were beginning to leave. It made sense. We had given them what they wanted. A fiery kiss was all they needed and now they have their cover story for the next day. Maxon and I's date was also coming to a close. We had almost finished a bottle of champagne and the plate of tarts was running on low. Plus the sun was setting and a breeze was beginning to send goosebumps across my arms.

"This was...surprisingly a lot more fun than I thought it would be," Maxon admitted, beginning to pack up the food into the baskets and cooler.

"Did you think that I would be boring?" I teased, popping the last bite of the last tart in my mouth.

"No! Uh—I just meant." He stopped blubbering as soon as he saw my mocking grin. "The idea of a fake date just seemed like it wouldn't be...fun. But it was."

"I had fun too," I smiled.

We were quick to finish packing up, Maxon putting away the dishes and me taking it upon myself to fold up the blanket.

Maxon took the blanket and placed it in the basket before hopping off the grass and extending me his hand. I took it and he pulled me to my feet, even steadying me when I stumbled the landing.

"Shall I walk you to your room, your majesty?" He offered grandly, even going as far as to bow.

"Sure," I shrugged.

I took his arm and held the picnic basket in the other. We walked in a comfortable silence to the palace and once we got inside we still remained quiet. There wasn't much to say. I think that the idea of it not being a real date removed the pressure of it all and I actually ended up enjoying myself. I've learned a lot about Maxon and he is actually a pretty interesting person. Could I fall in love with him... well that's a bit of a stretch. But if I had to be in an arranged marriage with someone, I suppose he wasn't all that bad.

But that didn't mean I was giving in. I was still looking for a way out of this, something, anything that I could do so that I didn't have to marry Maxon Singer. He doesn't deserve all this. And honestly, neither do I.

"America...? America!"

"Huh....what?" I shook my head, glancing at Maxon.

"You zoned out," He replied. "We're at your door."

"Oh," I mumbled, glancing at the door to my room. "Sorry, I guess I'm just tired."

"Well then you should get a good nights rest. Goodnight, America."

I twisted my door handle and took a few steps into the room. "Goodnight Maxon."

I closed the door and took a deep breath as if I haven't been breathing the whole time I was with him.

I have some serious thinking to do.

Hello from social distancing everyone! I worked hard on this chapter and I hope you all enjoyed it!

CHAPTER 16

I woke up to pictures of my own face.

Well actually, I woke up to Lucy gently shaking me awake while holding a warm cup of coffee. Not only that, but I woke up with a smile on my face.

"Good morning girls," I greeted, lifting myself onto my elbows.

"Good morning, Princess," Lucy replied. "Coffee?"

"Of course," I said and accepted the cup.

"And here is a magazine!" Mary exclaimed, swooping over to me with a devilish grin on her face.

"I don't read magazines, Mary..." I told her, giving her a weird look.

"Well here's a newspaper than," She said, brandishing one from behind her back.

"I don't read those..." I trailed off as I saw my own face staring at me off the cover of the newspaper. In vibrant color, was a photo of Maxon and I, looking into each other's eyes as our lips hovered millimeters apart.

"Oh my god," I whispered, taking the newspaper from her. I turned to the page and began to read aloud. " 'The news of Princess America's engagement came as a shock to all of us when it was announced a few weeks back. Our beloved future queen has been turning away princes and other suitors for years and now it all makes sense as to why. Though the couple was seen together on The Report during the announcement of their engagement, they have been dark ever since. But their date last night more than makes up for it'."

"Keep reading," Mary encouraged, bouncing on her toes.

" 'The couple was seen last night on a romantic picnic in the gorgeous palace gardens. An inside source tells us that the picnic was set up by Maxon himself.' " I looked up at Mary. "Inside source? What inside source? Where do they even get this stuff?"

She motioned for me to continue on.

" 'Her majesty,' I read. "and her fiancé enjoyed a Tupperware style meal prepared by the palace chefs and enjoyed conversation with each other for the duration of the date. But they couldn't stay away from each other for too long and the couple shared a passionate kiss at the end of the night. The chemistry is definitely there'. This is..."

"So cute," Mary said.

"This is what we expected," Anne reminded me.

"Yes, I know but I just wasn't quite prepared. Hand me my tv remote please."

Anne retrieved the remote and clicked the tv on before handing it to me. And I was greeted with Maxon and I kissing again. Ugh! This is obsessive! I wouldn't have kissed him if I knew this was going to be the result.

"The video is even spicier than the picture," Mary cooed.

I rolled my eyes. "It was a platonic kiss, Mary. It was my first so it probably sucked."

"Honey, with natural chemistry there is no need for experience. And you two, have chemistry."

I ignored her and clicked to the next channel. It was another news channel with Maxon and I as their top story. Don't any of these channels cover actual news?

"Where's my phone?" I asked.

"In your nightstand," Anne said. I pulled open the nightstand drawer and grabbed my phone. It was rarely used. I only use it occasionally to communicate with my friends from other countries. And I knew that Nicoletta and Daphne will have seen this.

I turned on the phone and was met with over 15 missed texts from Nicoletta and Daphne. The contents were basically them freaking out about the whole thing. I had explained to them about the arranged marriage after I had received a bunch a nasty texts when the engagement was announced. The content of these messages were more along the lines of how Mary has been acting all morning, obsessing over the date and kiss. That is until I read the last one.

"Oh no," I mumbled.

"What is it?" Anne asked.

"Nicoletta and Daphne are coming to Illea."

~oOo~

"Nicoletta, Daphne," My mother greeted, embracing Daphne in her arms. "We weren't aware that you guys would be visiting."

"It was very last minute, Amberley. But we saw America's big date last night and we couldn't wait any longer to meet her fiancé."

"Yeah sure," I murmured under my breath but Nicoletta caught it.

"America! It's been far too long since we saw each other," Nicoletta said, coming over to hug me.

"Yes I agree," I replied.

"We have much to talk about," She whispered in my ear in a sing-song voice.

"I don't think we do," I sang back.

"Oh. My. God. Daphne!"

I whipped my head around and saw Amara descending the last step of the stairs and barreling towards Daphne. They hugged each other full force and this is when I knew this was going to be a be a very long day. These were my three best friends, whom I love dearly, but they can be...a lot.

Especially when they're together.

"You saw it right?" Daphne asked Amara.

"Of course! I have 3 copies of the magazines and tea outside in the gardens, all ready for us," Amara told her excitedly. Daphne, Nicoletta, and Amara greeted one another, circling each other and whispering excitedly.

My mom laughed lightly and touched my arm. "I'll leave you girls to it."

"No mom please don't," I whispered after her but she just thought it was funny and walked away. Traitor.

"Come on America," Daphne called, the three of them already heading into the gardens. I took a deep breath and followed after them. Amara had a table set up in our usual spot and I begrudgingly sat down. On the table was a warm pot of tea and 4 cups, plus a few magazines with Maxon and I's faces staring back at me. They were actually 3 different magazines each with Maxon and I kissing on the cover.

It seems I cannot get away from my own face.

"This is a bit excessive, don't you think?" I pointed out.

"I think it's romantic," Daphne sighed,

"No," I warned. "I told you guys this is an arranged marriage."

"Yes, yes," Nicoletta said dismissively. "But it was intimate none the less."

"And you went as far as to kiss him," Amara stressed. "You didn't have to go that far."

"There we're cameras pointed at us the whole time. They didn't want pictures of us talking, they wanted a cover story," I said defensively.

"You've never been one to do what others want," Nicoletta said, lips pursed in suspicion.

"I was doing what I wanted. I want my father and all his advisors to leave me alone. And as you can tell, it's working. I have no stupid meetings or unnecessary etiquette lessons to attend, and instead I can spend time with you guys all day. Which I would be very excited about if only I didn't have to talk about this."

"America," Daphne reasoned, pushing one of the magazines forward. "Look at this. This is not a platonic kiss. A peck would have been enough to placate the so called 'cameras'. This is full on tension."

I scoffed. "Daphne..."

"America, may I be blatant with you?" Nicoletta asked, though it didn't matter what I said. I nodded my head.

She waved her hand over the magazines. "This, doesn't look like its for a camera. It looks real."

"I mean obviously we kissed each other. There was nothing fake about it. But there aren't any feelings there."

"I kinda wish there was. You deserve to be happy," Daphne said.

"I appreciate that, but I'm not going to get that from Maxon. We are being forced into this, and we are both trying to make the best of it, but this is not a situation either of us want to be in. We have to remember this is a forced union not a love story."

"Why does it have to be?" Amara spoke.

"Excuse me?"

"Who says this has to be a complicated mess where you're sad for the rest of your life? Who is saying you can't be happy?" Amara continued.

"She's right, America. You like Maxon correct?" Nicoletta asked.

"He's a nice guy. Very sweet and gentlemen like, funny too."

"Than maybe you two could actually be happy as a couple. There is no reason you have to be depressed while stuck in a marriage you don't want to be in, when you guys could be happy in a relationship together."

"You have to understand that he is only in this marriage because—." I almost just said my father but than I realized that they wouldn't understand that at all. That part of my life was one thing that I kept one hundred percent separate from my friends. The only people who really knew were my maids and Maxon, and he only knows to an extent. "For his family. He isn't interested in anything else."

"How do you know?" Daphne challenged.

"Have you two talked about it?" Nicoletta followed.

"No! What do you think Maxon and I talk about? The possibility that we could one day actually be in love is not on the list of topics!"

"Maybe it should be," Amara said.

I scoffed but couldn't help but imagine it. I've been thinking for so long about how I could get rid of this arranged marriage, just make it all disappear. Would it actually even be a reality that I could be happy while still being forced to marry him? Would that be giving in to my father or would it be letting myself be happy? Can Maxon and I even be together?"

"This conversation is over," I declared.

Daphne rolled her eyes. "Fine. So Nikki, I heard you've been talking to the younger English prince..."

I took in a deep breath and sagged into my chair in relief. It wasn't the end of the conversion but Nicoletta could talk for a long time. My eyes fell to the table and I looked at Maxon and I. I had been so worried about that kiss. I had been worried about how it would effect Maxon but I was also worried about myself. I give myself a tough time sometimes but at the end of the day I honestly think I do deserve to be happy. And when Maxon and I were on that date...I was happy. Our banter made me happy. Holding his hand made me happy. Even that kiss made me happy after I just stopped worrying about it and let myself enjoy it.

That's what Maxon did. He helped me to stop thinking about all of my constant worries and problems, and just made me happy. When I'm with Maxon, I'm not a princess. I don't have responsibilities. I don't have to act older than I am and I don't have to be someone else. Maxon doesn't care who I am. He actually just likes me.

"Oh god, how cliche," I sighed into my hands.

"What?" Daphne asked.

"I have to talk to Maxon."

~oOo~

"We have to meet in Italy soon," Amara was saying.

"You totally should," Nicoletta squealed. "And I've been dying to visit France again too."

"We will make a weekend out of it. Fly America and Amara to Italy, stay there a while, and then go back to Paris," Daphne added.

"My mom never lets me go on those trips with her when she goes with the royal family," Amara complained, disdain in her voice.

"I will request you personally next time," Nicoletta laughed. She looked over at me. "America, are you in for a girls week sometimes soon?"

I snapped out of my haze. "Oh, yeah of course. That sounds great."

Daphne suddenly stopped walking and the rest of us all stopped.

"Oh my god," She whispered. "It's him."

I looked past her and saw Maxon walking down the hallway unaware of the situation he was walking into.

"He's hotter in person than in the magazines," Nicoletta whispered, looking over Daphne's shoulder.

Maxon caught sight of us and gave a nervous wave and I waved back. And then he was walking over.

"You must be the fiancé," Nicoletta greeted, making herself look taller and more intimidating.

"Ciao, Principessa Nicoletta," Maxon replied, bowing deeply. It was exactly as Silvia had taught him and he executed it perfectly. No longer was he breaking protocol.

"And he speaks perfect Italian," She said approvingly.

"And French," Daphne echoed as Maxon bowed and uttered the same phrase to her. He slyly glanced up at me and I smiled in encouragement.

"Hey Maxon," Amara greeted. "We would really like to stay and chat with you, but we were just going..... going somewhere else."

"Oh," Maxon said, eyebrows raised. His eyes flickered to me and he awkwardly shuffled towards me. "Goodbye, my—uh my dear."

"They already know, Maxon," I laughed, pushing him away. "And I'm not going with them."

He sighed in relief. "Oh."

I smiled tentatively. "I was actually hoping we could talk."

"Goodbye America!" The girls called, walking away.

"So what's up?" He asked.

"Maxon, there is something I have to say," I announced officially.

"Okay..."

"You don't suck."

He laughed lightly, a confused smile taking over his face. "Uh, you don't suck either?"

"Thank you." I responded.

"I'm confused," He admitted.

"You've seen the magazines, right?"

"And the news, and the papers..." he trailed off.

"And all the photos. They're all so obsessed with this date we went on, but it was fake to us. I thought I would hate it and that I would be miserable the whole time. Instead I had fun."

"I did too," He confided.

"The point is, you don't suck. And that date didn't either. And I was thinking that maybe this situation doesn't have to suck either. What I'm trying to say is that...."

"You want to go on a real date."

"I'm just saying that we don't have to go through this whole thing being all sad about it when we can try and make the most of it," I mumbled quickly. "Just forget I even said anything. That was stupid."

He laughed. "It's weird seeing you nervous when you are always so put together."

I huffed. "I wish you'd go back to being nervous around me."

"I enjoyed that fake date too, America. I enjoy you. I think I'd enjoy going on a real one."

I breathed out in relief.

"Oh good. I've never done anything like that and I'm so relieved that it went well," I admitted.

"Don't let it go to your head. It wasn't your smoothest speech ever."

"How about 1 week from today?" I asked, ignoring that comment.

"I think I'd like that."

I smiled shyly. "I think I would too."

CHAPTER 17

I hope I can bring everyone a little bit of joy while you're stuck at home. Enjoy this chapter, which is the same as chapter 16, but from Maxon's point of view

Maxon's PovThe morning after Maxon and America's fake date...

I opened my eyes and stared at the white ceiling. Every morning when I woke up I had to remind myself of where I was and how I got here.

The palace.

Marriage.

America.

I'm getting used to mornings around here. My favorite part is not having to wake up early to go to school. I'm fact, not having school is a top highlight of being here. I could sleep in for as long as I wanted unless there was a specific reason otherwise and I had my own room, which is very different from the countless years I've spent with Gerad. My whole room is self-sufficient, complete with bathroom, closet, and tv which is also very different from my previous living environment. All I need is food, and that can be delivered right to my door.

The palace is basically the opposite of every aspect that I lived in my old life. It's big. It's plentiful. And it's lonely.

I miss my family.

Even on weekends when I was allowed to sleep in, Gerad always woke me up bright and early to play ball with him. Mom and dad were so supportive of me. My dad is my role model and my mom is my inspiration. Kenna and I used to sit together on the couch and talk about adult things, just her and I. I miss talking politics and school with her. May brought constant positivity and joy to my life. She was always talking and acting girly and being annoying. I miss her most of all.

Sometimes I think it would be better for us all to be together even if that did mean King Clarkson following through on his not so subtle threat against us. But then I remember May's letter that she sent yesterday.

I sleepily threw my hand at my bedside table until my hand came in contact with the drawer handle and I was able to pull it open. I felt for her letter, which I had thrown in there last night, and unfolded it to reread.

Dear Prince-to-be,

Hey Maxon! It is so weird not being able to talk to you every day and I totally miss you 1000%. But it is actually pretty nice around here and I really wanted to tell you about it. Mom said to send you a letter and I tried to tell her how completely old-fashioned that was, but after I thought about it, it seemed like something the sister of a prince does. So this is me writing a letter. OMG I wonder if you're hearing my voice in your head as you read.....You TOTALLY read that in my voice.

Well anyways, life is pretty great around here. It has been approximately 3 weeks since we left the palace and thing's have already changed so much. For starters, we have eaten a FULL MEAL literally every night. As in a full portion for everybody, seconds, AND it is not soup. It's actually crazy and I'm waiting to wake up from this dream. I mean I'm sure you're eating like 5000 dollar steaks every night and salad with gold leaves sprinkled on top, but for me, this is pretty amazing. The food isn't even the cherry on top though. The palace paid all our bills this month and we have been running the heater NONSTOP and mom hasn't said a thing. INSANE.

I'm sure that you are super interested in my personal life too so I'm going to tell you about it. Remember Brett? The really cute guy I told you about? Of course, you do. Well I was in math...and he turned around to ask to borrow a pencil...and then...BOOM. HE ASKS ME OUT! I know that you are totally against me being anywhere near guys, but guess what? You're in Angeles so you can't do anything about it!

I have also realized that with you gone, I am the oldest sibling in the house. But don't worry, I am using my power for good only (Ok that's kinda a lie. I got Gerad to unload the dishwasher for me yesterday) But I'm trying my best to be a good older sibling to him like you always were to me.

I really do miss you Maxon. And even though my life is pretty cool right now, I don't understand why you're gone. Dad said that I was too young to get it and that he would tell me when I'm older, but I think I'm old enough now. This whole arranged marriage thing seems pretty weird no matter how awesome it is that you're going to be King. Please don't forget about us little people when you're wearing a crown.

I love and miss you all the time. Try and get them to get us phones so that we can video chat sometime.

With love,

May Singer

(P.S. If there really is salad with gold flakes, can you get me some?)

I set the letter down and smiled. I really do love my sister. But this is why I have to stay here. Just hearing about how happy she is and how well things are going at home, is all I really need to get me through this. I'm doing this for them

And well, there was also America.

The Princess of Illea, the object of every guy's dreams and the envy of girls everywhere, was not who she seemed. America had always come off as different on TV. She always appeared more caring than other ones I've seen and she alway's seemed to ask the questions that no one else wanted to. She was special as far as royals went but there was more to it than that.

She isn't just a royal and that's what gets me every time. She is witty and sarcastic, with comebacks that leave me at a loss for words. She is mysterious and captivating in that way where you no she is keeping secrets that she will never tell. She is an amazing Princess too. After observing her for the time I've been able to, it is evident that she works her self to the bone to make other people happy. Her friends, her family, and now even I seem to have joined that list of people that she will put before herself. But there is an underlying brokenness about her.

And that's the other reason I stay.

I've noticed it in the way she pauses when she talks or the way she looks down at her hands and avoids eye contact. She is trapped here just as much as I am.

Jeez, this is way too much deep thinking before I've even gotten out of bed.

I hauled myself out of the sea of pillows and into the bathroom so I could brush my teeth and hair. Usually, around this time, I turn on the television and watch the old shows that I used to watch with May. Then a maid shows up with a list of things I have to do that day and helps me to get ready. The maids are all very friendly and we usually make small talk about both being in similar castes while they slick back my hair. I'm beginning to learn names.

The knock arrived today before I got the chance to turn on the TV however. I had to speedily spit the toothpaste out of my mouth and rush to the door to pull it open.

"Goodmorning," The maid greeted, bowing her head to me which I still found super weird.

".....Shea, right?"

"Yes," She smiled. "I have a few messages and things for you. The first is that you have a completely free schedule today."

"Free?" I repeated, the word foreign to me.

She nodded her head.

"No etiquette lessons or photoshoots or fake dates or anything?" I clarified.

"Nothing of the sort. The day is completely yours. That reminds me though. A guard wanted me to give you this." Shea pulled a magazine from behind her back and handed it to me. "He said that he is a friend of yours."

"Aspen Legar?"

She tilted her head in recognition.

"He also wanted me to tell you that he has the day off and that Avery and he will be up when you quote 'wake up from your princess nap'. His words, not mine."

I chuckled, shaking my head. "Thanks Shea. Is that it?"

"Yes, Sir Maxon. Have a good morning," She bid.

"You too," I said and gently closed the door. At first I had found these conversations unnerving. You're talking to a person, but there is no pleasantries, simply business. It's weird.

I tossed the magazine onto my bed. I don't understand why Aspen would give me a magazine. Wait...why would Aspen give me a magazine?

I picked the stack of glossy paper up and examined it almost dropping it to floor. That's....me. Well, my face. And America's. Together. Kissing. On the front of a freakin magazine. I held it up to the light, almost believing that it wasn't real. America had been very clear that the date was a publicity stunt but I hadn't expected this. I hadn't expected that kiss either though so it's weirdly fitting that it's plastered on said magazine. It was my first kiss actually which is super humiliating to say as an 18 year old man.

Rolling my eyes, I set the magazine away on a table and changed into a pair of sweats and a t-shirt that I had bribed a maid to get for me. No suits and ties for me today. I laid back on my my bed and clicked the tv on. I was immediately met with a video of America and I on our date, laughing and talking. The next channel was a talk show where the host was talking about our date with a celebrity guest. The channel after that was a women analyzing a picture of our kiss and what the different movements we made meant about our relationship.

This is...a lot.

There was a knock at the door, but the person didn't care to wait and threw the door open.

"Bro," Aspen boomed. "Did you get the magazine?"

"It's on the dresser. And the tv."

Avery followed in closely behind Aspen and actually took the time to close the door. Avery was a cool dude. He was much more polite than Aspen was and he was pretty funny. He has this wise aspect about him, like he has more experience at life in general and knows more than you do. He grew up here in the palace and is apparently pretty close with America. He goes by his last name though and I'm not sure what his real name is anyways.

Aspen's eyes watched the tv with great interest as the women explained that the way America's nose was angled meant that she felt insecure or something like that.

"Dude you made her feel insecure," Aspen bellowed, looking at me accusingly.

"How? We're not even in a real relationship, how could I have possibly done that? And how could you tell that by the angle of her nose!"

"Just remember that if you hurt her, I'll hurt you," Aspen warned.

"Whose side are you on?" I accused.

"Always the side of my country," He said seriously.

I rolled my eyes and turned my attention to Avery. "You have the day off too, Avery?"

He shook his head. "Only half. I have to guard the door tonight."

Aspen automatically became bored with the change of topic and reeled it back in.

"I can't believe you kissed her," he sighed.

"She kissed me. It was for the cameras only. So they'd have their cover story," I explained, gesturing to the women on the tv.

"I can't believe your engaged to her," He reiterated. "You know I had it all planned out, man. I made it to the palace and now all I had left to do was make her fall in love with me."

"I didn't choose this Aspen. You know how this works."

"If it makes you feel better," Avery pitched in. "America doesn't go for guards in the palace. She actually doesn't really go for much of anybody romantically. She is very friendly to guards and maids, but romance has never been in her plan. I don't know what her plans are but I guarantee that she will change the world."

Aspen and I were both kind of dumbfounded. There is a respect in his voice that was at a higher level than anyone I had ever talked to at home.

"You're actually kind of lucky to be engaged to her," Avery continued, looking me in the eye. "And you better know it because there isn't a single person who I've met at this palace who wouldn't defend her."

I was starting to gather that. You could count me as one of those people. Because in the short time I've known her, I've learned how amazing she is.

"So how does the whole arranged marriage work?" Aspen asked, calming down and sitting down in a chair by the window.

"So far its been a lot of prepping me for the future. I've been learning etiquette and all the other junk that's necessary for me to be king. America and I went on the one date but she sits in on different things with me so that we can get to know each other. It's.....weird. I mean there is no other way to put it. But the situation is strange and I'm just trying to figure it out."

"How do you feel about marrying her?" Avery asked.

I raked a hand through my hair, shaking my head. "I don't even know. It was daunting at first to think about spending the rest of my life with this women who I don't love or even really know at all. It's easier to think about now."

"What's changed?" Aspen inquired.

"Well....her. Like Avery said, she's pretty great and I suppose if I have to be stuck with someone, she's not that bad. The opposite actually."

"You sound like your starting to care about her," Aspen said.

"She is a great girl—."

"I don't mean like that, Maxon. You sound like your falling for her."

"It's not like that, man. This is a bad situation we're stuck in. She doesn't want a king at all. I'm just a thorn in her side that's distracting her from what she wants to do. I'm sure she wishes we never figured out about the switch and that we could just go back to how things were two months ago."

"Maybe she doesn't," Aspen shrugged. "I mean I'm sure neither of you want to be forced to marry each other. But that doesn't mean she may not be starting to feel a little something for you too."

"You're crazy man," I chuckled and we all laughed together. With that the conversation was over because that's how it worked with us guys.

~oOo~

We never breeched that topic again as we hung out that day, but that didn't mean I stopped thinking about what they said as the hours flew by. We spent most of the day together, catching up and I got to know Avery pretty well. Avery headed out around dinner to go do what he needed before his shift started at 8 and Aspen decided that it'd be best, with the French and Italian royalty in town, if he took up an extra shift.

I ended up walking with them down to the sub floor of the palace where they gave me an impromptu tour of the maid and guards quarters, along with the kitchen, laundry room, and everywhere else. The floor was huge and big enough to fit the whole staff comfortably, but the bustlings halls had a striking contrast to the loneliness of the three empty floors up above. After walking them to their room, a maid showed me a secret passageway from the sub floor to the third floor which would get me to my room, or anywhere in the palace, a lot faster if I ever needed. I thanked her as I stepped onto the third floor and she returned to her days work.

I was walking the short walk from the secret doorway to my room when I heard the gorgeous ringing of America's laugh. It seemed like fate or at least some sort of sign to me. I turned the corner and was met with America and 3 other young women walking down the hallway lost in conversation. I know one of them is Silvia's daughter Amara, who I've met a few times, but the the other two were unfamiliar to me. It only took a few moments for one of them, with blonde hair and fair skin, to notice me and stop the group in their tracks.

"You must be the fiancé," One of them addressed me, her words layered in a thick accent. I realized instantly that this must be the

Italian princess. I remember America mentioning that they were friends.

I bowed deeply, understanding instantly why Silvia forced me to take all those lessons on greeting royals. "Ciao, Principessa Nicoletta."

Her face went into shock and her eyebrows shot up. "And he speaks perfect Italian."

I bowed again to the last women with them, who I could only assume must be the French Princess.

"Bonjour Princesse Daphne," I murmured to her.

"And French," Princess Daphne echoed Princess Nicoletta's thoughts. I couldn't help but checking with America if I had done that right. It felt like a mini test but she just smiled and nodded.

"Hey Maxon," Amara greeted, giving me a small wave before pushing the two princesses past me. I tuned around in confusion to face them. "We'd would really like to stay and chat with you but we were just going...." she grasped for an excuse before finally deciding that it didn't matter. "Going somewhere else."

"Oh," I said dumbly. After a moment, it dawned on me that America was leaving with her friends and that I hadn't even addressed her nor was I making any move to say goodbye to her. Besides Amara, they think I'm her fiancé right? So I'm supposed to...... what?

I shifted towards her and awkwardly reached for her. "Goodbye my uh," I stuttered. "My dear."

America pushed me away from her, saving me from too much more embarrassment. "They already know Maxon. And I'm not going with them."

Both of these things were news to me.

"Oh," I sighed.

She smiled at me, rubbing her lips together and looking up at me with her crystal eyes. "I was actually hoping we could talk."

The way she said it was an invitation which was very out of America's style. She seemed different right now, a little bit more shy and tentative, which is a side of her so only get glimpses of sometimes. America is almost always fierce, always moving forward, and never stopping to take a breath.

America's friends said goodbye to us and retreated away. I was too caught up in her to notice.

"So what's up?" I asked, putting as much casualness into my voice as possible.

"Maxon there is something I have to say," She spoke, sounding more like the girl I was used to. This was an announcement even though I was already aware that she wanted to tell me something.

"Okay..."

"You don't suck."

I couldn't help but laugh because this was so random but seems so oddly fitting.

"Uh, you don't suck either..." I replied, though it came out a question.

"Thank you," She responded formally, not saying anything else. It's like she had suddenly forgotten to carry a conversation.

"I'm confused," I admitted.

She nodded as if this made sense. "You've seen the magazines right?"

I could only assume she meant the obsessive pictures of us everywhere. "And the news, and the papers..."

"And all the photos! They're all so obsessed with this date we went on, but it was fake to us. I thought I would hate it and that I would be miserable the whole time. Instead I had fun," She admitted and we shared a laugh over this.

"I did too."

There was a brief pause before something in America seems to snap and she started to spit out what she had to say. "The point is, you don't suck. And that date didn't either. And I was thinking that maybe this situation doesn't have to suck either. What I'm trying to say is—."

"You want to go on a real date."

I interrupted her in a burst of confidence because I finally understood what this was about. She was saying words and they were aligning with every thought I had today and that's when I knew.

"I'm just saying that we don't have to go through this whole thing being all sad about it when we can try and make the most of it," She rambled, trying to cover up the mistake she had thought she made. "Just forget I even said anything. That was stupid."

"It's weird seeing you so nervous when you are always so put together," I said.

Her face went pink. "I wish you'd go back to being nervous around me."

I knew I had to answer her before we started arguing and she stopped wanting to go on a real date with me. "I enjoyed that fake date too, America. I enjoy you. And I think I'd enjoy going on a real one."

She sagged in relief.

"Oh good. I've never done anything like that and I am so relieved that it went well."

"Don't let it go to your head," I teased. "It wasn't your smoothest speech ever."

"How about a week from today?"

"I think I'd like that."

She smiled and I think she may be the most adorable person I've ever met.

"I think I would too."

CHAPTER 18

The day of the date, I gave my maids the day off.

Or at least I decided that I am going to, but I haven't gotten to the point where I tell them that yet. I'm a little nervous for my life to be honest.

I knew how it was going to go. Mary, Anne, and Lucy were completely invested in my love life in a way that I couldn't begin to understand. It's as if it were them who were going on this date today and not me. I'll have to let them down easy, but I'm afraid that there may not be a way to do that.

The door to my room burst open at exactly 1' o clock, 2 hours before my date with Maxon was to begin. I had actually been napping in my bed because I was up late working, but the sound of my door handle bouncing off my wall woke me up.

"What are you doing?" I mumbled, rubbing my eyes. My maids faces blurred together before clearing up.

"America! Your date starts in two hours and you still have to shower and get ready," Mary rambled. "There is no time to wait, we have to draw a bath...."

"That won't be necessary," I cut in, blinking repeatedly to get full function back in my drooping eyes.

Anne's eyes narrowed. "What do you mean 'that won't be necessary"?"

I waved a hand in her general direction. "You guys have the day off."

"The day off?!" Mary screeched, her eyes going wide. "You have a date in two hours, now is not the time to be messing around."

"I'm not messing around. I don't need two hours to get ready for this date." I looked over at Lucy for help but she was standing aside, looking at the ground innocently.

"Your right. You probably need more so we better start making up for lost time," Anne agreed, flipping my sheets partially off me.

I glared at her and pulled them back.

"You guys are excused," I said.

"America, you are going to ruin this for us," Mary pleaded. "How could you do this to me?"

"To you? This is my date, Mary," I reminded her.

"Stop messing around, Ames," Anne sighed. "This is an important day for you. You're going to spend the rest of your life with Maxon, whether you like it or not, and this date could be your chance to be happy. We need to get you ready."

"I am ready."

"No....your not," Anne said.

"Yes. I am," I replied, throwing my legs over the side of the bed and standing up. I presented myself to them dramatically.

"What are you wearing?" Mary deadpanned, eyeing me.

"Jeans," I said simply, shifting around in them. "They're comfy."

"How did you get those? We make all your clothes," Anne accused.

"Lucy made them for me."

Anne and Mary's eyes shifted to her and Lucy's eyes widened.

"She asked me to," Lucy mumbled.

"You cannot wear jeans on a date! That's crazy!" Anne yelled.

"Jeans are actually perfect for what I have planned for the date. And it honestly doesn't matter because I'm a big girl and I can get myself ready," I spoke, sitting myself down at my vanity. "I'm thinking of wearing a ponytail too..."

"You can't be serious," Anne gaped.

I twisted my head and looked her in the eyes. "You have the day off ladies. Enjoy it."

Anne frowned and shook her head. Mary rolled her eyes.

I smiled. "You're excused."

Anne and Mary begrudgingly headed out the door, grumbling as they went. Lucy followed quietly behind them, giving me a small victorious grin, before gently shutting the door.

I looked at myself, in a tank top and dark blue skinny jeans, wondering if this is what I would have worn if I had been a five. I didn't really mind myself in it though it wasn't at all me. That America would probably pair this with a t-shirt or something. A cute blouse is much more my style. I walked over to my closet and selected one of my blouses that I usually wear with a pencil skirt when I'm working. Pulling it over my head, I checked myself in the mirror.

I was surprised. Smoothing my hand along my hips, I tilted my head. The jeans hugged around my curves and clung to every part of my legs. They were flattering, but comfortable in a way that I never could achieve by wearing a dress. Plus they went really good with my white blouse and I even think that I might be able to wear May's bright red converse that she had left here at the palace. I had contacted the Singers about sending them back but May told me to keep them.

I realized after throwing my hair back that I was done getting ready, and the date didn't start for almost a full two hours. I might have time to read that book that's been sitting on my dresser for a few weeks or maybe watch some tv. This is so much better than what I usually do. Why should I spend two hours getting ready when I can get ready in a few minutes and have some me time.

I laid back in my bed with a book and I continued to read it until I was halfway through and there was a knock on my door.

I ran to the door and pulled it open. Usually my maids do it and this simple task thrilled me.

"Did you eat before hand like I asked?" I said in greeting.

"Yes..."

"Good," I said, grabbing Maxon's hand and pulling him out the door. "Lets go."

"Woah," He called, simply stopping in his tracks and rendering it impossible for me to move. "This is already weirder than our fake date. Where are we going and why did you tell me to eat before I picked you up?"

"Because we aren't eating on the date. I thought we could go on a walk," I said, trying to urge him to follow me. He did so hesitantly.

"A walk? That's doesn't seem all that interesting," He replied, keeping up with my pace.

"Well I thought, you've seen the palace. You've seen the gardens. We already had a picnic, been there and done that. But there is a top secret part of the palace that very few have seen, and where we are definitely not supposed to go."

"Does it involve trespassing?" He asked.

"I technically own the palace so....no. And it's not really even apart of the palace. It's the woods behind it."

"Woods?" He asked, intrigued.

"Woods," I confirmed. "They're gorgeous and I used to spend a lot of time there, ripping dresses and getting mud all over me."

"That's sounds like fun," He commented.

I smiled, remembering times where I climbed trees so high that they would have to send herds of guards out to find me. I would giggle down at them as they called my name, a game of hide and go seek that only I knew I was playing. It got me into trouble but at that time, trouble only meant a scolding, and I'd forget about those moments after I'd receive them. Sometimes I would chase after birds or pretend I was the queen of the forest. When my father caught wind of my Tarzan ways however, they came to a swift close, but I spent many good years in the woods.

"They were," I reminisced. "As a kid, all the green grass and tall trees were magical."

"It sounds like it still is for you."

Flashes of the view from the top of a tree flashed into my head. "Well I guess we'll see."

I led him down to the lower floor of the palace and through a few different hallways that would take us to the back palace field where we often held events during the summer.

"Through there," I told him, pointing to a large set of French doors.

I dropped his hand to rush forward and push through the doors, into the large clearing.

Maxon stopped. "That was sort of anticlimactic."

"Just look forward. Past the field and out there."

His eyes made a path through the field and slowly reached the large expanse of woods that framed behind it for miles.

"Holy........" he trailed off.

"I know," I smiled.

"Are we even allowed to go out there?"

I glanced up at him. "Not technically but..." I shrugged. "No one really has to find out."

I tugged on his hand and began to pull him through the field and towards the trees beyond. It took us a few minutes to travel across the large expanse of grass but eventually we stepped into the trees, the ground switching from grass to dirt and leaves. There were trees in front and around me for as far as I could see. They reached up towards the sky and the sun peaked through the branches, lighting the ground with light.

"This is beautiful," I whispered, everything flooding back to me.

"You look beautiful," He replied.

I laughed, shaking my head. "That was cheesy....but thank you."

"The jeans are a new addition to your wardrobe I assume."

"You would assume correct," I agreed, smoothing my hand along the material. "I thought it better to wear more suitable clothes than to wear a dress. You never know if I may want to climb a tree."

"You're not going to climb a tree."

"You never know," I said, eyes twinkling.

He shook his head, a faint smile gracing his lips. "You are a mystery."

"I try."

The back of my hand brushed against his and I couldn't help but take it again, threading my fingers through his. He looked around the woods, taking it in.

"I want to take a picture of this," He said. "I wish I had my camera."

"I am working on that," I told him. "But I don't have it yet. So maybe we just take a mental photograph."

"I don't think that's how photographs work."

"No really," I said. "It's a picture in your mind and it'll be just for the two of us. We will always remember it but than it's just ours."

"Now who's being cheesy?"

"It's in the air," I replied.

"So do you have stories that go with certain trees? Or did you carve your and your secret lovers initials into a tree somewhere?" He wondered.

"I mean most of the trees look the same so there isn't any specific tree that I can remember with a story. And there was no initial carving, but I do have stories."

"Tell me some."

"I was so young when I used to play out here, I can't remember much of the specifics. But I do have a more recent story that's pretty fresh in my memory."

He looked at me, waiting patiently for me to say it.

"It's actually not the happiest story. I actually ran out here once and hid in the trees for hours."

"Why?"

"We were holding an event outside when rebels attacked. There is a swift passageway to the royal safe room that's around here but for some reason, I freaked. I got nervous and just sprinted into the woods and I ran and ran. Eventually I stopped and climbed a tree where I hid for hours before the guards found me."

"Wow," He murmured. "How old were you?"

"Like 15 maybe."

"That's insane. Like being a teen isn't difficult enough, you had rebels attacking your home constantly."

I looked down at our hands, frowning slightly. "It definitely wasn't easy."

"Well I'm just glad it didn't change you," He said. "Something like that would make a lot of people cold and distant, but you didn't let it get to you."

I had always assumed that it did make me that way, or at least that's how I always made myself out to be.

"Yeah," I mumbled. "I'm glad too. I think that I just grew up with the attacks so by the time I became old enough for them to effect me, they just became a regular occurrence."

"What happens to the maids during attacks?" Maxon wondered.

"Well must of them are usually on the sub floor. We have yet to have rebels who have figured out how to get to the sub floor so they're pretty safe down their. Those of the staff who are unlucky enough to be out and about during the beginnings of attacks, hide in smaller safe rooms around the palace. We built them just for them and they just have to locate one and hide. Once they're locked inside, no one can open the door without special clearance."

"It seems like it would still be risky though. Don't you worry about your maids? I know your close with them."

"I usually take them down with me to the royal safe room," I said. Memories flooded back to me. "But I haven't always."

He looked at me, his eyes questioning.

I frowned. "Mary, Anne, and Lucy haven't always been my maids. When I was a child, my maids were Anne, Jane, and Rosa. Mary and Lucy were still basically children themselves at that time, way too young to work at the palace."

"So why did you get new maids?" He asked, already knowing the answer.

"When I was 12, Jane and Rosa we're rushing me to the safe room. They got me inside but I suppose they didn't make it to a safe room in time and I never saw them again. The next day, I had two new maids, as if Jane and Rosa, two of my closet companions for 12 years, had never even existed."

"Oh my god, America..."

"Replaced by Mary and Lucy," I finished.

"That's terrible."

"It's kind of bittersweet. I would have never met Mary and Lucy otherwise and they're two of my best friends. But from what I can remember of Jane and Rosa, they were the sweetest women. Anne would always be hard on me about messing around and such, but Jane and Rosa were always reminding her that I was just a kid. I miss them."

"I'm sorry," He said.

"For what? You didn't do anything," I replied simply.

"But I'm sorry all the same." He squeezed my hand and his thumb traced along my palm.

I smiled meekly. "Well I think we've heard enough sad stories about me. Tell me something about you, preferably happy. What is high school like?"

"Not as fun as you'd think," He grumbled, rolling his eyes in memory. "People kinda suck, especially when they think your a stupid five. I tried to keep my head down and just be a good student."

"I said happy stories."

"My bad," He chuckled. "Well I have a lot of good memories with Aspen and my sister. Both of which loved you dearly."

I raised an eyebrow. "Do tell."

"Well you met May, and obviously she idolized you. She's been like that her whole life. It's always been 'look at Princess America's hair cut' 'look at princess America's dress' 'oh my god, did you see who Princess America danced with last night'. You were her role model in every way."

I smiled. I may have gotten that vibe from her.

"And Aspen...well he'd kill me if he knew I was telling you this, but he was in love with you through out all of high school. There was a plan and everything of how he was going to get you. Of course he didn't know you, and I'm sure that it was strictly based on your.......ahem, looks. But none the less, there was a definite crush."

"Oh my," I giggled, trying to keep from laughing. "Isn't it just stupid to long for someone you would have no chance of meeting?"

"He was most definitely not the only one who did so. And he did meet you, now didn't he?"

"I suppose you're right, but that was simply chance," I said.

He looked around, shrugging. "It happened none the less....America where are we?"

"What do you mean where are we? We're in the woods," I replied, looking at him.

"But where in the woods? We've been walking for a while, how do you know where we are?"

"Well I..." I trailed off, spinning around and seeing nothing but trees. "I don't."

"You don't!" He yelled. "America! You got us—."

"Don't say it—."

"Lost," He finished.

"I most certainly did not," I said defensively. "We came from this way so we just follow that way back."

"Which way America?" He asked.

"Well...that's another great question."

Maxon sighed and sat on the ground, leaning against a tree.

"Why are you sitting?"

"Well the guards will have to come looking for us eventually so I'm going to sit here and wait."

"We can find our way back," I argued.

"No we can't, America. We don't know where we are." He took a deep breath and ran a hand through his hair. "And this date was going so well."

He's right. It was going well and now I've gotten us lost.

"I messed this up, didn't I?" I sighed, collapsing softly onto the ground next to him.

"No, I mean yes, but the date isn't over," He tried to console me.

"We're lost in the woods," I deadpanned.

"Yes, yes we are," He agreed, looking around. He reached for my hand and I let him take it. I don't know why I was letting him console me, when 1) it went against everything I stand for and 2) I'm the one who messed this up, but I was beginning to learn that Maxon just made me a little different.

"What's the most princess thing you've ever done?" Maxon whispered, as if he talked too loud he would spook the woods.

"I once got off a private jet in Paris, attended a ball there, got on another private jet immediately after and flew to get a dress and tiara from Spain before flying home to attend another ball, in that dress, that my family was hosting."

"That's very Princess," He murmured. "What's the most normal thing you've ever done?"

"I brush my teeth twice a day," I replied.

He laughed lightly. "I do that too."

"See? Completely normal."

I leaned my head onto his shoulder because even though we were lost in the woods, and talking about brushing our teeth, and we're engaged to be in a forced marriage, this still felt like a moment. His arm twisted around me and rested lightly at my waist.

"How often did you get lost as a kid?" He asked.

"All the time. But then I would climb a tree and see where I should go."

"Resourceful."

"I am quite intelligent."

"America?"

"Yes Maxon?"

"Why don't you climb a tree now?"

"You told me not to."

"America?"

"Yes Maxon?"

"Climb the tree."

I grinned and pushed away from him. And he grinned in return. I stood up off the ground and brushed dirt off my jeans.

"It's been quite some time since I've climbed a tree," I said, my eyes examining the trees for the perfect one. "I'm probably a bit rusty. I hope I don't fall."

His grin faltered. "You haven't fallen before, right?"

"No," I replied. "But there's a first time for everything."

He rolled his eyes and stood up, following after me as I crossed to a tree that looked like it had enough sturdy branches.

"Help me up, please," I told him. "The bottom branch is a bit too tall for me."

"You're really going to climb this tree?" He clarified.

"That's the plan."

His eyes were weary but he still gently placed his hands at my waist and lifted me like I was nothing into the air. I reached for the nearest branch and hoisted myself onto it, trying to make it look like it was nothing even though I hadn't done this in years. I reached for the next branch, pulling myself up and straddling it. I looked down at him.

"You should climb the tree too," I called.

"I'm not crazy like you," He called back.

"It's not crazy. It's fun. Live a little."

"Living is the part I'm concerned about. I will not live if I fall off that tree. And either will you so I have to be here to catch you."

"I won't fall and neither will you."

"This is peer pressure."

I smiled. "Are you too wimp to climb the tree?"

"I am perfectly secure in my masculinity and you cannot get me to climb the tree by being insulting."

I leaned against the trunk of the tree. "You're probably right...you couldn't even climb the tree if you wanted to."

He rolled his eyes. "Yes I could."

"Mhmmm. Whatever you have to tell yourself," I taunted and climbed onto the next branch. It was only a few moments before I felt the tree shake slightly as he started to climb the tree.

"Oh," I said in mock surprise. "You've decided to climb the tree."

"I don't appreciate your sarcasm," He said as he sat two branches below me.

"I think I'm hilarious."

I began to climb higher and higher into the tree, like riding a bike, Maxon following a few branches behind me. The tree wasn't too tall but it was definitely not the easiest task.

"You did this as a tiny little kid?" He asked.

"All the time."

He stopped climbing and I did too. We we're only a branch apart and I could lean down and touch him if I wanted to.

"You're pretty amazing you know that?"

"Because I can climb trees?"

"No, you're just amazing."

I blushed slightly, a smile lifting the corners of my mouth. I couldn't help myself but lean down and close the gap between us, connecting my lips with his. I was highly aware of the fact that we were sitting on branches in a tree, but I had too. Because this was a real date and this is my chance at something, and I'm not letting it slip away from me. I'm not a romantic. I'm not an optimist. But I'm hopeful.

Because I really like Maxon.

I pulled away, my face hovering inches from him.

"What was that for?" He mumbled.

"I think you're pretty amazing too," I said.

He leaned forward, as if to kiss me again and I slipped past him, climbing onto the next branch. I grinned down at him and he shook his head at me. It wasn't long before we were back in a climbing rhythm and I noticed that the sun was getting brighter and we were nearing the top. I'm completely shocked that I managed to get Maxon to climb up this high. I'm shocked that I'm even still able to climb this high.

"Oh my god," I mumbled, my eyes getting a glimpse over the trees.

Spread out in all directions around me, was Angeles. Reaching past the trees was the main city, bustling with people and lights. It was a glow with activity, and it never stayed still for more than a second, before you saw a light blink and it was all moving again. But from up here in the trees, you could see the more calm part of Angeles, past the major city and into the towns and fields past. When I think of Angeles, I always think of the palace and the city, but there is much more to the province than that.

"Do you see it?" I asked.

"The palace? Yes, it's that way."

"No. Everything else," I said.

"Of course I see it. It's gorgeous," He said. I could feel his presence on the branch below me, but he was tall enough to still peek out into the sky.

"This is why I fight so hard for my throne," I told him. "All these people are just trying to live there lives to the best that they can, but they are always fighting. There is always something that these people have to work for or work against, because no ones looking out for them. I want to look out for them. It's all I want."

"You're going to make a really good Queen than," Maxon said. "And I think that Illea knows that. I certainly do."

"I'm trying to fight so that they don't have to." I glanced at him. "I originally saw you as something I had to fight to reach that goal."

"You fought the marriage? I always kinda thought you just went along with it," He admitted.

"I've learned to accept a lot of things, but this...." I gestured between us. "Marrying you was something I wasn't willing to accept for a while."

"And now?" He asked.

"I still don't like it. There's just no choice in the matter and I will never accept something entirely that I didn't have a say in originally. But I do like you. And that has made it a lot easier to handle."

"It wasn't exactly the easiest thing on my end to leave my family behind. I've never really gone without them. But May sends letters and you've given me hope that being King isn't going to suck entirely."

"It'll suck, but I hope that it'll be pretty fulfilling too," I said.

"We know what direction the palace is. Do you think we should get out of the tree?"

"Gentleman first," I said and he slowly lowered himself back down onto the branch below. Going down was much easier than up if you didn't look at the ground too much. There were branches coming at you from all directions from different trees and it wasn't difficult to go from one to the other. Maxon was a bit slower than I was but I didn't mind waiting for him. Eventually he slid off the last branch and his feet reconnected with the ground. He looked very happy to be there. Looking up he stood at the base of the tree and held his hand out, silently asking if I needed help down. I took his hand and he pulled me out of the tree, and I crashed into his arms completely ungracefully.

"Sorry!" I yelped.

"It's fine," He laughed, setting me gently onto my feet.

"Do you remember which way we're supposed to walk or should we climb the tree again?"

"It was that way, no tree climbing necessary," He said, beginning to walk. He stopped though and grabbed my hand, and we started walking together.

We didn't talk much on the walk back. The sun was beginning to set through the trees and we both watched it as it went. It was luckily pretty easy to find our way back and we did it without much effort. Eventually we reached the clearing again and then we were back in the palace, heading to my floor where Maxon would drop me off at my room.

It was quiet as we approached and I felt kinda sad about the night having to end. It's like I've been walking on a cloud for the past few hours. I've felt different, acted different, completely separate from the way I usually am.

"This night has been really weird," I spoke. "But really good."

"I climbed a tree."

"Is that the only thing you're going to remember about today?"

"Well...." The corner of his mouth lifted slightly. "I also kissed a pretty girl."

I raised my eyebrow.

"And I'm wondering how said pretty girl would respond if I did it agin."

"I suppose you can't really know unless you do it."

"I wouldn't want to—."

"You talk to much," I said and stepped forward, tilting my face to meet his. The kiss was short and sweet, just what you would expect for a kiss goodnight. It was all I could have really asked for.

"Goodnight Maxon," I said.

"Goodnight America."

I opened my door behind me and looked at his face one more time, before shutting it quietly behind me.

"So?"

"Oh my god!" I screamed, clutching my chest. I glared at my maids as they waited expectantly in various places around the room. "You scared me half to death."

"How was the date?" Mary asked.

"It was..." I took a deep, calming breath and smiled in spite of my racing heart. "It was really really good."

Aweeeeee. Wasn't that just such a sweet chapter? In others news... WHO HEARD ABOUT THE SELECTION MOVIE COMING TO NETFLIX!!!!!!!

CHAPTER 19

"Did he give you his jacket?"

"It is spring in Angeles and it was midday. Neither of us were wearing jackets."

"Did he walk you home?"

"We live in the same place, Mary. There wasn't much of an option in the matter."

"Did he kiss you goodnight?"

I looked down, a giant blush coloring my cheeks.

"How romantic," She sang, mock swooning and landing on the bed next to me.

Anne sighed. "Mary, get up and do some work."

"Let her be, Anne," Lucy said quietly. "This is really big for America."

"Are you going to go see him?" Mary asked.

"What do you mean?"

"Like, today. Are you planning on seeing him?"

"I hadn't even thought about it....am I supposed to?"

"Yes!" Mary yelped.

"Do whatever feels right for you," Lucy said.

"I hate this," I grumbled, falling back against my pillows. "It's so complicated. There is so many little things you have to worry about and check up on."

"That's called dating."

"We're not..."

"You kinda are," Lucy spoke. "There really isn't any other way to put it."

"We're engaged."

"That should make it easier, if you think about it," Mary pointed out. "A lot of people have to worry about where the relationship is going. You're going to marry him no matter what, so you don't have to worry."

"It's not that simple," I said.

"It could be."

"He's going to stop by your room this morning," Lucy mumbled.

Mary and I's head both whipped around to face her. "What?"

"Well I was talking with Aspen—Officer Legar—before I brought you breakfast. And he had come from Maxon's room, and said that Maxon was planning on stopping by your room to say hi."

"What!" Mary screeched. "She's basically in a robe and slippers!"

"I'm in a day dress and flats—."

"Might as well have just woken up. Needs makeup and—."

"Mary I look fine," I interrupted. "I wore jeans on a date last night and your worried about my dress? Would you prefer I wear an evening gown?"

"Yes."

"I swear—."

"Hi Mr. Singer!" Lucy squeaked, gathering our attention.

I looked at the door, and saw Maxon hesitantly peaking his head into the room. Why do I always leave that door open?

"Uh hello......" Maxon trailed off.

"Lucy."

"Hello Lucy."

Mary scrambled off my bed and next to Anne and Lucy.

"I apologize. I know we've met but I don't think we ever introduced ourselves," Maxon spoke.

"Mary, Anne, and Lucy," I told him, pointing to each of them respectively. "They were just leaving. They have lots of sewing and dusting to do."

"Actually—."

"Dresses to sew, downstairs, away from here," I continued.

She pouted and Anne whispered harshly to her. "Quit pestering her. She wants to be alone with him."

"I feel like she's replacing us with a man," Mary mumbled to her dramatically. I rolled my eyes internally and gave her a small push towards the door.

"Minutes ago you were campaigning for said man," I heard Anne say.

The two of them quite noisily left the room, Lucy following quietly behind and gave me a small smile before leaving.

"They're an exuberant bunch," Maxon said.

"You have no idea," I mumbled, hopping off the bed. "So what's up?"

I said this casually but I was anything but casual in every other way.

"Oh well I wanted to stop by and....."

I raised my eyebrow. "And?"

"And....." He shrugged. "Say good morning."

A grin slowly took over my face.

"Good morning," I said.

"Good—."

I cut him off by stepping towards him and bringing my face towards his. It felt like I hadn't kissed him in days even though it had only been a simple nights rest since. I don't know who this was but I had confidence—

And then something hit me.

I stepped away from him.

"America?"

Who is this girl? Giggling and laughing like a teenager in love, going on dates and kissing boys, wearing jeans and converse. Thinking about a boy instead of her work.

But who am I supposed to be anyways?

I once knew a girl who made her own rules and followed her own path. She was fierce and fearless, and had dreams of what she could be. She was whoever she wanted to be. I also knew a girl who was the perfect princess. She spoke only when spoken to and did only what she was told to. She was who everyone else wanted her to be.

But now? Who am I now? I'm happier, thats a given. But am I worse than either one of those people, because I'm giving in. I'm letting my dad force me into something that will change my life completely.

I've somehow said yes to marriage as if it's not the most important decision I'll ever make.

Sure things with Maxon have been fun. They've been pretty amazing if I'm being honest. But marriage is the rest of my life not just a few dates. Love is one thing. I've always imagined I'd be happily married in the future, but this isn't love. This is a trap set up by my father and I've fallen right into it. He did this to me and I let him. I've become exactly who he wants me to be.

A dumb, bubbly, complacent girl who will sit by while someone else rules the country that I've dedicated my life too.

And I won't have it.

Even more then that, Maxon doesn't deserve it.

He puts on a brave face, and I'm sure he actually is okay with it, but he doesn't realize the life he's committed to living. He'll be drowning in work, he'll be destroyed by choices he has to make where there's no good decision, he'll rarely see his family. Life as a five isn't easy, but as long as my father is around, it'll be better then being a one. I'm privileged and I live a comfortable life. He would too. I can't deny that fact in any way. But it comes down to more than that. This place will destroy him.

And I can't let it.

"America are you okay?" Maxon asked, his hands still holding my shoulders.

"I...I need to go," I mumbled to him and stepped around him.

"What?" He said. "Did I do something?"

"No, it's not you. I just need to do something."

He was still looking at me with confusion and slight hurt. I didn't want to hurt him. I'm trying to help.

I muttered a quick goodbye and didn't look back at him, as I left him standing in my room. I needed to talk to my father. There has to be someway that I can reason with him. He's a human being. There has to be a person in there who would listen. I just had to reach him. I found myself at his office, turning the handle, before I could convince myself otherwise.

"Father?" I called out, peaking my head into the room.

"Yes America?" He replied, not looking up from what he was reading.

"I was hoping that I could talk to you about something," I said, stepping hesitantly into the room and closing it behind me.

"I'm very busy America," He said, still not looking up from his paper.

"It's important," I said. "It won't take very long."

He sighed deeply and set down his paper, folding his hands on top of it. "Well get on with it then."

"I want to talk to you about the arranged marriage with Maxon Singer."

"Schreave."

"Excuse me?"

"Well he's to be Maxon Schreave in a short matter of time," My father reminded me.

"That's what I wanted to talk to you about actually," I said, standing awkwardly next to one of his sitting chairs and trying to decide if I should sit down or not.

"I don't see what there is to talk about."

"I know that you think it's the best idea, but I think that we should revisit the subject and try to find an alternative option."

"I thought you were done with this, America," He sighed, rubbing his face. "It's happening."

"But it doesn't have to. We announced it but I don't see why we can't just stage a breakup. The press would eat that up."

"My blood runs through his veins," My father said coldly. "Which means he will be the only one creating the next generation of Schreave's."

"No one will ever know," I argued.

"It would take a simple blood test to bring that all down. What would happen if your blood test got out America? Stop wasting my time with all this jabber."

Clearly this is not working.

"Don't you care about me Dad? I don't love him. Why don't you want me to be with someone that I care about?"

His eyes narrowed at me. He knew what games I was trying to play.

"You two looked pretty cozy during that picnic in the gardens. I think you'd be very happy together."

"He's a five though Dad." I was disgusted with these words even as they left my lips. "Is that really what you want representing our great country?"

"It's actually proven quite helpful. The people love seeing someone like them in rule."

"Even the twos and threes?" I prodded.

We were playing a game of cat and mouse, avoiding the others questions like a sport. If you read between the lines than you can tell what we're really saying, but we were pretending like we couldn't. I had to be forward because obviously this wasn't working.

"I don't want to marry him," I said.

"Clearly."

He rolled his eyes and stood up, crossing over to his tray of glasses and liquor. He began to fix himself a drink.

"I'm not marrying him."

His hand stopped moving and he slowly turned around to face me.

"Excuse me?" He said coldly.

I lifted my chin up, staring him in the eyes.

"I. Am. Not. Marrying. Maxon. Singer," I said slowly.

His mouth was set in a straight line and he tilted his head to the side. "I think you want to rephrase that."

"Actually, I don't," I spit.

He was at my side in an instant, his hand gripping my arm tightly and his nails digging into my skin. "Watch your mouth."

My back burned in distinct lines, warning me that I needed to stop. He doesn't take well to me talking back to him. He never takes well to to me talking back. Stop. I need to stop.

"Make me," I said instead.

He threw my arm away from him and I crashed to the floor. I looked up at him, his face so angry. I crawled back until my back was flush against the wall. I could of avoided this. I could have stopped. He towered over me, staring down at me with hatred in his eyes.

"You need to be reminded of which one of us is in charge."

GASPS A cliffhanger ending! I think we can all assume what happens next...In other news, I am almost done prewriting this story. If any of you are curious, I actually pre-write chapters and I'm usually about 10 chapters ahead of what I've posted this week. I've almost finished and I think their will be about 31 chapters and an epilogue, so that's what you all have to look forward to :)

CHAPTER 20

Disclaimer: Some words taken or paraphrased from The Elite by Kierra Cass.

I knew it was a mistake, leaving my room and trying to get to the hospital wing, but my maids weren't back yet and I had no choice.

The wounds hurt worse once the blood dries.

I was able to get a shawl over my shoulders, though I can't remember how I did it, and somehow I got myself out of my room. The hospital wing, located on the first floor of the palace, was supposed to be hidden. No one wants to see the sick and injured when they come to visit the palace, so it's out of the way, so even the wandering person couldn't find it unless they were seeking it out. I can't go there for this, but my maids usually go there for the supplies I need, conveniently kept in a box. We are always prepared for if this happens. But it's been a while, and I suppose I'm out of practice.

That's usually a good thing, being out of practice at bandaging your-self up.

I hissed as I straightened myself out and tried to appear as normal as possible as I passed staff throughout the hospital wing.

"Princess America, are you alright?" A maid asked.

"I'm fine," I replied, waving her off, the simple task almost making me black out. "My maid cut her finger and I'm getting some bandages for her."

"One of us could—."

"I can handle it myself," I cut off. "If you could open the door for me though..."

"Of course, Miss," She said, bowing and pulling open the door.

The hospital wing appeared to be relatively empty. There was no one initially in the first room and all staff seemed to be elsewhere. I suppose they really only stick around when there are patients to be taken care of.

I was thankful to be able to take a minute to breath because it was becoming almost impossible to get air through my lungs.

I hobbled over to a shelf stacked with supplies and prayed that the box would still be where my maids left it when I was younger. Hidden behind boxes of cotton swabs and marked with my name on a piece of tape. No one was going to mess with something that was labeled as the Princess's property.

I felt the cool metal handle against my finger tips and steadied myself against the shelf, as I griped it and lifted it up. My back burned with the movement and a few stray tears slipped down my cheeks, that I quickly wiped away. I moved as fast as I could towards the door, which was quite sluggishly, and pushed the door open. I squeezed my eyes shut through the pain of the movement and had to stop to collect myself. But then someone suddenly crashed into me, immediately trying to catch me but brushing my wounds with their hands and holding them there to steady me, sending fire across my skin.

I groaned and pushed whoever it was away roughly.

"America?"

I didn't dare look at him for fear of how he was looking at me.

"What are you doing here Maxon?"

"I was looking for a library," I heard him say but it sounded like it was miles away.

"This is the hospital wing," I hissed, my tone of voice hurting me more than anything else.

"Are you alright?" He asked, ignoring my attitude.

"Fine," I said shortly. I was having a difficult time standing and I knew Maxon could tell.

"Do you need help?"

"No," I answered quickly. "I'm just heading to my room, I—."

I heard the shouting just as Maxon did and my slow brain could hardly make sense of the sound. It was fighting and we had to move. I think.....it's an attack. This is an attack and the hospital wing is not far off from the doors to the palace.

"We need to...." I mumbled. "We need to move."

"Sound the alarms!" Someone yelled.

"Guns at the ready!"

"Alert the king!"

I tried to pull him away but I couldn't move and I had to grab his arm to keep myself standing.

"Maxon—."

"Your majesty!" A guard called, racing over to us. "We have to get you and Sir Maxon to safety."

I'm sure he hadn't meant to but the guard pushed me roughly away from the action, and I cried out, the metal box clattering to the floor.

Maxon picked up the box and examined me for whatever was wrong. He looked as if he thought the guard had driven a knife into my back, which I suppose was justified with the noise I made.

I shook my head.

"I won't make it to the royal safe room, Lark," I said.

I was sweating like a pig and my whole body was going into shock. Everything hurt.

"Yes mam," He said grimly, and placed an unsuspecting hand on my back to lead me to a servants safe room. I didn't cry out but it was all I could think about as he took Maxon and I down the hallway. He was moving quickly but I was slowing everyone down. Eventually we reached a dead end and Lark opened the invisible door. I walked in without a second thought and collapsed on the floor.

"Tell my mother that Maxon and I are okay," I told him. "Do that before anything else, Officer Lark."

"Of course, your majesty. Right away," He spoke and pushed Maxon into the room. I could hear the siren sounding before the door clicked shut and everything went silent. I looked around. It appeared to be one of the better safe rooms by far.

"Help me up," I told him.

Maxon hesitantly approached me and placed his hands under my arms, lifting me up. It wasn't not painful but at least he didn't touch my back, so I suppose there's that.

"What's wrong?" He asked.

"Nothing," I said quietly and limped over to the bench in the middle of the room. I sat down, my whole body sighing in relief.

"I'm guessing those were southern rebels?"

I nodded. Was that alarm fast enough? How long would Maxon and I be in here for? How long could I last before I had to take care of my injuries?

"Are we safe here, America?"

"Yes," I forced out, clenching my teeth. "This is where the servants hide during attacks. They're relatively safe down on the sub floor but if their running about doing chores, than it's best that they hide in one of these rooms. They also work in a pinch for anyone who can't make it down to the big safe room."

"Do the rebels know?"

I winced. "They might but they have no way of getting in even if they do. After the door is sealed, you can't get out for at least 24 hours, or with a keycard...which I don't have on me."

Maxon was looking at me and I knew he knew I was in pain. But I had to push through this. I leaned forward and hissed. My dress has to be soaked through and it's only a matter of time before it gets to the shawl and then there's no hiding anything.

"America?"

"I can't take it anymore. Maxon, please help me with my shawl?"

Maxon jumped up and stood in front of me, where he tentatively lifted my shawl from my shoulders. He crumpled it in his hands and set it aside.

"The back of my dress," I told him. His eyes widened and he hesitated. "Please Maxon."

He slowly walked around the bench and I closed my eyes tightly as I heard his sharp intake of breath.

"America...your dress is soaked with blood."

I looked down at my hands in my lap, trying my best not to cry. My lip quivered.

"Please," I whispered. His gentle hands fumbled with the buttons on my dress and my own hands shook as if I was undoing them myself. I could feel the material sticking to my skin and I could only imagine what Maxon was seeing. Well I knew, because I'd seen it before. The back of my slip would be in tatters, long rips slicing through the material and into the skin underneath. 6 gashes this time, with a countless number of them scarred underneath.

The silence between us was deafening. I could feel him staring and a stray tear rolled down my cheek. The truth was that I was ashamed of it. I had considered what I would tell someone if someone were to ever find out, but I could never come up with something. The scars were red and ugly, some faded because of time and others puckered because they weren't taken care of correctly. Each time my father caned me added a new layer of awful marks across my skin that made me look away from the mirror when ever I saw them. My maids could cover them up as much as possible but I knew they were there.

I heard him walk away and I looked up, following him with my eyes as he retrieved a wash cloth from a shelf on the wall and soaked it in water from the sink. He came back and set the cloth aside.

"The slip is in the way of me accessing the wounds," He mumbled, looking at me unsure. "But I don't..."

"I have a bra on, it's just unhooked so the strap doesn't bother my back. But you can do what you need to. I trust you."

I maneuvered the straps across my shoulders and uncertainly let the dress puddle around my waist. He felt around the collar of my slip and then gripped it in both his hands, ripping the remains down the center of the back. I lifted my knees up to my chest and hugged myself tightly. I felt so vulnerable, my back bare to him, everything I had worked so hard to keep from everyone on display.

"This might sting a little," He warned.

"It's okay," I whispered. "I'm used to it."

I knew it was coming but I still pulled away as the ice cold wash cloth dabbed at the first gash extending across my shoulder. His hand hovered inches away from my back and I nodded for him to continue. I didn't flinch the second time. It wasn't until he moved onto the next gash that he said anything, and I'm glad he did because I'm not sure how long I could take of hearing him say nothing.

"Does anyone know?" He asked.

"Not really. My maids do but that's it."

"Not the doctor? Or..."

"No," I said as the dabbing continued. "Damn that stings." His hand froze for a second but I ushered him to keep going. "These things take a while to stop hurting, especially if you're determined to take care of them on your own."

"America I..."

"You can't fix me up if you're worrying too much," I said swallowing.

"Do you think there is any bandages in here?" He asked and looked around the room.

"The box," I said.

I heard the click of the clasps on the box, and the metal creaked as the lid was flipped open.

"Why did you go after this box?" Maxon asked. "Don't you keep bandages in your room?"

"No, mostly out of sheer pride. I didn't want to have to use them again."

"Who did this—."

I interrupted him. "There should be a disinfectant solution in there. It hurts but works miracles."

I heard him looking for it and I shook my head. How long until he asked the question that was slowly killing me? What would I say?

When the ointment made contact with my skin, I grunted, but kept minimally quiet. It only made it worse when he knew I was in pain. But like magic, my tension eased as the medication did it's job and did all it could.

"I knew this secret would come out eventually but I was hoping that I would have a stellar excuse by then. Any ideas?"

"I've heard the truth works."

"Not my favorite option. Not for this anyways. I even tried to lie to my maids about it, but I'm sure you can imagine how that went."

Maxon held the bandages in his hand. "I can't get around..."

I dropped my knees and cast away the ripped slip. With a little bit of my help, we were able to get the bandages wrapped over my bra and around my torso, without flashing Maxon.

"I think I'm done."

I twisted and bent a little, testing the waters. It felt...fine. It still hurt and it wasn't like I was magically healed, but I felt 100x better. I finally looked at his face for what felt like the first time all day.

"Thank you, really. It's great. Better than any job I've ever done."

"Anytime."

I slipped my dress back over my shoulders and Maxon wordlessly did the buttons up again. The silence grew now. What was there to say except the truth? But I wouldn't say it until he asked.

"America I—."

"I know. You can ask."

Maxon faltered. "Who did this to you?"

I closed my eyes, shutting everything out for a second, before opening them.

"My father."

CHAPTER 21

Disclaimer: Some words taken or paraphrased from The Elite by Kierra Cass

A/N: There has been a very weird but also super awesome influx of people reading my stories lately. My notifications for Wattpad are blowing up all day everyday and I don't understand why everyone is in the mood to read the Selection fan fiction as of late, but I am not complaining. Enjoy the chapter.

Maxon faltered. "Who did this to you?"

I closed my eyes, shutting everything out for a second, before opening them.

"My father."

He didn't look surprised and I suppose he wasn't. There are only a few people who have enough power to do this to me, and there is only one with enough hatred in his heart to do it. This is the truth I never told. We can play house all we want. We can play father and daughter. But you can't fake this.

"I don't...know what to say," He said.

I tucked a strand of hair behind my ear, and stared at my lap.

"I don't really know either. The truth works right?"

He was staring at me and I didn't want him to. I didn't want to know what he was thinking. Did he see in me what I always saw in myself? He knows everything now. Does he see the ugly and the flaws? Every inch of skin that I covered in makeup, every scar that I wrapped in silk. Every imperfection that I have layered diamonds over so that something shines brighter than everything wrong with me.

Does he see it all now?

"How did this happen?" He whispered. He sat down next to me on the wooden bench, a foot of space between us.

I fiddled with my thumbs. "I've always been a little different than my mother and father. It all makes sense now but there was no explanation for it then. When I was kid, it was different. I played in the trees and I was just being a kid. I tried to pitch in at a meeting, and everyone would laugh and talk about how adorable I was. But eventually I grew up, and knew what I wanted. I wanted to be queen.

I wanted to make a change and fix everything that I saw was wrong. I went after what I wanted and I fought for it. I've always fought for it. But when I'm fighting against my father, he always wins. But he can't ever just win. He has to put you in your place. This is how he puts me in my place."

Maxon made a sound of disbelief and my lip quivered. I bit down on it. I'm not going to cry.

"Your mother doesn't know?"

"I would never tell my mother or even give her a reason to suspect at all. She knows father is stern with me, but I don't want her to worry. I can take it."

He stared at me.

"He's not like this with her," I promised. "She gets mistreated in her own ways, but not like this."

"What are the old ones from?" He asked, then shook his head. "Never mind, that's rude."

"Things I said or did. Things I know. There's no end to the expanse of things but..." I shrugged.

He hesitated. "...How old?"

"I was 13, I think. Around that age at least."

"Why ever....how...I'm sorry, I just."

"It was because of a meeting. My dad had trusted me with this great responsibility of going to an important meeting. I was so excited. But I said something wrong, I can't even remember what it was now, but he was furious. It was his way of training that habit out of me and eventually it worked. It's been a while since the last time, but I've been a bit mouthy as of late, and this was his reminder of where I'm supposed to be."

"America...I can't even begin to imagine what it was like growing up in that environment."

"It ripped apart my views on my father forever. He went from my role model to my biggest fear. That was quite confusing for a 13 year old. But I've learned to deal with it as best as I can. I know where the line is and what pushes him over it. I've been very careful not to put myself in that situation. But a lots changed lately and I guess I forgot to be careful."

"What happened?"

I covered my face with my hand. "I don't want to tell you."

"You don't have to—."

"It's not that," I mumbled. "You'll hate me after I do."

He reached out and gently lowered my hand from my face and wrapped it in his. His touch was warm and comforting. "I don't think at this point I could ever hate you."

I took a deep breath and nodded. I really hope that's true.

"It was right after you stopped by my room and we were kissing and I stopped. I got confused because it's so unlike me to be giggly and flirty...that's not me. I was so happy after our date, I thought it wasn't right. I was giving in and bringing you into this place where my father was going to take control of you, like he did me. So I went to him and I told him I wasn't going to marry you, and he reminded me that I had no choice."

"You did that...for me?" He murmured.

"I was born into this life. And it can be good. But it can also be terrible. I don't want you to have to see the side of me that is broken, the side of my father that is evil, or anything else that is going to make you someone who you're not. That's what my father does. He makes you who he wants."

Maxon's hand was still in mine and he looked down at our hands before talking.

"I don't think your who your father has created you to be. Because he's terrible and he would make you terrible. But you're not. You're you, and I think you're pretty amazing."

Another rogue tear slipped down my cheek but Maxon caught it before I could, gently wiping it away with his thumb and holding my face.

"It is so difficult," I broke, an ugly sob racking through my body. "I try so hard to be a perfect princess, and not make him angry, and be a good daughter for my mother so she suspects nothing. But I'm also trying to fight for what this country needs, because it's so messed up and I'm scared that even with a crown on my head, I won't be able to fix everything my ancestors have done. I try to be a good friend to those who always stick by me, but I'm always lying to them and that hurts me more than anything. I'm silenced but I have so much to say and no one to say it to. Sometimes I just can't."

Maxon stopped trying to catch the tears and instead rested his arm low enough on my waist as to not bother my wounds, because he's that thoughtful, and pulled me close to him while I talked.

"And living with him makes me sick. He treats me, my mother, the staff, the country, everyone, like scum on his shoes and he gets away with it. And I can't do anything about it and I just feel so helpless. I know you didn't live an easy life, but your lucky that you weren't born the Prince of Illea. There is so much good in you, and I don't know who you'd be if we weren't switched."

"It didn't ruin you, and I like to think it wouldn't have ruined me either." His hand lifted from my waist and hovered over my bandages. "Those scars should be on my back, not yours. I'm supposed to be the Prince. He should of been beating me. You don't deserve this."

I looked up into his eyes. "I'm glad that it was me and not you."

His hand lifted to cup my face and I turned my face into his palm, kissing it. He than traced the side of my face and dug his hand deep into my hair, pulling my lips to his.

I don't know how Maxon and I became so close, so fast. He knows so much about me that I haven't told anyone and I only met him a few short months ago. But from the moment we met in the gardens that day, he understood what I was going through and I understood him. We definitely aren't always on the same page, though that is mostly my fault, but I can see myself being happy with Maxon. If I had to be stuck marrying anyone, I'm glad it's him.

I pulled away slightly, my face inches from his.

"You're not going to run away again, right?" He teased.

I smiled. "There's no where to go. Besides I...I don't think I want to."

"I'm glad," He replied and brought my face towards his again. We shifted somehow, so that he was laying across the bench and I lay on top of him. He kept on running his hands through my hair and I became obsessed with how soft his lips were. I could do this whenever I wanted now and I think I will be partaking often.

Maxon pulled away.

"Is your back okay?" He checked.

"Better than ever," I mumbled against his lips, kissing him again. I'm not sure how long we kissed for, but for a person who only started this whole kissing thing a short while ago, I can tell you that Maxon is a really good kisser but I didn't hear any complaining on his end either. I can also tell you that making out is one average teen experience that I'm very sad I missed out on.

Eventually we did stop but for no reason other than the fact that the bench was uncomfortable and definitely not big enough for the both of us.

I straightened up and sat on the bench.

"You look tired," He murmured, his hand reaching towards my face and tracing under my eyes.

"Long day," I sighed. "I always forget how much energy this takes out of me."

"You should sleep," He said.

I laughed. "Where? On the bench? I don't think so."

"There's blankets in here, right?"

I nodded.

He stood up and walked over to the shelves against the wall, shuffling through them. He collected a few blankets and some pillows and set them on the floor.

"You hungry?"

I shook my head.

He grabbed a few granola bars anyways and two bottles of water. Then he built a makeshift bed out of blankets. The floor was still concrete but it was sweet of him anyways.

He presented his work to me with a big grin. "Well?"

I smiled. "Thank you."

We laid down together on the cold concrete and I couldn't help but curl up closer to him for added warmth. Not that he minded much. I was tired but we talked still with his arm around me, careful of my back, and me cuddled into his side with my head on his chest. He had eaten at least 3 or 4 granola bars and he got me to eat one too.

Eventually I had to ask a question that was bothering me at the back of my mind.

"How many girlfriends have you had?" I asked tentatively, stifling a yawn.

"None."

I glanced up at him. "Really?"

"You sound surprised."

"I mean, you go to school with a bunch of girls and live in a town with a bunch of girls and you're pretty easy on the eyes, so I would just think..."

He stared at the ceiling, his arm tracing up and down my arm. "There wasn't much time for that. It's not like no one was ever interested....I just had a job and a family to help provide for. No room in the schedule for other distractions."

"Oh," I said.

"What about you? You've had suitors knocking on your door you're whole life. You had a chance for a Selection, there are princes all around the world who want to marry into the Schreave family. Why haven't you dated any of them?"

"I kind of always hoped for something more than any of that." He looked at me questioningly. "Think about it. With the selection, 35 random people are arbitrarily selected to court me and 1 of them is just supposed to be my true love. What are the chances that any of them actually would be? And with princes and such, it's like you said, they want America Schreave not just, me."

"You want real love," He stated.

"I don't know about true love or any of that, but at least someone who wants me and not my crown."

"I get that," He said.

"I know you do," I mumbled, my eyes fluttering closed and open again.

"You're tired. You should go to sleep," He whispered in my ear.

"I don't want to," I mumbled. "I want to keep talking."

But even as I said it, my speech lagged and my eyes dropped close. I didn't open them this time.

"Goodnight, America," He breathed.

"....Goodnight, Maxon."

CHAPTER 22

All of you guys are literally so sweet, I'm just sitting her crying because I have so many supportive readers. Some of you just read for the story and I get that, but for those who always support me, thank you so much. Enjoy the chapter

The sound of the door creaking open, woke me up, and the light that filled the room was so bright, I had to shield my eyes.

"Your Majesty?" Someone called. "Oh God, I've found her! She's alive!"

There was a sudden flurry of people to the entrance of the safe room, all of them staring into the space at us. Maxon was slowly waking up and I blinked a few times, trying to come too. I felt my back pull and everything came back.

"We're you not able to get downstairs, your majesty?" Markson asked.

"No," I mumbled, shaking my head. "An officer was supposed to tell my parents. I told him to go there first."

Maxon was awake in a second, hopping up off the floor and offering me his hand to pull me up. I accepted it.

"Which officer?"

"It was Officer Lark," I said.

"He didn't make it, your majesty. We lost about 25 guards and a dozen staff."

I covered my mouth with my hand. "What?"

Officer Markson nodded grimly.

"What about my maids? My parents?"

"All fine, Mam. Your mother is worried sick though."

"Is she out of the safe room yet?" I asked, beginning to lead the group out of the safe room, Maxon following closely next to me.

"Everyone has been for a while. We were doing a sweep of the smaller safe rooms hoping to find you and Sir Maxon. A guard went to get your parents."

Maxon's hand grabbed my own and forced me to stop and look at the palace around me. Everything was in chaos. There was horrible damage all around us, leaving no mystery of what went on here while we were hiding. Deep red stains in the carpet showed where people had once been and there were huge gouges in the walls, as if someone had tried to claw they're way through them. It was sickening. Lights flickered, trying to hold on to some semblance of life, and glass coated the floor near where windows used to be and now only empty holes remained.

"Amy!"

I looked up and dropped Maxon's hand as my mom rushed down the hallway, my dad following behind her.

She enveloped me in her embrace, tucking me into her like a puzzle piece. My back, in desperate need of new bandages and more ointment, screamed in protest but I ignored it. I closed my eyes and squeezed her back, tightening my arms around her body. Pulling away slightly, she examined me for damage.

"I was so scared," She murmured.

"I tried to send for someone to tell you but they didn't make it," I explained.

"We're just glad your okay," My father spoke, appearing next to us and placing his hand, comfortingly against my back.

I gritted my teeth. "I was with Maxon the whole time. He got me to safety. I wouldn't have made it there if it wasn't for him."

"Well I'm grateful he's okay too," My mom spoke, smiling at him. "You should rest."

"I just woke up," I told her.

"But this is extremely taxing and we all need to stay in our rooms, while they fix the palace up."

"Of course. I'll see you at dinner then."

My mom nodded.

I looked back at Maxon. "I'll see you then too?"

"Maybe even before."

~oOo~ 1 week later ~oOo~

I unzipped the back of my dress and peeled back the bandages, twisting around to examine my wounds in the mirror.

"These are healing well," Anne observed. "He did good work."

"Will they scar much?" I asked.

"I don't think so," She replied. "And it looks like they've stopped bleeding so I think we can take the bandages off."

"I still can't believe you told your father that you weren't going to marry Maxon," Mary quipped from my bed, flipping her magazine.

"Mary!" Lucy chastised, shooting her a look. She rummaged through the medical box and handed Anne a few things.

"I don't mean it like that! I just mean that her and Maxon have basically spent every waking moment since then together. It seems like she wouldn't be that bothered by marrying the man."

"Maxon is really sweet," I agreed as Anne stripped the bandages from my body and began applying ointment to the healing skin. "But I don't know if I want to marry him! We've only been actually together for a week. And you know it's about the choice, Mary, not whether I'd do it if I even had the option."

"I just want you to be happy Ames," She sighed.

"Thank you Mary. I know you do. I know that's what all of you want. It's a complicated situation but I'm figuring it out."

"You don't have to figure it out alone," Lucy reminded me.

"I know."

Anne's swift hands zipped up the back of my dress and straightened it out.

"Please," Anne scoffed. "America can't even get dressed by herself. She needs us."

"Right," I laughed, shaking my head. We all giggled together good-naturedly as Anne hid the box away in my closet, something we all agreed was for the best.

There were three swift knocks at the door.

"Maxon?" Lucy asked.

I tilted my head. "Maybe...but he's early."

Mary shrugged and hopped off the bed to get the door. She pulled it open and immediately sunk into a bow.

"Your majesty," She muttered.

"My mom?" I asked, peeking around the door. I was shocked to see Father standing there, his face like stone and his foot tapping impatiently.

Anne and Lucy dropped into identical curtsies as my father strolled past Mary and into the room.

"Oh, hello Father," I stuttered.

"You're excused ladies," He nodded at my maids. They curtsied again and scurried away immediately.

"Who do I owe the honor of your visit?" I asked, sitting down on the edge of my bed.

He wandered around the room, looking around at everyday things as if they were foreign objects to him. He picked up a tv remote off my dresser and then tossed it back onto it.

"I wanted to inform you that I will be taking a trip to New Asia to discuss the war with some of the officials there."

"Will I be coming with you?" I asked.

"No."

I narrowed my eyes. "Why not?"

"Because I no longer think your mature enough to come along," He spoke smugly and ran a hand over my piano.

"Excuse me? I have a right to be at all war meetings. I'm as involved in this war as you are and I'll be the one who is making all war related decisions when I become queen," I argued. "I have to be there."

"No," He said. "You don't. That's a right that you have to earn."

I stood up. "I have earned it! I've gone with you on very other trip to New Asia!"

"But that's before you decided to throw a hissy fit over your little marriage situation. War meetings are much too serious for children, and until you stop acting like one, you don't get to go to them."

I gritted my teeth, my hands clenching into fists.

"This isn't fair."

"Life's not fair." He strolled back to the door. "You can continue going on trips with me when you learn to act like you're old enough."

I watched him, resisting the urge to scream and cry like the child he's treating me as.

"I'll see you in a few days, America," He said and went to close the door but then stopped. "Oh! Maxon."

I lifted my head up.

My dad grinned and looked back at me. "Your fiancés here."

He than walked away, revealing Maxon to me, whose eyes were darting from me to my father. I just shook my head and stood up, walking over to him. We both watched my father walk down the hallway and didn't say anything until he turned onto the next one.

"Are you okay?" Maxon asked immediately, checking me for damage.

I waved him off. "Yes, yes. I'm fine. My father was just grounding me."

Maxon followed me into my room. "Grounding you?"

"Basically. He told me that I can't go onto a business trip with him."

"Are you upset about it?" He asked. I sat on my bed.

"Actually...I don't really think I am. I'm actually kind of glad I don't have go on that boring trip. I think I'd much rather hang out with you than be packing right now."

I reached out and grabbed his hand, pulling him to sit next to me. I gave him a quick peck and smiled.

"What do you want to do today?" I asked.

"I'm not really sure. I haven't thought about it much."

"We can go on a walk around the gardens," I suggested.

His eyebrows raised high. "In the rain?"

"It's not raining..." I trailed off and ran to my balcony doors, throwing them open.

"America!"

I stepped outside and a light warm Angeles sprinkle hit my skin, making me smile. It was nothing but a few droplets but it meant rain was coming.

"What are you doing? You're going to get all wet!" He said, standing by the doors hesitantly.

"I know! Isn't it great?" I laughed, spinning around.

"I'm confused," He admitted.

"It's starting to rain," I told him as if it should be obvious. "You're from Carolina, it rains all the time there."

"I know," He said, a crease forming between his eyes. "It sucks."

"What?" I gasped. "Take it back."

"I'm so lost," He sighed. "Use your words America."

"I love the rain. It never rains here in Angeles and it's probably the one thing I would change."

"It rains most of the year in Carolina and it's never something that I exactly look forward to."

"But it's like the changing of season, you know? Rain washes everything away from the day before and leaves it all clean..."

"...And wet and muddy," Maxon finished.

"No, it leaves it new," I corrected.

"But also wet and muddy."

I waltzed back inside just to smack his arm. "Don't be rude to the rain."

"It can't hear," He said.

I went to smack his arm again but he caught my wrist and pulled me close to him, kissing me deeply. I melted into him.

He pulled away.

"I love the rain," I repeated.

He shook his head. "You're weird."

"Come with me to the roof."

"The roof?"

"Yes."

"Uh, is that safe?"

"Very."

I grabbed his hand and pulled, urging him to follow. After a second, he did. I ran with him out of the room, and led him up the stairs to the fourth floor. I then entered the parlor and found the unused fire place which would be our entrance. I could only smile wide as I undid the latch and led us through another series of passageways. I stopped outside the door.

"You just led us through a bunch of secret passageways as if it was nothing," Maxon deadpanned.

"Well how do you think we get to the roof?"

"That's..." Maxon trailed off and hesitantly pushed on the door, revealing a wall of rain.

I smiled and stepped forward reaching into the water. Droplets of warm water collected on my skin and ran down my arm. I looked back at Maxon, awaiting his reaction.

"The roof," He mumbled, taking a step forward but both of us were still protected by three walls. And then he laughed, a childlike grin taking over his face. I giggled along with him. And then he shoved me out into the rain.

In the time it has taken us to get here, the rain had drastically picked up, and I was soaked instantly. I couldn't be bothered though. Turning around, I grabbed his arm and he smiled as he pretended to fight. His hair fell in strands into his eyes and he was instantly drenched as well.

I looked into the sky, blinking water out of my eyes, and smiling contently. I reached for his hand and he took mine.

"Isn't it peaceful?" I asked.

"There is nothing peaceful about rain pounding down on us," He responded.

I sighed, shaking my head. "You just don't get it."

"You're right, I don't. But I don't have to. As long as you understand it than I believe it too," He said.

He randomly lifted our conjoined hands above my head and twirled me around. I laughed as he spun me out and then whirled me back into his arms, hugging me and rocking me gently from side to side.

I giggled and tilted my head back into his neck. I felt so happy and my mind wanted to self destruct and reject it all, but I'm learning not to do that. I have to just be happy.

"You've learned to dance," I commented.

"It's part of the mandatory etiquette lessons. Though you are a much better dance partner than Silvia. Especially when she tries to lead."

I laughed. "Oh you poor thing. Imagine what she would say if she saw us up here in the rain."

"She'd throw a fit!"

"She'd loose it," I agreed

He twirled me around so I could face him while we talked, and we still swayed left to right in a hug.

"I think I like the rain better," He said.

"You see the magic?" I asked.

"No, not in the mystical way you see it but in a normal way. Angeles rain is much warmer and softer than Carolina rain. It's freezing cold and pelts you hard there. Maybe that's why you like rain. Because you've never felt true rain."

"Stop trying to ruin rain for me," I fake pouted. "I like all rain."

"We will see about that when I take you to Carolina for real."

I smiled. "I'd like to see it for real someday. I hear about it so much from you, I feel like I know you're home town, but I'd like to actually visit there. You know, see where you grew up. I mean you've seen where I've lived my whole life but I've seen nothing."

"One day," He promised. "We will go."

"I could finally meet Kenna!" I gasped.

"She wants to come so bad but it's difficult with her job and she has a baby on the way."

"That's great! Give her my congratulations please and send the rest of your family a hello too."

"I will."

"Speaking of your family...there's been something I've been meaning to ask you about," I told him.

"What is it?"

"You haven't mentioned him at all, so I haven't really brought it up, but I know about Kota."

He pursed his lips. "Oh. I see."

"It's perfectly fine if you don't want to talk about it, but I was just wondering why I have a biological brother that no one seems to want to tell me about."

He sighed. "It's a rough subject."

"You don't have to—."

"No, I want to. Just...let's sit away from the rain," He said.

I nodded and we sat down under the ledge of space by the door. I let my feet sit in the rain.

"Kota is the oldest brother, only a little bit younger than Kenna is. We don't talk about him anymore because we don't really know where he is. He comes around when it benefits him but for the most part he stays away. Which were all glad about."

"What happened?" I whispered.

"He had his heart set on being a two and he was willing to do anything to get that far. One day he had a sculpture that sold, to the palace if I'm correct, and he got paid pretty well for it. Instead of helping out the family though, he kept all the money for himself and set out to be at two."

"Do you think maybe that's why you chose to stay at the palace?" I asked.

"What do you mean?"

"You've mentioned that sometimes you think being with your family would be best even if my father were to put you in a bad situation. At least you'd be together. Do you think that maybe the reason you stayed and agreed to marry me is because you want to give your family what he never could?"

He looked down at his hands and I reached out and grabbed them.

"Maybe," He said.

I rubbed my thumb across his hand, trying to comfort him. It was sad to know that my brother was a real piece of work, but it wasn't really my burden to bare. I've never even met the man.

"I'm surprised he hasn't reached out to me. Now that I'm in line for the throne, you'd think he'd try and get back in my good graces."

"Well the mail list is pretty strict at the palace. But I'll make sure he's on the no mail list for sure," I said.

"No—don't. If I ever get a letter from him, I'd love to send one back and give him a piece of my mind."

"As long as you let me say a few things as well," I agreed.

"Deal."

A comfortable silence settled among us and I looked out past the roof and the palace, and out to the city of Angeles. The lines of the roads and angles of the buildings, mixed with bright sparkling lights, surrounded by a barrier of rain.

"I could stay out here all afternoon and night," I murmured.

"We'd probably get hyperthermia," Maxon said.

"We have the best doctors here."

"Well then I see no reason not to."

~oOo~

"Miss wake up," somebody said, shaking me awake.

I blinked my eyes open and expected bright daylight but instead was met with pitch darkness.

"What time is it?" I mumbled to Lucy, rubbing my eyes.

"One in the morning."

"Then why am I awake?" I asked

"There's an emergency. We need you downstairs."

"Did they get my father...." I trailed off. Oh, he's in New Asia. "My mother?"

"Just you."

My brow furrowed. "Alright."

I threw off my covers and slipped my feet into my slippers. Lucy brought me my robe and ushered me out the room. I ran down the halls and stairs as quickly as I could, probably looking like a crazy person to all guards and definitely having slipped twice.

There were a few guards standing in the foyer and I walked straight toward them, wrapping my robe tightly around me.

"What is it?" I asked.

"There are rebels in the palace," Avery informed me.

"What?" I shrieked. "And you called me down here? Why aren't I hiding?"

"They aren't here to attack. It's just two," Avery explained.

"And why are they here?" I accused.

"They're unarmed and say that they are from the northern camp. They said they will only talk to you."

"What about my father? He's not here. He should be here."

"They said you and only you, your majesty. Your fathers on a trip anyways. Will you talk to them?"

"I'm in my nightgown," I said, looking down at myself and touching my hair.

"They're pretty informal."

I nodded, weighing it in my head. I'm not sure I want to talk to rebels. Even unarmed, they're far deadlier than I could ever be. But this may be my only chance to ever talk to the rebels, and there are so many things that I need to know.

"Okay," I said. "Okay. Lead the way and keep your holster unlocked, just in case."

"Of course, your majesty," He answered and lead me around the corner to the great room, where two people were standing surrounded by even more guards.

"Could you call off your dogs?" One of the rebel's asked.

He was tall and slim, with blonde shaggy hair. His outfit showed that he was maybe a six or seven, and a compass hung from his neck on a long chain. He wasn't what I expected at all. He looked rugged and mistreated, but not like a threat in anyway.

The girl with him, even more surprisingly, looked like she was trying to be fashionable while still holding true to whatever they're caste was. Her hip jutted out to the side and she seemed confident, even in such a situation.

"We've come in peace," The man said. "We are unarmed and your guards have searched us. I know asking for privacy would be inappropriate, but there are matters with which I wish to discuss with you, that no one else should hear."

"What do you want?"

"Again," He said, almost playfully gesturing around the room. "These guys need to be out of earshot."

"How do I know that I can trust you?"

"I know you're skeptical of us, and for good reason too, but we mean you no harm. We have no cause to hurt you. We just want to talk."

I deliberated for a minute. "Fine. All of you, please stay back so I can speak to them in private." I turned and spotted Avery. "But not too far off."

The guards stepped back, wordlessly forming a barrier around the room, their eyes never leaving the two rebels as if they'd be ready to shoot if they so much as breathed too close to me.

I gestured to a table in the room, and the man and women took their seats.

"I suppose introductions are in order," The man said, offering me his hand. I stared at his hand and eventually he retracted it, eyeing me nervously.

"I suppose," I agreed. "I'm America Schreave, your sovereign."

The man chuckled. "Honored, madam."

"And you are?"

"Mr. August Illea, at your service."

CHAPTER 23

Disclaimer: Some words taken directly or paraphrased from *The One* by Kierra Cass

"Mr. August Illea, at your service."

My mouth fell open.

"You heard me right. I'm an Illea. And by birth too. This one will be by marriage sooner or later," August said, nodding to the girl.

"Georgia Whitaker," She said, her voice like jingling bells. "And of course we know all about you, Princess."

She gave me a small smile and I lifted my chin. I wasn't sure I trusted her but she seems nice, which is odd considering what I had always considered rebels to be.

Then something occurred to me.

"So my father was right then. He said you would come for the crown one day. Well, I have a news flash for you, I'm not giving it up that easily."

"I don't want your crown," He assured me.

"Good because I intend to lead this country. I was raised for it and you can't just waltz in here claiming to be Gregory Illea's great—."

"I don't want your crown America!"

"Princess America," I corrected coldly.

"My bad, Princess America. I have no ill intent towards your throne. Destroying the monarchy is more up the southern rebels alley, don't you think? We have other goals."

Georgia looked around at the guards surrounding us. "What does a gal have to do around here to get something to drink?"

"Would you like some coffee or tea?" I asked, my upbringing coming out.

"Coffee?" Her eyes lit up.

I couldn't help but smile and I waved Officer Woodwork over.

"Yes, your majesty?" He asked.

"Could you tell a maid to bring us some coffee. And to please make it extra strong."

"Of course," He said and headed away.

"I can't even begin to imagine what it is that you are here for. But it appears you've made a point of coming to the palace while everyone's asleep, maybe even while my father is away, so what is it that you want? I can promise that'll listen but that's about as far as your demands may go."

"That's all I ask," August replied. "We have been looking for the diaries of Gregory Illea for decades. The northern rebels mean the monarchy no harm, in fact, we quite like a few people here." He looked pointedly at me. "We have no issue with having a sovereign leader, particularly if that leader is you."

"Thank you," I spoke, a smile that I couldn't help spreading across my face. It was nice to hear it from someone besides myself.

"What we would like are other things. Particularly, elected officials and the end of the caste system," He said, leaning back in his chair as if these were simple inconveniences that I could have taken care of in a jiffy.

"You act like I'm already the queen. Even if that was possible, I couldn't simply give you what you're asking for."

"But you're open to the idea?" August countered.

"What I'm open to is irrelevant right now because I'm not the queen."

August sighed, preparing to speak but I placed a silencing finger to my lips. A maid, Lucy, stepped towards the table and placed down 3 cups, pouring coffee for the three of us. She gave me a questioning look and I motioned to her that I'd tell her everything later. Georgia was already downing her coffee and I raised it to my lips, taking a delicate sip. I like my coffee like I like my wine, meaning, I do not like coffee at all. But it would do the trick at keeping me awake.

"Why do you want the diaries?" I asked, hardly waiting for Lucy to get out of earshot. I'd tell her it all later.

"We're looking for evidence that Gregory is who we've always heard he was. If we had it then maybe we could negotiate for the officials and the end to the caste system."

I took a swig of coffee, no cream. "I'm unsure of what you want me to do with that information. You're asking for things that only a King can provide and there isn't one here."

"This was deliberate timing."

"I assumed so. But if you don't want the crown and only want things I can't give you, then why are you here?"

August and Georgia looked at each other, perhaps preparing to make their biggest request of all.

"We came here to ask you these things because we know you are a reasonable woman. We've watched you your whole life, and we can see it. I see it now. You don't like the castes either. You don't like the way your father holds this country under his thumb and laughs while they struggle to get free. You don't want to fight unnecessary wars, and more than anything you want peace in your lifetime."

"You seem to know a lot about a person you've never met," I said curtly.

He ignored me. "We're guessing that once your Queen, things could really change. And we've been waiting a long time for that and we're prepared to wait longer. We just want your word that when the time comes, you will work towards freeing your people and giving them the chance to live the lives they choose. All we need is a sign and we will do everything we can to help you lead, peacefully and fairly. Give your people a chance."

"What kind of sign? Money?"

"No, we don't need money. We have more of it than you'd think," He said offhandedly.

"How?"

"Donations," He said cryptically.

That meant that there are people who are knowingly supporting this cause, donating to them, and helping them out. Enough people to the point that they don't need anything from me. Has sitting pretty in the palace all my life meant that the rest of Illea knows more about this rebel cause than even I do? We are supposed to have all the information so that we can make the proper decisions but we don't even know anything about these people who attack us regularly. Now I know more than even my father does and I have to admit it made me happy.

"Answer a question for me," I told him.

"My knowledge is all yours," He smiled.

"The northerners are trying to help, then what are the southerners doing. What do they want? Just to kill us all?"

"So much of the country is oppressed. I like to think that you're not ignorant of the world outside the palace walls, but in case you are, it kind of sucks out there. And with this, has come the idea that some people could lead better than you could."

"It's not as easy as it seems," I said.

"I'm sure it's very difficult to make decisions that affect the whole country, but I get the feeling that you don't make all that many decisions. And that someone is keeping you from making them."

I stared at him, not confirming nor denying. I nodded at him. "Go on."

"As I said, they think they can rule better than you but I can promise you that they wouldn't. They just want the wealth, and then they'll obliterate all good that's left in this country and make promises that they can't keep, and leave everyone in Illea in the same, if not a worse place, than they are now. They'll try and create a semblance of removing the castes, but instead of giving the lower castes what they deserve, it'll leave all the castes with nothing. It would be like your ancestors but worse. The southerners are prepared to be way more cutthroat than any of the Illea's or Schreave's have ever been. It would be the same oppression, under a new name, and your people would suffer more than ever before."

"I don't want that," I whispered.

"None of us do. We hate the southerners just as much as you do and we want to help you stop them. But we have our demands."

I stared at both of them, scrutinizing their faces and body language. They seemed legitimate. I mean, August seems far too cocky for someone who is in my home, surrounded by guards who do what

I say and making demands with me. And Georgia seemed more interested in her coffee then the business at hand, but they didn't seem like they were trying to trick me.

"You know, you have a lot of nerve coming here," I spoke.

"There was a chance we'd be shot on sight," He replied. "We came anyways."

"Asking me," I continued. "To go against my father and promise you things I'm not even sure I could ever accomplish. Things that are treasonous."

"But...?" He trailed off.

"If I become queen, I can promise you that my people will be free and without any numbers determining who they are," I proposed.

"If?"

"A lot of things are up in the air right now," I said hesitantly.

"Would that have anything to do with Prince Maxon?" Georgia spoke up.

"He's not a prince yet, last time I checked."

"Oh really?" August asked, raising his eyebrow. "Because I've heard differently. Does the phrase, blood test, ring a bell to you?"

I stood up, sending my chair to the ground and all the guards around me to attention. I waved them off.

"How do you know about that?" I muttered lowly.

"We have people," He said.

"So does the whole rebel organization just know all my personal business—."

"No," August interrupted. "It is extremely confidential information that only the two of us and the person who told us know."

I gritted my teeth. "That doesn't make me feel better."

"We have no wish for that information to get out. We couldn't have hand-selected a better princess than you, whether you were meant to have that role doesn't matter us."

Georgia sneakily switched her and August's cups of coffee and began drinking it. She addressed me. "So you think that you won't be queen for some reason?"

"It's not that I don't think I'll be queen. People just like to jingle my role in front of me sometimes, and threaten to take it away."

"Your father?"

"Can we talk about the attack last week?" I asked, obviously changing the subject. They allowed it.

"That was the southern rebels, not us," He said, raising his hands up non-threateningly.

"I know that. But I agreed, so the northern rebel attacks end, correct? And you'll work towards helping us stop the southern rebels as well?"

August and Georgia locked eyes, silently communicating with one another in their own language. It was sickeningly adorable.

"Yeah," Georgia said. "I think we can do that."

"We promise that when, not if, you become queen, we will stand by your side."

I nodded my head and offered him my hand. "And you will do it freely, with no caste."

He pumped my hand twice and smiled.

"You know you're quite reasonable for a spoiled brat princess," He commented.

"And you're quite put together for an off the street rebel," I replied.

"Why thank you," He said.

Georgia grabbed his hand. "Babe, this coffee is really nice."

"I know, but these guards are looking a bit too trigger happy for my liking. We should go," He said.

I nodded.

"Would you like a coffee to go?" I offered.

"You can do that?" Georgia asked, her eyes going wide.

"I'm sure it can be arranged. Come with me to the foyer and I'll see what I can do."

We stood up from the table and the guards parted ways as I approached. August and Georgia followed behind me closely, eyeing the guards. I noticed Aspen standing duty at the door and he was talking quietly with Lucy.

"Lucy," I called, motioning her over. She said something to Aspen and he smiled before she walked quickly over.

"Yes, your majesty?" She asked, curtsying deeply.

"Could we get some sort of to-go coffee for our guests?" I asked.

"Of course," She answered. "I'll get right on that, Ame—your majesty."

"Great," I said.

Georgia was looking around, admiring the beautiful architecture. "I rarely ever have time to look around when I'm here. And I never get offered coffee."

I rolled my eyes. "You joke about it, but the attacks have been quite traumatizing to my life. You scared my fiancé's family half to death when they were here."

"What's it like being in a fake engagement?" She asked.

"Georgia," August mumbled.

"What? I'm just asking!" She said defensively.

"No, it's alright," I told him. "It's quite confusing at first. But it's not all that fake anymore."

"Woah! Plot twist much? How did that happen?" She asked.

"I couldn't even tell you if I tried," I sighed.

It felt weird talking to Georgia as if she hasn't broken into my home multiple times. But she was so normal that it felt good to talk to her. It made me feel kind of normal as well.

"How quick can I get that coffee?" Georgia joked, eyeing a few of the guards.

"Depends on the maid, but Lucy's a good one."

"You know them all?"

"I try my absolute best to know every maid, butler, and guard here," I said proudly. I should be proud of that.

"You're a good Princess," She said.

"I've made a lot of mistakes," I murmured.

"And those actions have had consequences right?"

"You have no idea."

"And you probably knew they would. But you acted for those who couldn't speak for themselves anyways. That's special."

I blinked a few times, staring at her. I wasn't used to this type of praise. Maxon gives a lot of compliments, which is nice, but this is different. She doesn't even know me.

"Thank you."

"Coffee?"

Lucy appeared next to us with two paper cups of coffee. I'm not sure why the palace has them, but we have everything here I suppose. Lucy handed one to Georgia and one to August, who then handed his right back over to Georgia.

"We really should be going," August said.

"Of course," I agreed.

They walked toward the door and I followed them with my eyes.

Georgia turned around as if a second thought. "See you around, America."

"Princess America."

"Yeah sure."

And then Aspen pulled open the large door and they were gone. It almost shocked me when I saw it was still dark outside. It felt like we had talked for hours.

"Are you okay, America?" Lucy asked, placing a hand on my shoulder.

I jumped and looked at her. "Um, yeah. I'm just tired."

"Don't you wanna go back to bed?"

"I don't think I can."

CHAPTER 24

"Your hand is shaking," Maxon said gently, squeezing my fingers.

"That's because I'm nervous," I murmured and snatched my hand from his.

He gently took it back and looked at me with concern. I stared at the large palace doors with fear, praying that they wouldn't open.

"Why are you nervous?" He asked once he realized I wasn't going to tell him on my own. "You've met them before."

"Because they're your family. And my family. Oh god, this is a mess. How am I supposed to talk to these people? Like my boyfriend's family? Or like my long lost parents who raised my boyfriend, which is actually really messed up, and who I completely ignored last time they visited."

"Those are valid concerns," He coaxed gently.

"Not to mention, I'm meeting your older sister. Who is also my older sister? I'm not even sure, and I'm just really scared."

"Is that all?"

I rolled my eyes, pushing his shoulder and almost causing him to fall off the bench we were sitting on. "I'm serious. I feel really bad about being so cold to them the last time, but I'm not even sure this time will be any different. I don't know how to act around them and I'm worried I'll just seize up and go all ice princess."

"I'm sure they're just as nervous to see you again. They're very excited to be invited back though."

"To see you, not their emotionless excuse for a biological daughter."

"You're being dramatic. Everything will be fine. And if it is isn't, then I'll just keep you guys away from each other for the time they are here," He joked.

"You might have to make good on that promise," I said seriously.

He shook his head and pulled me closer into his side, kissing my head. "I have full faith in you."

I smiled and snuggled into his side. "That faith is misplaced but thank you."

He tilted his head down to kiss me but I dodged and slid off the bench.

"Do I look okay?" I asked, smoothing my dress.

His forehead crinkled as he looked at where I just was and over to where I now stood in front of him. "Did you just kiss block me?"

"Yes, now focus. Is my dress okay? Does it say, I'm really sorry for being a heartless brat when we last met, but I really like your son and we are also blood, so maybe we can move past that?"

"Can the dress talk? I think you may have to say all that on your own."

"Maxon!"

"You look beautiful," He said. "And my family is going to love you. So kiss me."

I pursed my lips to keep from smiling and stepped in front of him. He pulled me between his legs and I wrapped my hands around his neck.

"Am I acting crazy?" I asked.

"Completely, but I like crazy."

I kissed the tip of his nose. "Thank you."

I was about to step away but he grabbed my waist and pulled me back, bringing my lips to his in a real kiss. I grinned against his lips and relaxed for a moment, before pulling away and sitting back on the bench. We spoke for a few minutes about meaningless things before the guards at the door finally alerted us that Maxon's family was entering the palace gates.

He stood up, a new excitement entering his eyes as he pulled me to my feet.

"I didn't even ask you about how you're feeling about seeing your family," I said guiltily.

"Don't feel bad. You were nervous. I'm just excited to see them," He said.

"Do you miss them a lot?"

"Yeah, but I'm a grown adult. I can handle being away from them. I'm glad they're here though."

I smiled and slipped my hand into his as the doors were pulled open from the outside and the Singers stepped into the foyer. Maxon was immediately bounding away from me and towards his family, but I hung back hesitantly.

I watched him hug his Mom and observed the way she looked up at him and excitedly asked him questions.

"I've missed you so much," She told him, fixing his collar happily.

"Let the rest of us see him a bit, Maggie," Shalom said to her, placing a fatherly hand on Maxon's shoulder and nudging his wife aside gently. "Hey, son."

They shook hands and then hugged lovingly, saying a few things I didn't quite catch. Gerad was saying something too and Maxon was kneeling down to speak to him. Maxon's face was completely lit up, which as I was slowly learning as of late, was something that also made me happy. I know, I find it weird too.

That's when I took notice of May, looking around excitedly at the palace, and the two adults standing next to her, who were listening with interest as she spoke.

"Kenna!"

The woman, who had reddish-brown hair and a round belly, looked up and smiled. "You look good, little bro. You clean up nice. Who would've guessed."

"I'll take that as a compliment and not as what I think it was meant to be," Maxon grinned and crossed over to hug her. It was sweet for a moment before May jumped onto his back.

"I'm so happy to be back here!" She squealed in his ear.

"Aren't you also happy to see me?" Maxon teased, looking over his shoulder to see her as best as possible.

"Well of course," She said, ruffling his hair. "But the palace is way cooler than you'll ever be."

I felt like I was waiting too long to say anything. I don't think they've seen me yet so would it be awkward to say hi now? Should I wait for Maxon to say something? Maybe I'll just leave...

"Ames!" Maxon called, his eyes all big and unaware of my inner turmoil. He waved me over and I just about died walking over to his family who all look just like me.

"It's so good to see you again, Princess," Magda mumbled, unsure of what to do so she kind of just bowed her head awkwardly.

"Just call me, America, please," I said. Because that's what you're supposed to say. And apparently I didn't say it the first time we met.

"Of course," She said.

I reached out my hand to shake and she awkwardly took it. I then shook Shalom's hand who mumbled a quick greeting. I was spiraling, suddenly noticing that his skin was the same shade as mine and his nose had a slight upward curve that was so familiar. I stepped back, looking at Maxon but he seemed unaware.

"America, your dress is so gorgeous," A high-pitched voice squeaked. May's red hair flashed into my view as she appeared next to me and I took a deep breath. May was exactly what I needed. She was so sweet and oblivious that her presence instantly made things calmer, which seems ironic with how much energy she seems to have.

"Thank you," I mumbled, fiddling with the edge. "That's very sweet."

"Though you always look so amazing," She continued. "Did you know that red heads are supposedly more likely to be left handed? I'm left handed. What about you?"

"I'm left handed as well."

Mays eyes went wide as if this was the most interesting thing she'd heard all year. "My moms right handed though, so who really knows."

"May," Magda cut in, reaching out towards her and gently pulling her away from me. "Your rambling and I'm sure America could care less about which hand we write with."

"I'm left handed as well," Shalom laughed nervously. "But I don't have red hair."

"Me too," Gerad piped in, looking around in confusion.

"Gee, this is a riveting conversation," Kenna spoke sarcastically. "I'm right handed and I'm going to use said hand to shake America's hand. It would be nice if you all would move aside so I could do so."

Kenna broke through her family and her eyes scanned me from my high heels to the roots of my hair. And then she smiled, laughing lightly, and holding our her hand for me to shake.

"I don't understand how I've never seen it before. I feel like an idiot. James, come over here," Kenna said, releasing my hand and waving the other man over. "She looks like the perfect mix between May and I. How have we never seen this before?"

"Well you wouldn't have known to even think about it," The man said, his voice quiet, as he slipped a hand around her waist.

"It just seems so obvious now. It's very nice to meet you, America. I'm Kenna and this is my husband, James," She grinned.

"It's very nice to meet you, Kenna."

"You as well. Now I'd love to stay and chat so we all can continue this big awkward greeting, but I'm jet lagged and very pregnant. So if someone could kindly show me to where I can sleep, that would be great."

"I'll show you guys to your rooms," Maxon offered and picked up May's bags for her.

"That is why he's my favorite," Kenna announced and handed her bags to James, who just smiled lovingly.

"Hey!" May yelped.

"Don't worry, May-bug. Give it time and he'll screw it up."

Maxon rolled his eyes and then suddenly turned to look at me. I had hung back as inconspicuously as possible as they all began to head towards the hallway, but Maxon noticed and then his whole family was looking at me.

"Are you coming, Ames?" He asked.

I wanted to because I could tell he wanted me to. But this was a lot, too much, too fast. Kenna seemed really cool. And May is really sweet. Gerad is so innocent. And Magda and Shalom mean well. But there my blood and I can't get past the way they all interact as one big family, when it was me who was supposed to be there at the center of it.

"I can't," I said. "I have a meeting I have to get to."

Maxon knew that wasn't true. I had planned on spending the day with him and his family. We talked about it earlier.

"Totally slipped my mind," He said, like it was nothing and set the bags he was holding down so he could come over to me. He leaned forward, kissing my cheek sweetly and whispered in my ear. "Thank you for trying."

"I'm sorry," I mumbled.

"I get it," He said and squeezed my hand. Our fingers slipped apart as he returned to his family.

"It was nice seeing you again, America," Magda called.

"You all as well."

~oOo~

Avoiding the singers became my number one objective over the next week. It appears that my meeting schedule had filled up, or at least my 'hide in my room while Maxon tells his family I'm at a meeting' schedule. I felt bad about it. They seemed very sweet but I've been trying to work on being a little warmer and less unapproachable, but I can't seem to get past this. They're my family but they're not. I have a family. Or at least a mother.

And Maxon's been great about it. He understands though I don't think his family does. It's not that I wouldn't like to get to know them. May seems so sweet and I think Kenna and I would get along really well. I can tell Shalom and Magda would like to get to know me and I'm not sure about Gerad, but I think he may just be too young to understand much of what's going on.

I also realize that I will have to get to know them eventually. Not just because they are my blood, but because their Maxon's family. And he is my fiance/boyfriend/complicated whatever and I know how much he wants me to get to know them. And I will. Just not today.

Or at least that was the plan.

I was in the middle of a "meeting" where I was really catching up on some reading, when their was a knock at my door. Maxon and I were supposed to have lunch.

I dog-eared my book and set it aside, heading for the door and pulling it open.

"You're early—."

I snapped my mouth shut as two identical pale faces with tiny button noses and icy blue eyes, stared at me accusingly.

"You've been lying to us for a week," Kenna announced, waddling past me and into my bedroom. My eyes followed her and then flick-ered to May as she did the same.

"And you were probably going to lie to us for the next few weeks we're here," May spoke.

"Um...I—."

"Which we understand this is messy, it's messy for us too," Kenna continued, gesturing between May and her and taking a seat on the edge of my bed. "But you can't just avoid us forever. Because not only are we your future sister-in-laws, but if we get down to the nitty-gritty, we're actually sisters. So no more 'meetings'."

"Plus," May piped. "We're not that bad. Mom and Dad can be a lot, but we just want to get to know you."

"So do they," Kenna added.

"May I talk now?" I asked.

"Proceed."

"I'm sorry for avoiding you, but this is also really confusing. From the minimal amount of time I've spent with either of you, all I've done is notice every similarity between us. The three of us could pass for triplets."

"Well—."

"And I grew up with no siblings," I interrupted. "I've always wanted some but it's never been a reality for me. I don't know how to act around either of you. And because of my title, I've never lived in the same family dynamic as all of you have grown up in. I don't know how to be apart of a big happy family, who have lots of inside jokes and spend loads of time with one another. That's not how things work around here. I just don't know how. And with the added stress of Maxon being my fiance...It was just easier to avoid you all together."

I took a deep breath and stared at the two of them, waiting for what they had to say. Kenna turned to May.

"She has the Singer rambling trait," Kenna observed.

"And she plays music like mom," May said, pointing towards my piano.

"We just want to know you. There doesn't have to be anything else to it than that," Kenna sighed. "But see it from our side too."

"What do you mean?" I asked.

"You view this whole situation differently than we do. I assume it's because of your upbringing and the whole Princess thing, but it is all just an inconvenience to you. It would have been better if you never knew your real family," Kenna said this, and looked me in the eyes. "But my parents, see this as a loss. They never knew their daughter and they want to. This isn't an inconvenience to them. It's a second chance to know you, like they should have in the first place. Let them know their daughter."

"Let us know our sister," May murmured.

I didn't know what to say. Every fiber in my being, everything I had ever been taught, all the walls I have always put up. All of it, was telling me no. But maybe I should stop listening to that part of me all the time, because she isn't who I was meant to be in the first place.

Being Queen is all I want, but that doesn't mean I can't get to know these people. I missed out on being a sister and having a big happy family. But it isn't too late.

"Okay," I mumbled.

"Okay?" May repeated.

"Okay."

"Jeez, I didn't think that would work," May said, releasing a breath.

"Yeah. Aren't you supposed to be like a really bad-ass princess? If it's that easy too convince you than I think Illea should be worried," Kenna agreed.

"Hey!" I yelped. "You're the one who was trying to get me to agree-."

"Were just teasing," Kenna interrupted, grinning. "Sisters do that sometimes."

I couldn't help but smile and I hesitantly approached my bed, balancing daintily on the side. "I'll try my best to be sisterly or whatever, but I don't think it's going to be an instant change. I'm kinda stubborn and this goes against everything I've told myself in the last few months."

"Well if your stubborn then you'll fit right in. We get that trait from our mother and let me tell you, no one win's monopoly in our family."

"Monopoly?"

"It's a board game," May explained. "You like buy and sell properties to become rich. It's fun, but it can go on forever when you play with competitive and stubborn people. We should play sometime, though I'd warn you that the Singer's don't take well to loosing."

"Neither do I," I said, raising an eyebrow.

Kenna grinned and was about to say something when there was a light knock and my door edged open slightly, Maxon peeking in.

"America? You ready for lunch?"

His eyes landed on the three of us, sitting on my bed, and his eyebrow's shot into his hairline.

"Kenna? May? What are you guy's doing in here?" He asked, opening the door and stepping into the room.

"We were just chatting with America," Kenna said innocently.

"If you need me to make them leave..." Maxon trailed off, his eyes flickering to me.

"Hey!" May said and grabbed a pillow off my bed, throwing at his face.

He caught it, looking at it like it was a foreign object.

"I'm fine, Maxon," I assured him. "Can we reschedule lunch for tomorrow?"

He still looked confused. "Of course."

I stood up and walked over to him, wrapping my arm's around his neck. "Thank you. And I'll come see you tonight to make up for having to reschedule."

"It's no problem," He said distractedly, his eyes flickering to his sisters.

"Good," I smiled and leaned forward to kiss him quickly. As soon as my lips met his, his sister's sounded off with a synchronized ooh that had Maxon and I rolling our eyes simultaneously and separating from one another. "Bye Maxon."

"Goodbye America," He said, walking backward's out the door, still not quite sure what was going on.

I shut the door behind him and turned to Kenna and May, who both giggled.

"He's so nosy," Kenna sighed. "Has been since day 1."

I laughed. "I'd love to hear about that."

"Baby Maxon? Oh I have so much to say. He was almost as annoying as May," She shot, and reached over to pinch May's side.

May yelped and slapped Kenna's hand, and they laughed about it. I laughed along with them and sat contently back on the bed next to them, a weird warm feeling settling in me.

"When Maxon was five..."

I took a deep breath and laid against my pillows.

Okay.

CHAPTER 25

"Okay we need to get serious," I announced. All 3 of my maids looked up from their various tasks.

"About what?" Lucy asked.

"I think we've been avoiding the topic for years and it's time we truly confront it," I continued, a smile slowly creeping up my face because I couldn't contain how silly I was being.

"Oh dear, this sounds bad," Anne said, setting aside the clothes she was folding. "What is it?"

I took a dramatic deep breath and laid out a magazine on my bed and placed next to it the photo from my bedside table. "Is my color green or blue?"

Anne groaned and rolled her eyes, picking up the laundry again. "You had me thinking this was something serious."

Mary mock-gasped. "Watch your tongue, Anne. This is completely serious."

"I agree," I laughed. I tilted the photo towards Mary and picked up the magazine. "Blue, as seen in this photo, really brings out my eyes. But this magazine article clearly states that forest green makes my hair pop. And I simply can't decide which one I agree with."

"It is a difficult decision," Lucy laughed.

"No it's not!" Mary said. "The answer is obvious. Blue and only blue. We put her in it most and that's because it brings out her eyes, compliments her skin tone, and contrasts her hair. It's perfect and she always looks good in it."

"I like green," Lucy mumbled shyly.

I grinned. "I know why you like green, Lucy."

A light flush crawled up her neck and tinted her cheeks. "It's a nice color."

"It's also the color of Officer Legar's eyes," I sang playfully. "How'd you describe them? Like two sparkling emeralds."

"No!" Lucy yelped, her face going full red but she was smiling anyway. "Well yes...but that has nothing to do with than. Green makes you look dramatic and fiery. It contrasts your hair in a more striking way then blue and also makes you look very elegant. I like green."

"Biased!" Mary yelled.

"I'll count it," I cut in. "Anne? What do you think? You have the final say."

"You guys can be so ridiculous sometimes. Why does it matter?" Anne asked.

"It needs to be decided."

"You look good in both. You look good in all colors. We make you look good in all colors. Case closed."

I groaned. "That's no fun."

"Why don't you ask Maxon?" She replied, a devious twinkle in her eye. "I'm sure he has an opinion on what colors you look good in."

"He thinks she looks good in everything," Mary chimed in. "He thinks she walks on water."

"Does not!" I gasped.

"Why don't you ask him?" Anne said.

"I wish I could," I mumbled, falling back against my pillows dramatically. "But he's been super busy with his family. I've been trying to spend time with him and them, but we don't really get any alone time when we're with his younger siblings and parents."

"When are you supposed to see him?" Lucy asked.

"I think tomorrow night..." I said, not really sure. "I feel bad because I know he misses his family when they're gone, but I can't help but be a little selfish and want him to myself for a little bit."

"Well the first step in a healthy relationship is to talk about things like that," Anne advised.

"Oh god no. He can spend as much time with his family as he wants. I'm the whole reason he is apart from them in the first place. They'd all be home playing monopoly in Carolina if I wasn't around."

"That may be true but it isn't a good thing to have looming over your relationship. That's not a way to start a marriage," Anne said.

"Also," Mary said. "Of course he misses his family. He's going to be far away from them for a long time with only small visits in between. Have you guys even talked about that or the arranged marriage at all?"

I frowned. "Well, no...but everything's been so good. I don't want to mess it up. What if I tell him some of my insecurities and it freaks him out?"

Mary shrugged. "Well, it's not like he can break up with you—."

"Mary! That's not the point!"

"I'm just saying," She said, putting her hands up defensively.

"I think all of this can be solved by talking to him," Lucy said quietly. "You do have a very complicated relationship. If you don't talk about the important things, you guys will never really be happy. I'm very happy that you and Maxon decided to try and make this work for real. But it won't work if you guys aren't honest with each other."

"Jeez! I just wanted to know if I looked good in blue or green! I wasn't expecting a therapy session," I said.

Lucy shrugged. "You guys should talk."

I waved it off. "We will. We are very open with one another, but I don't want to bother him with heavy subjects when he is so happy."

"If you say so," Anne shrugged. "There's a new dress in the closet for you to wear tomorrow if you do see him."

"Thank you," I said. I placed the picture frame back on my nightstand so that the picture of my mom and I faced towards me. I picked up the magazine and began flipping through it. I liked reading these magazines because I learned a little bit about the world outside the palace from them. But it was mostly celebrities and other twos and threes in them. I just wish learning about the other castes was as easy as flipping a few pages.

~oOo~

The Angeles air was quiet and for a while, I just laid there, listening to the sound of Maxon's breathing.

"I can't remember the last time I just looked at the stars," I murmured, staring up at the twinkling orbs. "You know, just for fun I mean."

"As opposed to for what?" He wondered. I noticed that from where we laid in the center of the balcony, Maxon's foot extended to the railing and he was dangling it off.

"Well to study them," I said.

It was quiet for a second before Maxon burst out laughing. I pushed him away and shook my head.

"I'm serious!"

"You've studied the stars?" He chuckled.

"A tutor had me practice astronomy a few years ago. You can't really tell without a telescope or a very trained eye, but the stars are actually different colors."

"You've never just looked at the stars for no reason at all? They are quite pretty," Maxon said.

"I've never really had time. My schedule was rather packed before I met you. But ever since we found out about the switch, my father's been limiting my schedule to unimportant things. Anything he can get away with me not attending, he will. I think he's mad that even now I'm not really listening to him, after how many times he's threatened me."

"Do you miss going to all those meetings and stuff?"

I settled closer to him on the blanket, trying to keep warm in the cool Angeles night.

"A little bit," I decided. "I think I miss being involved, but not the meeting's as much. I mean budget consultations and infrastructure committee meetings aren't exactly fun. Oh, and war strategizing which, by the way, I am terrible at."

"What else are you terrible at?" His hand was stretched behind my back and the hand closest to my shoulder drew lazy circles on the skin there.

"What kind of question is that?"

"I just feel like I still know so little about you. And you seem perfect all the time, it's nice to know you have flaws."

"I'm impulsive and ill-tempered. Not to mention the fact that I can be cold and mean. I close myself off, I'm over-opinionated...I don't think I need to go on. If anyone's perfect, I'd say it's you."

He waved me off. "Those are just parts of your personality. I mean like thing's your bad at, besides war strategy."

I pursed my lips. "Hmmm...well I must be a terrible cook. I've never tried so I can only assume."

"Never?"

I grinned. "Yes never. You might not have noticed, but the teams of people who are keeping you well-fed? They feed me as well."c

"Really? I would have never guessed," He laughed, rolling his eyes. A cool breeze blew past us, sending shivers across my skin. I subconsciously shifted closer to him

"Are you cold?" He asked, his hands reaching to rub across the goosebumps rising on my arms.

"A bit," I admitted.

"We can go inside, maybe watch a movie?" He suggested.

I smiled thankfully. "I think that'd be lovely."

He grinned in return and leaned forward to kiss me quickly. He pulled away but I leaned forward again, kissing him a little longer.

"Okay. Now we can go inside," I decided, pushing myself into a sitting position. Maxon was quick to stand up and offer me his hand, which ended with us kissing again when I stumbled into his arms. He folded the blanket like a true gentleman and followed me inside.

"What should we watch?" I asked, sitting on the edge of my bed.

"I have no idea."

"Well, there isn't really a limit of options on the palace streaming service. Your wish is my command," I said, clicking on the tv and handing him the remote.

"What kind of movies do you like?"

"I enjoy a good rom-com or just a pure comedy. Actions are okay but they have to have a good plot. I can enjoy a good musical, but the criteria are pretty tough. I mostly enjoy anything though so you pick."

He laughed. "That's a foreign concept to me. When I watch movies with my family, it's a complete war to decide. May likes musicals, but Kenna likes rom-com's. All of us guys like actions, and my mom will only watch The Notebook."

I smiled and went to reply when my mouth went dry and I remembered what my maids said earlier. About Maxon and I needing to talk and that if we didn't, it would ruin our relationship. I think that's a bit dramatic, but they're not wrong.

"Hey, Maxon?" I asked.

"Yeah?" He asked, shuffling through the movies.

"Can I ask you something kind of serious?"

He looked over at me from where he was standing by the tv and his forehead creased with concern. "Yeah, of course."

"It's nothing bad," I said, folding my hands in my lap. "I just feel like we haven't really talked about how you're doing with this whole arranged marriage thing."

"What do you mean?"

"I mean, with you being forced to marry me and being apart from your family. I want you to be able to talk to me about it," I said shyly.

"It's not a big deal," He shrugged, setting the remote aside. "I mean I've adjusted and it's all been pretty good."

"That's not the full truth though. Please talk to me, Maxon. We have to talk about this."

"'Well...if I'm being completely honest, I really miss my family. All the time. And it's been pretty hard being apart from them."

I nodded, encouraging him to continue.

"It's weird to say because I live in this huge palace, but I miss my house. This place gets kinda lonely. It's just so big. And I'm actually really nervous about becoming King. I mean, me? A king? I'm just a five from a nowhere town in Carolina and now I'm going to be making laws and marrying this super intimidating woman. It's all really crazy and it's happening so fast, it's hardly been half a year since we found out about the switch."

I squeezed my hands in a futile attempt at calming myself down. I will not spiral right now.

"I'm not gonna say that this is what I had planned out for my life, but it's been getting better. I'm settling in here, and my family visits so that's good. I think I'm getting a hold of the etiquette and talking to you has already helped me envision what I would want to do as a King...America? Oh god, I've freaked you out. America, say something."

"It's not too late," I whispered.

"What?"

"We can still do something. We will figure a way out of this, we are just not trying hard enough."

"Ames, that's not what I meant at all. You've already tried to reason with your father, numerous times, and it hasn't ended well for you."

"We won't involve him. I can get you and your whole family on a plane to Italy before he would ever know. And then you'll be out of his reach."

"And leave you here?" Maxon burst. "America, your father will beat you near to death. I've seen what he can do and I won't have it happen again."

I stood up fiercely, a few tears slipping down my cheeks. "I'd take those beating's again and again if it meant that I'd never had to worry about you receiving one too."

"America, I'm not leaving and letting him hurt you."

"Maxon please," I sobbed, breaking down. "You need to get yourself out of this. You're just going to become another one of my father's pawns, who he can yell at and beat. You need to get out of this marriage before your stuck in it."

Maxon grabbed my wrists, holding them in front of me. My fake engagement ring caught in the moonlight and all I wanted to do was rip it off and throw it off my balcony.

"You are so broken," He whispered, almost as if he was just saying this to himself.

I saw the reflection of myself in his eyes. I looked a mess. I am sad. I am angry. I am desperate. I am afraid. I am afraid for Maxon. Maxon made me feel again and now I need to save him before he ends up an empty shell of who he is.

"Think about what it's like to be a little girl and to have your home broken into and destroyed by rebels. To be a little girl who worships the ground her father walks on but then he beats her until she can't walk. And then having to keep it a secret."

"Just think about being afraid in your own home. I wasn't afraid of monsters under my bed. I was afraid of the monster that lived in my home. The monsters that broke into my home and tore apart my stuffed animals. I was afraid of even moving. Picture what that does to a person, to a little girl. This palace. These people. This job. It breaks you, Maxon. And I'm stuck but you have a chance to get out. You have to figure this out."

"Don't you realize that I'm stuck too! I'm stuck in this relationship because it's no longer an arranged marriage. There are feelings and I know we both have them. I can't just leave and let you face your fathers anger when I do. Because I care about you America and this isn't just an arranged marriage anymore."

I made a sort of sound that was a mix between a laugh and a cry. "But you said it yourself. I'm broken. I am one of the most powerful people in this world. I have everything I could ever want at my fingertips. And what do I do with it? My people are starving and living on the streets and are separated by a number that they cannot control. I am one of the only people in the world that can help them and I do nothing! How can anyone possibly care about me?"

"I care about you America," He said fiercely. "Which is why I'm not going anywhere."

A sobbed racked through my chest and I almost collapsed, but Maxon's arms circled me in a tight embrace. My body molded against his as I silently wept into his shoulder. His chin rested on my head and his hands wrapped around my hips, and it felt right to be there in his arms for at least that one moment.

"Maxon," I whispered. "I...I think I might be falling in love with you."

His hand moved from my waist to my back and pulled me impossibly closer. I looked up into his eyes and our foreheads rested against one another.

"I think I might be falling in love with you too."

CHAPTER 26

"Please do not be a 9. Please do not be a 9," I pleaded, shaking the dice in my hands and eyeing the hotel on the property.

"Please be a 9! Please be a 9!" May chanted, watching me intently.

"Please don't be a 9. I swear, do not be a 9," Maxon said.

"Max!" May yelled. "Whose side are you on?"

"America is scary when she's angry," Maxon shrugged, unapologetic.

"Does she get angry when she loses?" May taunted.

"I don't know. She never loses," Maxon said.

"And I'm not gonna start now," I said, flicking my wrist and sending the dice rolling across the board. I held my breath as the dice rolled and tipped before finally settling on 8.

"Yes!" I screamed, grabbing Maxon's face and kissing him. There was a loud ew from Gerad. I pulled away smiling wide. "I love monopoly!"

"Kenna and I both still have more money then you," He reminded me.

"Not for long! I'm playing to win!" I yelled and moved my piece around the board. I smiled at the hotel on the square in front of me. Not today, May, not today.

"I needed that money to get ahead," May pouted.

"Don't worry, May. We can get Maxon to land on that square," I assured her.

"Ames!" He yelled.

"I'm sorry, but this game is everyone for themselves," I grinned. I leaned forward and kissed his cheek.

He shook his head, grabbing the dice and throwing them back down. He rolled an eleven and moved accordingly.

"Your the richest, so your the enemy," I shrugged.

"He won't be for long," Kenna quipped. "That's my space, pay up Max."

"Doesn't even make a dent, Ken," Maxon taunted, handing her a few bills.

"Slowly closing the distance," She replied, counting the bills and handing them to James, who sorted them into piles next to him.

"Be nice kids," Magda warned, taking her turn. "I think that's your property, America. How much do I owe you?"

"Your not supposed to remind her, Maggie. If she would have forgotten, you wouldn't have had to pay her," Shalom told Magda.

"But that's dishonest. And she's the princess, I don't think were supposed to lie to her," Magda said.

"It's a capital offense," I nodded solemnly. We locked eyes and I broke out smiling.

She laughed. "How much?"

"100."

Magda frowned down at her funds. "That'll bankrupt us, Shalom."

Maxon turned to Kenna and they high-fived.

"Well maybe I could reduce the price because you were honest—."

"No America! That's how you win. They have to go bankrupt," Maxon explained.

"But—."

"Thank you America, but it's fine," Magda cut in. "You can stop being a princess for a few minutes, it's just monopoly. Shalom and I are used to to loosing anyways. Kenna and Maxon are relentless."

"I win too sometimes!" May yelled.

"Of course honey," Magda said, patting Mays arm reassuringly.

Shalom helped Magda get to her feet and they sat on the edge of my bed to watch.

"I'm bored. Can we turn on a movie?" Gerad asked, throwing his money and properties next to him.

May and Kenna immediately went after all his assets like hungry animals and I laughed.

"Sure, Gerad. The remotes on the side table. You can watch whatever you want," I told him.

"Yay!" He yelled and took a running start to jump in the center of my bed.

A soft knock sounded at the door. Gerad was jumping up off the bed to get it before I could say a thing.

"Hello!" He greeted the person.

"Who is it, Gerad?" I asked, standing up and smoothing out my dress so I could get the door.

"A maid," He chirped.

He slid away from the door and I pulled the door open wide so I could see who it was.

"Oh hey Veda, what's up?"

"Good morning, Princess America. I have a message from your father."

"What is it?" I asked distractedly, glancing back at Maxon to make sure he wasn't stealing my money. I wouldn't put it past him at the moment.

"Your father has requested that you and Sir Maxon meet him downstairs in the parlor by the women's room," She said. "Silvia and your parents are waiting for you there."

"Oh um..." I peeked behind me. "I'm sort of in the middle of something."

Her mouth dropped open and she shut it quickly. "Um...I—Uh. The King said it was urgent, your majesty."

What did I just say? Did I just say I was in the middle of something? Literally, I have no idea who I am.

"Right, of course. Thank you, Veda, I'll—. I'll be right there," I mumbled, closing the door. I shook my head, muttering to myself.

"In the middle of something? I don't think I've ever said that in my life!"

"America?" Maxon asked, rolling the dice. "You alright?"

"We gotta go, Maxon," I sighed, walking over to my vanity and fixing my hair. "Miss Silvia and my father want to meet with us."

"About what?" He asked.

"I'm not sure," I said, grabbing a lipstick and applying it quickly. "I'm so sorry about the board game everybody."

"I'm not!" Kenna yelled, holding up her stack of cash. "I'm in the lead right now which means I win!"

"That's not fair!" Maxon accused. "The games being cut short! We need a rematch, or we will continue playing later but—."

"Max, let it go," May sighed. "She won. She always wins."

"I am the oldest, hear me roar!" Kenna yelled, tossing her money.

"Ken—," James tried to cut in.

"Clean that up Kenna Renee Singer!" Magda chastised.

"Orders, Ma! Kenna Orders!" Kenna groaned.

"Not when you're acting like that," Magda quipped. "Clean up the money you threw around."

May laughed at her and I smiled, running to grab a pair of heels.

"Somebody help the very pregnant women up," Kenna called out.

"So people just summon one another here?" I heard May whisper to Kenna.

"It's the palace, May. Of course they summon each other."

"M' lady," Maxon said, holding out his arm.

I took it and waved to the singers. "Goodbye everyone. Monopoly was great!"

"Bye America," They chorused.

I closed the door behind me and smiled.

"I love your family," I sighed.

"They love you too," He said. "They talk about you all the time."

"My mom has been talking about you all the time since you had tea with her the other day. She loves you!"

"I think it's sufficient to say that we are both in with the in laws," Maxon said, pulling me close and kissing my cheek.

I high-fived him, clasping our hands and leaning my head on his shoulder.

"What's this?" Maxon asked, gesturing to the painting we were passing of my mother and father.

I examined it, remembering the story that went along with it. "That is a painting recreation of the first photo my mom and dad took together."

"Why do I recognize that dress...?" Maxon trailed off, glancing back at the painting.

I rolled my eyes. "That's the same dress I wore for our engagement pictures. The selected used to wear that exact dress when they took their official photos with the Prince. Cream, with a slit on the left thigh and a modest v-neck. It's been that same dress for generations."

"If you don't mind me asking, why didn't you have a Selection?"

"For the exact same reason that I've been fighting marrying you for so long," I admitted. "It would be just another part of my life that everyone else would be controlling."

"But wouldn't you have a choice in who you married then? I thought that's what you wanted."

"The Selection would hardly be my choice. I'd be surprised if I even got to choose who won it. The truth about the Selection, is that's it's all fake. Anyone can apply but the people who make it to the palace are each hand selected. Either they have connections that would benefit the palace, or they are breathtakingly beautiful, or they are of a lower caste to make it seem like it's all random. But none of it is random. Everything is carefully orchestrated, from the people who are picked to when each girl leaves to the person who wins. And I could only imagine how much worse it would have been with my father controlling it all."

"That is...sick. Is that how it was for your mother and father?"

"Undoubtedly. I do think my father loves my mother. He's despicable but he takes care of her. But none of that would have mattered if she didn't have other valuable things going for her. And I despise that about the Selection."

His eyes were wide as he took all this information in. I'm sure that from any citizens point of view the Selection may have seemed romantic, but it was anything but if you knew the truth.

"So how'd you get out of it then? Isn't the Selection a tradition that's been carried down for generations since the beginning of Illea? I remember reading that King Gregory Illea's son was the first." I had to bite my tongue to keep from ranting. You don't even want to get me started on Gregory Illea and his stupid diaries. "I know your crafty, but how'd you manage that one?"

I peeked around to make sure no one was listening to what we were saying. Maxon knew more about me and my family then I suspect anyone, even my dad's closest advisors, knew. I trusted Maxon with anything. I trusted Maxon more than I think I've trusted anyone, but I wasn't going to dwell on how much that scared me because then I'd go spiraling to a place I try to avoid going. But I didn't trust everyone in the palace and we had to be careful with who was listening.

"Last year, on my 17th birthday, my father brought up the idea of us beginning to prepare for a Selection. The country had been asking about if I would have one and my father was all too happy to provide the people with my misery. And I outright refused."

"It was that easy?"

"Oh god no. That began a month long process of my parents trying to get me to plan different things in regards to the selection. The Selection had always been women, so the guest rooms needed to be more masculine and they wanted me to pick between green and blue drapes. They wanted a feast for the first night and I needed to choose the meal. But I refused to do anything. They couldn't get a peep out of me. My father punished me for it and ultimately they just started making the decisions without my input."

His thumb rubbed across my palm, soothing me.

"So I went to my father and I made a speech that I still remember every word of till this day. I think it's the only time it ever worked. I told him that no matter what he did, I wouldn't talk to a single suitor in this palace. I wouldn't go on the report and talk to Gavril Fadaye. No dates. No kisses. No nothing. I was not going to put on a show. He could kick and scream and beat me until I was bleeding on the floor, hanging on to my life, but I was not going to participate in the Selection."

I took a deep breath, thinking about how scared I had been when I confronted him. He had been so angry, I honestly think that if he got the cane out he never would have stopped.

"And it worked. He had no choice and for once I got my way."

Maxon lifted our conjoined hands, waving them in celebration. "Well cheers to that!"

"...And now I'm in an arranged marriage so the tables really have turned," I sighed. "But I'm happier now, thanks to you. Happier then I've ever been."

"I'm glad," He murmured, leaning down to kiss me quickly.

"We're here," I mumbled against his lips.

"Do we have to go in?" He asked. "Silvia and your father both scare me."

"We have to," I said, pulling away and reaching for the door handle with the hand that wasn't holding his. I pushed the door open and was faced with a parlor that probably hadn't been used in years, but looked like it had been hit by a tornado. Every surface was covered in papers and books and magazines, and there was so much clutter that I didn't even have enough time to dwell on what any of it was.

"Mom? Father...." I trailed off looking at where my parents sat on a love seat. Silvia was filing through some of the clutter on the coffee table. "Miss Silvia? What is going on in here? It looks like someone converted the parlor into a library."

"No jokes right now, America," My father reprimanded.

My brow creased. "My apologies...I didn't realize this was serious. I assumed it was just something about the arranged marriage."

"It is," Silvia confirmed.

I glanced back at Maxon who looked just about as confused as I did.

"Amy, Maxon, why don't you two sit down?" My mother said, watching me wearily.

My mother has always been a dead giveaway and that's when I knew I wasn't going to like this at all. Maxon squeezed my hand, immediately sensing that my mind was already beginning its spiral. His hand in mine grounded me though, and I just calmly led us to to the loveseat opposite of Mother and Father's.

"What is going on?" I asked, taking Maxon and I's conjoined hands and folding them officially in my lap.

"The whole country is upset," My father grumbled. "The rebel attacks have only been increasing in number, and unrest amongst the castes is at the highest it's been in a 100 years." I looked at my father and over to Maxon. It was shocking that he would say any of this in front of Maxon. Maxon would be dealing with this in a matter of years, but Father never liked to admit to anyone that his country wasn't perfect. "If we don't do something quick, it will only be a matter of time before everything begins to crumble."

"Okay..." I murmured, trying to think of how we would approach this. "Isn't this something that we should be addressing with the advisers?"

"We've already talked with them," He said as if I should have known. Fantastic. Another meeting that I wasn't present for. "The people are unhappy. And what we need is something to cheer everyone up."

I narrowed my eyes, biting my tongue to resist telling him everything that was wrong with that statement.

"And what do you have in mind?" I asked.

"In the past, what has always worked best is a selection. But obviously that is not an option. So we're doing the closest thing that we can. We're shortening your engagement as much as we can. We want the two of you married as quickly as possible."

My jaw dropped open and that's when I realized what I was surrounded by. The room was a mess with bridal magazines. And books with pretty destination landscapes and photographs of wedding dresses.

Oh my god, I think I'm going to be sick.

Why can't I get a moment of peace around here? I am finally just beginning to come to terms with everything. I'm finally beginning to let Maxon and his family in. I'm actually in a good place in my relationship and I really like him. Nothing can ever be still though. As soon as my life begins to look like it's getting better, it all comes crashing down. My father can never just let me be. I'm hardly even eighteen and now were talking about marriage.

It was going to be a long engagement. I was going to have time to be with Maxon and get to have a normal relationship with him before we were to marry. I was looking forward to getting to know his quirks and flaws. The things that made him tick and the things that made him laugh. What he liked about me and what I liked about him. It was a long engagement when it was convenient to my father for us to get to know one another, and now it'a going to be cut short to suit his needs.

This is my life we're playing with! How many more times am I going to be pulled in different directions? How much more of this do I have to take before I can make my own decisions? Will I wake up tomorrow and have the wedding postponed again? Will I wake up tomorrow and there will be no wedding at all?

This is my life and I don't even get a say in what's happening in it.

It's not that there is a difference between marrying Maxon in 3 or 4 years and marrying him tomorrow. At the end of the day, we will be married. I just hoped that Maxon and I would almost get to have a real relationship, instead of something that has been fake since the beginning. I don't even know why I pretend like this could have ever actually ended any differently.

It's just another thing that is out of my control. I want to choose when and where and who I fall in love with.

And damnit, I want that person to be Maxon.

"I...um," I mumbled. "Okay. Well I..."

"Would you mind if I speak with America alone?" My mom spoke.

"Amberley we are on a tight schedule—."

"What I meant to say is that I am going to talk to my daughter," Mom interrupted sharply. "This is marriage, Clarkson. It is the rest of her life. And I am going to take a moment with her to talk about it."

His jaw audibly snapped closed. "Well uh...ahem. Of course, my dear."

Father stood up, brushing himself off and clearing his throat bashfully. I almost smiled.

"We will wait in the hall," He muttered and crossed to the door.

Maxon's hand was still in mine and he squeezed it, reminding me of his presence. He brought our hands to his lips, kissing them, and then let go to follow my father and Silvia to the door. He looked back at me and I could feel all that he was trying to convey to me, but I was too shocked to really comprehend. The door clicked shut behind them and it was just my mother and I.

It's always just been my mother and I.

"Amy," She whispered, sitting down on the same loveseat as me. She tucked her feet underneath her and reached for my hands. I let her take them. "Say something."

"I don't really know what to say. I'm trying to not freak out or scream and cry," I admitted. "It's not like I didn't know this was coming. I just assumed I had a few more years."

"Hey," She called, capturing my attention. "Scream and cry and throw things if you want. Do whatever you need. I know it doesn't seem like you have much of a choice, and I suppose you don't, but that doesn't mean you can't be upset about it."

"I'm pretty sure your the only one who feels that way. Father and Silvia would like it best if I just nodded my head and started picking out flowers."

"That not true," She murmured. "Your father...he, I...we haven't been the best parents lately. I haven't been the best mother lately and I'm so sorry Amy. I'm sorry that you got stuck in this situation and I'm sorry that everything is so crazy for you. I should have been there for you but I was worried that you blamed me. But that's no excuse..."

"I don't blame you, Mom." She looked up at me unbelieving. "Not at all. In all honesty, I think this whole experience has been something I needed to go through by myself."

"You've grown from this. With all that's happened, I wouldn't be surprised if you just gave up. I know I would have. I would have given up a long time ago, but you? You are so unbelievably strong. My little girl...You've grown up so fast and I didn't even realize it happened. You will make such an amazing queen. Much better then I am."

"The people love you, Mom."

"They do but I can see it in your eyes," She touched her hand to my face, rubbing her thumb across my cheek. "You have big plans and you will do great things. You'll do more for them." She looked away, lost in thought for a moment. I could imagine what she was thinking about. The things she should have done better, the things she did wrong. She shook her head, her eyes focusing on me. "But that's not what this is about. This is about you. And that handsome young man outside. And the rock on your finger."

I instinctively touched my engagement ring, big and flashy and most definitely not my style. My father had picked it out I'm sure, and an advisor had been the one to give it to me before we announced the engagement. There was no proposal. There will never be a proposal.

I curled my feet under myself too, mirroring her. "I'm afraid. To be a queen, but I've been preparing for that my whole life. More so then that, I'm afraid to be a wife. I'm still so young Mom, hardly even a legal adult, and yet everyday I think about getting married and having kids and carrying on the stupid Illean bloodline. How do I balance ruling a country and caring for a husband and then kids, oh god kids, before I'm even in my twenties? I don't know what to do. Maxon will just end up hating me because I don't know how to do any of this."

"You just have to take it all one day at a time. You are not getting married tomorrow. You don't have to think about kids for a very long time. Just get through today. Then tomorrow. Then the day after that. I know it's all terrifying but...your better. You look happier and you glow now. You never glowed before. So I don't know if your in love with Maxon, and I know even if you are that marriage is a big step above love. But I hope you keep glowing. And I hope your really really happy."

There was a few things that I'm sure of. I was never gonna "meet the family" because Maxon's family and mine were interconnected. There wasn't a first kiss because that had all been for show. I was never going to see where he grew up because who knows if he will ever go back there, and there was never going to be a proposal because we were already engaged. We were never going to have any of those moments and the thought did make me sad.

But did any of that matter?

I...I love Maxon Singer. I want to marry him. I want to spend the rest of my life with him.

Who cares about the rest of it?

"Thank you, mommy," I murmured, throwing my arms around her.

Her hand pulled me tighter to her and the other hand reached up to stroke my hair. She tucked me into her arms, resting her chin on my head and holding me.

"I am so proud of you, Amy. More then you will ever know. I love you to the moon and back."

"I love you more."

We pulled away, laughing weakly and dabbing at our eyes.

"That turned out more emotional then I meant for it too," My mom laughed. "And your Father has been standing in the hall with Maxon and Silvia this whole time."

I pushed off the couch and went to open the door, taking a deep breath. Silvia and my dad walked right past me, but Maxon peeked at me with concern. I grabbed his hand.

"So are we done here?" Dad asked, glancing at his watch. "I have work to do."

"Of course, your majesty. We will begin planning immediately," Silvia said, reaching for her clipboard.

"How okay are you with this?" I whispered to Maxon, leading him back to the loveseat.

"I'll meet you at your room tonight and we can freak out together," He replied, squeezing my hand. "Right now I believe we are picking out a venue."

"This is really scary," I mumbled.

"Absolutely terrifying," He agreed.

I smiled as Silvia started talking about flowers and guest lists and how the royal wedding was going to the biggest event of the decade. I was really scared to marry Maxon so soon. I'm terrified to pick out a wedding dress. I'm petrified to spend the rest of my life with this man who I've only known a short time, and yet I have very big, very real feelings for.

But he's scared too.

So at least we're in this together.